DONE

GOOD GIRLS STAY QUIET

JO CASSIDY

MONSTER IVY
PUBLISHING

ISBN (Paperback): 978-1-948095-11-2

ISBN (eBook): 978-1-948095-12-9

ISBN (Audio): 978-1-948095-13-6

For Mom & Dad. Thanks for giving me a stable, happy home in this crazy world.

CHAPTER 1

I ran my fingers along the white eyelet canopy surrounding my bed. Daddy said it would protect me at night while I slept but still allow me to breathe. Sometimes I liked to sit on the bed with the canopy closed, soaking in the comfort and safety it provided.

I'd already finished my homework for the day. It was always the first thing I did when I came home from school so I'd have the evening free to spend with Daddy.

My leg bounced, my fingers drumming along with the motion. I glanced at the twin bell alarm clock on my nightstand. Only twenty more minutes until Daddy came home and unlocked my bedroom door. I could hold my bladder that long. I'd done it before. I needed to distract myself so I wouldn't think about it.

I leaned over the side of my bed, the canopy draping over my hair, and retrieved the journal tucked under my mattress.

Noah, my stuffed elephant, cleared his throat, which did nothing for the rasp in his tone. "Oh, Cora dear. You know not to write in that during the day. *He* may come home and see it."

I glared at the elephant sitting on my bed, his bright, blue eyes staring back at me. "I know that, *Noah dear*. I was just seeing how much room I had left." I thumbed through the empty pages in the back. "I'll have to steal another journal soon."

Noah guffawed. "So you can write more thrilling stories about me?"

Whoever manufactured the stuffed animal didn't bother with getting the facts straight. I'd never seen an elephant with blue eyes that sparkled. It certainly didn't match with Noah's sometimes rough and sarcastic demeanor.

Daddy had bought him for me when I was eight. He'd said the elephant's eyes matched mine. Little did he know, he'd brought me home an elephant with a soul that came alive when we were alone.

"Or is this about brushing up on your shoplifting skills?" Noah asked.

I put my hand on my hip. "Please don't judge me. There are extenuating circumstances."

"Keep telling yourself that." He laughed louder, though his stuffed body remained completely still on the bed.

I was about to flick his trunk when I heard footfalls in the hallway. Daddy was home early. Shoving the journal back under my bed, I surveyed the room to make sure nothing had been left out that I didn't want Daddy to see. I fumbled to refasten the top button on my shirt so only half of my neck was exposed. Then I rolled down my sleeves and buttoned the cuffs. Daddy liked his little girl to look a certain way.

"Are you going to start hiding me?" Noah asked.

Daddy didn't know about my relationship with Noah, and I wanted it to remain that way. Luckily, I was the only one who could hear Noah. It was the main reason our relationship was special and why I confided in him so much.

Right as the lock unlatched on the outside of my door, I

settled into place on my bed holding a regency book I'd brought home from the school library. At the last second, I moved my braid so it rested on my right shoulder. The door opened, and Daddy stepped inside the room. He still wore his blue work coveralls, and I immediately took in the scent of grease and sweat. I noticed his pomade had held his perfectly brushed hair in place all day.

Even though his presence caused unease to swirl inside, I plastered on the smile he loved so I wouldn't have to deal with his explosive anger. It was why I referred to him as Daddy in my head. I never wanted to accidentally call him something else to his face.

"Hi Daddy!" I set the book on my nightstand and went to him. I put my arms out to hug him, but he took a step back.

"I need a shower." He rubbed at his tired eyes. "My last appointment was a bit of a mess."

"Why don't I cook dinner while you wash up and then you can tell me all about your day over our meal?"

Daddy leaned forward and kissed my forehead, his dry lips causing my stomach to roll. "What would I do without you, Cora?"

"Not be such a creepy old man?" Noah offered in a haughty tone.

It took everything in me to not turn around and scold Noah. He shouldn't talk about Daddy like that. Thank goodness Daddy couldn't hear him, or we'd both be locked in the basement for the night.

"I could really use a decent BLT," Daddy said.

"Consider it done." My tone was as sweet as honey, but my insides were heavy like molasses.

He turned to leave, but then faced me and raised his eyebrows. "Make sure the bacon is crispy, but not over-cooked." He placed his hand on my arm and squeezed as a small storm brewed in his eyes. "Last time it was practically burnt."

I clasped my hands tightly in front of me so I wouldn't flinch from the pain. "Of course, Daddy."

The storm in his eyes retreated, and Daddy left the room. I wanted to yell at Noah, but I really needed to use the bathroom. It had been hours. As soon as I finished, though, I headed back into my room.

"Don't say things like that about him," I hissed. When it came to Daddy, Noah and I didn't see eye to eye. He didn't like the way Daddy treated me.

"The truth?" Noah whistled. "Fine. I'll feed myself lies like you do."

Going to the bed, I put my face in front of his. "Being nice to him makes him happy. He's done so much for us, Noah." I poked his trunk. "Remember that."

"That's right. All the things he does out of *love*. Well, if you want him happy, then you should start dinner and stop lecturing me."

I gave him one last glaring look before I went into the kitchen to prepare dinner. I put on an apron so the grease wouldn't splatter my shirt. That would make Daddy real mad. I kept a close eye on the bacon, making sure every inch turned brown but had no hint of black. Once it was perfectly cooked, I took the plate of bacon and gently placed it on the table. I used a towel to wipe away a drop of grease on the edge of the plate.

After smoothing out a wrinkle in the tablecloth, I used my hand to measure the length of the material hanging over the edge, double checking it was even all the way around, just how Daddy liked it. We had a round table so the chairs could be spaced perfectly apart; far enough so Daddy could look at me, but not too far so he could reach out and touch me if he needed to. It had been almost a year since I'd stepped out of line at the dinner table and he'd sent me to timeout. I planned on keeping it that way.

The white ceramic plates and bowls were on their place-mats, with a fork on the left, fork above for the salad – even though we weren't having salad, it always had to be there – and a spoon and knife to the right. The glasses were up and to the right, with the cloth napkins flawlessly folded in a standing triangle on the center of our plates. It was perfect.

"Smells delicious, angel," Daddy said, joining me in the kitchen. He'd switched to his usual button-down shirt tucked tightly into his casual slacks. His shirt was buttoned all the way to the top like mine. My chest tightened at the sight of his leather belt.

He wrapped his arm around my shoulder and kissed the side of my head, my hair creating a barrier between his lips and my skin. His sweat and grease stench had been replaced by soap and Selsun Blue shampoo and his brown hair hung down, still wet from the shower. I preferred that look to his perfectly sculpted hair. It made him appear carefree.

"So, tell me about this last client of yours," I said, hanging up my apron in the pantry and softly closing the door.

Daddy grabbed a bottled beer from the fridge. "Not much to tell. A guy inherited everything in his dad's garage, which included some tools that hadn't been used in a very long time."

Keeping my hands steady, I pulled out his chair for him. He sat down, his thin lips turning into a smile as he did. I returned the smile, though my stomach fluttered. I hoped I cooked the bacon just right.

"Did you get them working again?" I sat down and tucked my napkin into the top of my shirt, just like Daddy had done. Then I made sure my braid hung over my right shoulder.

He winked. "Always do."

I grabbed two pieces of bread and spread mayo on them.

"Never leave a client unsatisfied."

He laughed. "So you *do* listen to me."

I tilted my head to the side and winked at him. "Always do."

The laughter reached all the way to his eyes and some of the tension released inside me. His eyes were much kinder when they weren't housing a storm.

I loaded up his sandwich with bacon, lettuce, and fresh tomatoes I had picked from the backyard the day before. I tried to keep my hands stable as I placed the BLT in the center of his plate.

Clasping my hands in my lap, I waited patiently for Daddy to take a bite of his sandwich.

"It's perfect, angel." He wiped his mouth with the napkin and nodded at the bread. "Go ahead and make yourself a sandwich now."

My heart calmed. "Thanks, Daddy."

"You deserve it," he said. "Having you gives me a reason to wake up every morning."

Tears welled up behind my eyelids. I was lucky to have a father who loved me so much.

After dinner and cleaning up under Daddy's watchful eye, I grabbed the playing cards from the closet in the hall. It was tradition to play every night. I let him win all the time because he hated to lose. The last time I won, he didn't let me out of the basement for two whole days.

~

*O*nce Daddy locked me in my room for the night, I switched to my long sleeve crew neck shirt and cotton pants. It was what Daddy liked me to wear to bed. They were comfortable, so I didn't mind. I waited for him to go to bed before I pulled out my journal. I sat down on the floor next to the large dollhouse and used the flower-shaped nightlight as my guide.

I wrote in my journal every night. I recounted everything that happened to me during the day, not leaving a single detail out. At the end of the entry, I'd sketch a drawing of my favorite event from the day, whether it was something that happened or someone I saw that I thought looked interesting. Sometimes I wrote poems or song lyrics imagining myself in a happier life.

"Don't forget to mention my charming personality," Noah said from the bed.

"Hush!" I whispered.

"Why?" he asked. "It's not like someone else can hear me." He raised his volume. "I could shout all night long, and nothing would happen. Maybe I'll sing you a few songs. Except I'd have to make up the words since you can't listen to music."

I reached for my backpack, fished out an eraser, and threw it at Noah. "You're distracting me. Now please be quiet."

He grunted. "Was that necessary? Hitting me? Please don't turn into your precious *Daddy.*"

His words punched me right in the gut. I was trying to be playful with him, not intentionally harm him. I never wanted to resort to violence to get my way. Noah had just proved that words could be more powerful than actions.

Suddenly the latch on the outside of my door lifted. Daddy. I wasn't close enough to the bed, so I stuffed the journal inside my backpack and pulled out my math book as the door opened.

Daddy flicked on the light and stared at my empty bed. He was still in his regular clothes. He never liked me to see him in anything less.

"I'm here, Daddy," I said.

7

He turned his attention to me on the floor, his voice coming out low and rough. "Were you just talking to someone?"

I held up my math book, holding tight so my hands wouldn't tremble. "I have a test tomorrow, and I wanted to review the material one more time. It helps me to repeat it out loud."

His eyes scanned the room, looking for anything out of place. He folded his arms. "Why are you doing it in the dark?"

I thumbed the pages of my math book. "I didn't want to wake you, Daddy. You work so hard for our family, and I wanted you to be able to have a good night's sleep for work tomorrow."

The strain in his face relaxed. "That's very thoughtful of you. But it's late. You also need your sleep."

I stood, hoping my legs didn't look as shaky as they felt. "Of course, Daddy."

He waited until I climbed back into bed. He tucked in the sides of my sheets, snuggling me in. "You're smart, angel. You'll do fine on your test." Grabbing my braid, he pulled it forward to its proper place. He kissed my forehead, but dark clouds flew into the back of his eyes as he squeezed my shoulder. "I never want to catch you outside of bed at night again, do you hear me?"

A painful lump landed in my throat, and it took me a second before I could speak. "Yes, Daddy."

"Sleep tight, my angel girl." His low, breathy voice caused me to shiver.

Once Daddy was out of the room, I took Noah and held him in my arms. His soft fur was soothing to the touch. My heart thudded in my chest from how close I'd been to being caught. Daddy would be furious if he knew I had journals that held our family secret.

He could never know I had them.

8

*D*addy's blue van sidled up to the curb minutes before school started. He never wanted me to have time to linger before first period. That would give me time to socialize and form friendships, and that was high up on the list of things I couldn't do.

"What are you going to do today?" Daddy adjusted himself in the driver's seat so his body and focus were turned toward me. His work coveralls had been washed and pressed. Looking at him – hair, outfit, and smile in perfect place – no one would ever think he housed a dark side.

I hugged my pink backpack close to my chest. "Only talk to students in my class if it's required for an assignment." I broke that rule daily with Jenna, the girl who sat next to me in French. But it would be rude to ignore her. "Be respectful to my teachers and answer questions correctly when called on."

"Are you going to talk to anyone during break or lunch?" He kept his strong hand on the passenger side headrest, letting me know he could touch me in a heartbeat.

"No." My thumb brushed along Husky, my Beanie Boo

keychain on my backpack zipper, clinging onto the comfort he offered me. Daddy had given him to me when I first started public school so I'd have a friend. One he'd authorized. "I'll keep in a spot where no one can see me so they won't get suspicious."

"We can't have anyone asking questions, can we?" His eyes were a calm blue, the dark gray nowhere near the horizon. I wished they would stay like that forever.

I shook my head in response.

"Have a great day, Cora." He leaned over and his cold lips found my forehead. "You're my perfect angel girl."

With my head down, I positioned my braid so it rested over my right shoulder, walked up the stairs and into the old brick, two-story school. If I avoided eye contact, the day was always easier. I had my school persona down to a science. To my teachers, I appeared quiet, yet hardworking and smart. To my peers, I was invisible.

I didn't mind being invisible. The few times I'd had to socialize for school projects had never gone well. I always ended up saying something wrong, and I'd get the strangest looks or worse – they'd laugh at me.

If it hadn't been for a new neighbor that moved in next door, I may have never had the chance to go to public school. Before that, Daddy had started trusting me and letting me out of my room more, but he didn't like the idea of the world tainting me, so he kept me locked up at home during the day while he went to work. He'd done a good job of keeping me hidden from all the neighbors.

Then the Roberts moved in, and one day Mrs. Roberts saw me getting into the van with Daddy. She ran out of her house and flagged us down before we could even pull out of the driveway. She rambled on for at least ten minutes about how she didn't know Daddy had a daughter and that I reminded her of her daughter who was away at college.

Daddy concluded that with Mrs. Roberts being so nosy, she'd certainly notice that I stayed home all day by myself while he went to work. So he called the high school and arranged everything. Plus, Daddy hadn't been able to teach me anymore. He'd never graduated high school.

I'd been terrified and exhilarated at the prospect of going to school. So far, all had gone well. But as Daddy had once said, good things always came to an end.

~

*M*y day went smoothly until I arrived in fourth period. My teacher assigned a project, picking our groups for us. We had to arrange our desks so we were all next to each other.

Sydney grunted as her thin frame moved her desk toward our group. She wouldn't let go of her cell phone to do it. I tried not to stare at the rips and holes in her jeans. Daddy would be furious if I ever allowed my pants to get that way. Her shirt also seemed a couple sizes too big and hung past her bottom. Half of her long brown hair was up in a sloppy bun. Maybe her family didn't have a lot of money.

"Are you new here?" Sydney asked, flopping down in her seat. She'd barely taken her eyes off her phone to ask me. But she did pause long enough to take in my long sleeved buttoned-up shirt and braid. She held her phone up toward me, her eyes narrowed in concentration before she relaxed as her fingers flew across the phone. I tugged on the braid, wishing Daddy liked my hair a different way.

"No," I said quietly.

Julien snatched Sydney's phone from her hands and threw it in her backpack. "No cell phones in class." He smiled at me, and it reached all the way up to his deep, brown eyes. Julien was a talker. He laughed and smiled more than anyone I'd ever known. He had a lightning design shaved into the side of his black hair. Another thing Daddy would hate. "And Cora's not new. Pay attention, Syd."

I couldn't believe he knew my name, or that I even existed. Maybe I didn't do as well at staying invisible as I thought.

"Whatever." Sydney slumped in her chair and folded her skinny arms.

The last one in our group was Dalton. His green eyes flickered toward me before his gaze landed on his desk. He wasn't much of a talker, either. His shoulder length brown hair had a wave to it and almost never looked brushed. A lot of the times it would cover his eyes, but he never seemed to care about that.

Julien stretched out his long legs, kicking over my backpack in the process. "Sorry about that, Cora." He grabbed it and set it upright.

Bending down, I reached for my backpack but stiffened when I noticed my journal inside. I couldn't believe I hadn't seen it before. Or that I'd forgotten I'd placed it in there. I'd have to put it away the second I got home. If anyone knew I had one, I could get in big trouble with Daddy.

I glanced at Julien, but his attention was back on the teacher. I stuffed my journal into the very bottom of my backpack and zipped it closed.

During lunch, I snuck into the back of the library and found a corner on the floor. I made sure I was alone before I got my journal and finished my entry from the night before. For the sketch, I drew Daddy standing in the doorway, his thunderous eyes staring at the empty bed where he'd hoped to find his little girl.

When I finished, I wrote down everything that had happened in fourth period. I'd never risked bringing my journal to school before, but I found it nice to write in it with everything fresh in my mind.

The sound of the bell startled me so bad that my blue gel pen made a long, squiggly line down the page. I shoved my journal into the bottom of my backpack and booked it out of there.

I didn't stop thinking about having my journal with me until I arrived in sixth period. French. I sat next to Jenna. She had large round brown eyes that were always full of excitement. She loved life. So, the opposite of me. If I had the chance to be someone different, I'd want to be like Jenna. She wore bright colors and bold styles that matched her personality. I stared down at my bland shirt and pants. I guess my clothes matched my personality as well.

She'd opted for a lighter look today, with lavender skinny jeans and tennis shoes, and a peasant top. All her eye makeup, multiple earrings, and necklace were light purple as well. She usually chose a color and ran with it.

Her hair was usually braided, but unlike my plain style, she always did creative styles like the waterfall, lace, and feathered braids all throughout her hair. Today she'd made bows with her hair, and it looked amazing.

"Hey," Jenna said as I sat down in my seat. "Do I have anything in my braces?" She spread her lips apart, showing me the wire on her teeth.

"Nope." I set my backpack on the floor next to me but kept my hand wrapped around the top strap so it wouldn't fall over again.

I loved that Jenna never looked at me like my clothes and hair were different. She accepted me for who I was and talked to me like she would anyone else.

She rubbed her top brace with her finger, her many lavender bracelets clinking together at the movement. "Good. Jess Freeman was staring at me last period, so I thought maybe something was in my braces." She ran her tongue across her teeth. "But I guess she was just being her usual weird self."

A guy walked down the aisle between me and Jenna to get to his seat. She watched his back the whole way. When he was in his seat, Jenna leaned over.

"What do you think?" she whispered. "He's like a seven in my book. He's cute and smart, but he's missing a little spark, you know?" Her wide eyes searched mine with so much hope.

I couldn't help but smile. I threw out a number. "Maybe a six." The only guy allowed in my life was Daddy, so I never paid close attention to the ones at school. Daddy told me guys would cause bad feelings to take over my body and the thought terrified me.

She twisted her lips to the side as she stared at the guy. "Maybe. I've heard other students say mean things about him, but he's real sweet once you get to know him. He's just quiet at first." She wiggled her eyebrows at me. "This is *so* going in the journal tonight."

Jenna kept a journal like I did. She wrote in it every night as well. But I had a feeling our entries were nowhere near being the same. While she wrote about cute boys and troubles with braces, I wrote about being locked away and acting perfect so Daddy wouldn't hurt me.

I'd never tell Jenna what was in mine. I had no idea how she'd react. Daddy always said no one would understand our relationship and they would try to tear us apart, which I didn't want. Nothing scared me more than being alone.

"Any plans this weekend?" she asked.

"Nothing exciting," I said. "Chores, homework, and spending time with the family." She must have thought I had the most boring life. My answer was pretty much the same every week.

"I'm going to the movies with a few of my friends. Heather's parents have been fighting, and she desperately needs to get out of the house and have some fun." She twirled a gel pen on her desk. "Not sure what we're going to see yet." She turned to me. "Wanna come?"

Her eyes held an unwavering eagerness that pulled at my heart strings. It suddenly hit me why Daddy didn't want me to have friends. Friends talked and shared everything with each other. They hung out and did fun stuff. Daddy didn't want that for me. He always said that friends would end up breaking my heart, but family would be forever.

"I really wish I could."

She frowned. "Next time, Cora. I'm not taking a no then." Her frown evaporated, and she pointed at a guy two seats over. "What about him?"

Next time I'd have to come up with yet another excuse. Maybe I needed to be less friendly with Jenna. But her personality made it difficult to ignore or be rude to her. Plus, I really liked the idea of having her as an actual friend. Even though I'd seen girls fight with their friends at school, I didn't think Jenna capable of treating me like that.

As soon as the bell rang to end class, I hurried out and rushed to the van so Jenna wouldn't try to talk to me again. I couldn't risk Daddy catching us chatting like we were friends.

After Daddy dropped me off at home, I waited patiently in my room until he locked the outside of my bedroom door. He always picked me up, took me home, and then went out on another appointment.

With a sigh, I took in my overly pink room. Daddy had decorated it when I first came home. I was six at the time. Any time I asked if we could update the room, he would get that storm cloud look in his blue-gray eyes. So, for the past nine years, it remained the same. Down to the pink dollhouse in the corner and the pink fuzzy shade perched atop a dress-shaped lamp.

Staying close to the edge, I watched out the window, waiting for Daddy's blue van to leave the driveway. Once he was out of sight, I counted to thirty to make sure he wouldn't come back. Then I undid the top button of my shirt and flipped my braid to the back. I kept my sleeves down since I wasn't as warm as usual.

"Why do you do that every day?" Noah asked. "Watch and wait?"

I turned my attention to him. He was on the bed in his usual spot, leaning against two pink pillows in the shape of flowers. He looked so comfortable and relaxed.

"Just making sure he's really gone." The tension fluttered away when I had peaceful time to myself. No peers, no Daddy. Just me, Noah, and our wild imaginations. Well, Noah didn't have much of an imagination. In fact, neither did I. But we were free to be ourselves.

Grabbing my backpack from the floor, I smiled at Noah and then set my bag on the bed. "What should we do today, Noah? After I finish my homework, of course."

I zipped open my backpack.

"A game of cards, perhaps?" he suggested. Cards were a huge hit at our house. They were fun, easy, and cheap. Playing with Noah gave me chances to win for once.

"We did that yesterday," I said, rifling through my backpack. I felt the bottom of my bag, but nothing was there. Confused, I dumped everything out onto my bed. I shuffled through the binders and textbooks, searching frantically.

Fear knocked into me so hard it almost sent me to the ground.

My journal was gone.

CHAPTER 3

*L*etting out a long breath, I slammed my dresser drawer closed, rattling the ballerina figurines on top. "Who would do this?"

Every inch of my room had been searched. The rational part of me knew that it had to have gone missing at school, but the irrational part hoped that maybe it had fallen out of my backpack when I came home.

"Oh, Pandora-Cora." Noah sighed. "Maybe you misplaced it."

I glared at him. "I've searched everywhere. It's gone." Panic bubbled up inside. Losing it meant exposing my secret. If anyone found out . . . I smashed the panic down, squishing out the fire before it started. It could destroy everything in a matter of seconds.

Glancing at my backpack on my bed, I noticed Husky judging me with his huge eyes. I scowled, warning him not to get involved in the conversation. Thankfully, Husky was the silent type. I couldn't handle them both grilling me at once.

"I told you to never bring your journal to school," Noah said in a sing-song voice.

"I know!" Closing my eyes, I took slow, deep breaths. I couldn't lose control. "It was an accident."

"An accident." Noah grunted. "That shouldn't be considered an accident. It's just a journal. Is this really how you want to live the rest of your life?"

Running my fingers over my braid, I tugged on it and focused on my breathing. The life Daddy had built for me was the only way I knew *how* to live.

"Maybe it's time you made a friend," he said, his tone saturated with sarcasm to the point it practically oozed from his cotton.

My gaze snapped to his blue sparkly eyes. "You know I can't have friends. They'll ask questions and want to come over." I glanced at my white dresser with pink flower knobs. Each drawer had been labeled with a drawing of what went inside – socks, shirts, pants, or pajamas. The underwear drawer had been left blank.

Someone being in my room would definitely reveal a flaw in me.

"Just a thought," he said, his tone telling me to not be so touchy. "Now, what are you going to do about your missing journal?"

I sat cross-legged on the bed and closed the canopy curtain, the *swish* a comforting sound. Warmth and security embraced me, and I hugged it close. I breathed in my room, letting the smell of old books, lilac, and paper calm my soul.

"For starters, I need to find out who took it. Then I can decide what to do from there." Since I'd had it during lunch, it had to have been lost between fifth period and the end of the day. It all depended on who knew I had a journal. One that was worth taking.

"Maybe it just fell out. Is your name in it? No one will know it was yours."

"I wrote my name in the front and back." My name

shouldn't have been in the journals. But if I had to remain under Daddy's care until my last breath, I wanted someone out there to know my story. Know that I had once existed.

"Let's just hope they see your name, turn it in, and don't read it."

Taking him into my arms, I held on tight. I pushed my face into the back of his head, and then pulled back when I got a good whiff of sweat. It was thanks to me. My sleep was rarely peaceful, and I woke up most mornings covered in sweat. "Smells like you need another bath."

"Yay!" His tone was beyond sarcastic. "Another dousing of air freshener. What will it be this time? Rain? Lilacs? Oh, is there a rustic smell we could try? Wood or something?"

I ruffled the fur on his head and then hugged him.

"Let's say someone finds the journal," I said, getting the conversation back on track. "They could turn it in to the front office. Someone in administration could read it. Or they could call the house to let me know they found it. Daddy would know about it then. There's no positive outcome here. I need to be prepared for the worst."

I'd never been so careless and reckless in my life.

"Can you ease up on the strangle hold?" Noah rasped. "I can barely breathe."

I loosened my grip around him, rolling my eyes in the process.

The door swung open. "What are you doing, angel?"

Daddy stood in the doorway, his arms folded and his back perfectly straight. He held his chin up in a way that let him command the room like he always did. It made him appear larger than he really was. It also took away the attention from his dirty coveralls.

I'd been so lost in thought, I hadn't heard him unlock the latch on my door. I held Noah in front of my chest with one hand and used the other to quickly fasten the top button of my shirt. I flicked my braid back up front. I'd never been so happy about leaving my sleeves down.

"You're home early," I said in the sweetest voice I could muster.

Noah grunted. "Oh, goody."

I placed my hand over his mouth, though it wouldn't stop his thoughts. But maybe it would warn him to stop talking so he wouldn't distract me.

Daddy opened the canopy, the *swish* slashing through my comfort. "My last appointment cancelled. I thought we could go out to dinner tonight."

My eyes widened, and I tried to hold back the smile that wanted to explode across my face. We rarely went out to dinner. We rarely went anywhere. "Can we go to the pizza place downtown?" I'd heard students raving about it at school.

A dark mist clouded Daddy's eyes. "Cora, is that the appropriate response to my invitation?"

The thought of my journal being stolen, our secret being revealed, had left me unfocused. I quickly stood and hugged him, letting Noah fall to the floor. Noah grunted when he landed on the carpet. If Daddy hadn't been in the room, I would have apologized.

Daddy's scent attacked me. Sweat and grease once again, but not as bad as the day before.

"I'm sorry, Daddy. I got overly excited. If you think going out would be a good idea, then I would love to accompany you wherever you'd like to go."

He ran his hand down my braid. "That's my good girl." He kissed the top of my head, lingering a second longer than usual. "Pizza does sound good, though."

A smile spread across my face. "Thanks, Daddy!"

He laughed, the corners of his eyes crinkling. "Anything to see that beautiful smile of yours. Be in the entryway in twenty minutes. Make sure you use the bathroom before we go." He held up a finger. "And bring a light jacket with you. There's a small chill in the air."

My long sleeve shirt should have been enough, but I would never argue that with him. I waited for Daddy to disappear down the hall. Picking up Noah from the floor, I gave him a quick peck on his trunk and set him back on the bed. "We'll continue this conversation later."

"Looking forward to it," Noah said. "Just don't keep me up all night. I hate pillow talk."

~

*D*addy drove away from our house and toward downtown.

I loved to stare out the window and watch the homes pass by, pretending like I knew who lived inside. In my head, they were all happy and perfect families with two parents, a couple kids, a dog, cat, and maybe even a hamster.

It was a nice suburban area, with all the brick homes blending well together. I wished I could've gone on walks after school while Daddy was at work so I could smell the crabapple trees and geraniums planted in people's yards. Daddy left our yard as clean and plain as possible. Would he ever let me plant flowers outside? What would the dirt feel like in my hands?

"How was your day?" Daddy asked. He'd turned off the radio so we could have 'Cora time' as he called it. The questions rarely changed.

"It was great," I said, moving my attention to him. If Daddy found out about my lost journal, or that I even had a journal, I'd be in timeout for weeks. Maybe months. I couldn't afford to miss that much school. Plus, it was cold in the basement.

We turned onto the main road leading toward the shopping areas. The lanes expanded and Daddy stayed in the right lane and drove slowly, both hands gripped tightly around the wheel. He always said the world would still be there when we arrived, so there was no need to rush.

"How are your classes going?"

"Good. I really like my teachers." My answers rarely changed, either.

He honked at a car that flew past us. "They need to slow down." He chanced a glance in my direction. He rarely took his eyes off the road. "You're keeping your grades up, I hope."

"Of course, Daddy. Still have mostly straight A's." With almost all my spare time being spent locked up in my room, I had nothing else to do except homework and reading. Well, and hang out with Noah. But he usually helped me study.

"That's my girl," he said as he pulled in front of the pizza place. He rolled down the window, placed his palm on the outside of the door, and stuck his head out, making sure he was perfectly between the lines. He'd never once had to correct his parking job, yet he always checked.

When my hand slid to the handle, Daddy snapped his fingers. "Wait for me, angel."

I'd hoped he'd grow out of the 'opening the door for me' phase when I started high school. He didn't. I waited for him to come around and open the door for me. He swept out his arm. "A prince always gets the door for the princess."

Pointing out the fact that I'd never have a real prince would cause him to take us back home, so I let it go and smiled sweetly at him. It was his favorite smile of mine. It was also my most acted and forced.

He beat me to the door and held it open. The yummy smell of garlic and pizza washed over me. Daddy casually took a menu from the hostess stand on the way to a table, not making eye contact with anyone. He found a booth near the window so he could still see the van. We were supposed to wait to be seated, but Daddy liked to pick his own spot.

I tried to focus on Daddy, but fear crept back in and paralyzed me. I'd been so stupid by leaving the journal in my backpack. I should have put it back under the mattress as soon as Daddy had left my room. But I'd been too scared to be caught out of bed again.

The waiter strolled up to our table, taking me from my thoughts. He retrieved a pad of paper and pen from the black apron tied around his waist. "Hey – Cora, right?"

My cheeks flared. I balled my hands into fists under the table and hoped Daddy didn't read too much into it. I forced myself to look at the waiter and tried to pinpoint how I knew him. He went to my school. He had his red hair in a fohawk. I licked my lips. "Yes."

His blue eyes almost matched mine. The waiter smiled brightly, revealing his straight teeth. "I sure hope your French is better than mine. I'm barely passing."

It hit me. He sat two rows over in my French class. Even though Jenna loved to talk about boys, the big guy next to me in class blocked my view of the waiter, so he had never made it into our conversations.

"She's fluent." Daddy had his jaw clenched tight.

"Really?" The waiter gently tapped my arm sending a jolt of energy through me. "Why are you in the class then?"

"A language class is required," I said quietly. I kept my hands balled into fists so I wouldn't rub my arm where he'd touched me. The only guy who'd ever touched me was Daddy. What would it have felt like if my sleeves were rolled up and he'd touched my skin? "I know Spanish and German as well."

Black clouds soared into Daddy's eyes, and I squirmed in my seat. He didn't like anyone touching me. "Aren't you a little young to be working?"

23

The waiter chuckled, clearly not noticing Daddy's anger. "I've been working here for years. Parents own the place. I actually turned sixteen at the beginning of the year." He wiped his hand on his apron and held it out to Daddy. "I'm Brendon."

I didn't think Daddy would shake his hand, but he surprised me by taking Brendon's hand and giving it a firm shake. The image burned in my mind. The two of them, locking eyes, Daddy trying to peer deep into Brendon's soul, and Brendon finally registering that maybe Daddy wasn't very nice. Even though my journal was gone, I'd have to sketch the moment later that night. Otherwise it would stalk my dreams.

When Brendon pulled his hand away, he shook it out. Daddy had probably held it real tight.

"I'm Cora's father, Mr. Snow."

"Nice to meet you, sir." Brendon flexed his hand. "What can I get for you tonight? If I could offer a suggestion . . ."

"No." Daddy folded the menu. "We'll take a large pizza, half pepperoni, half pepperoni and mushrooms."

Brendon's eyes flashed to mine as he took the menu from Daddy's hands. He stuffed the menu under his arm and took a step back, creating a distance between us, and scribbled down our order. "Anything to drink?"

Daddy relaxed now that Brendon was farther away from me.

I needed a drink badly since the whole interaction had left my mouth dry. "Is it okay if I get water?"

My eyes were on Daddy, but Brendon answered. "Sure. Would you like a lemon?"

I hated all things sour. They made my insides churn. I slowly shook my head, my focus sliding to the table. "No, thank you."

Daddy had somewhat composed himself. "I'll have a beer. Anything on tap."

"I'm going to have to see an I.D." Brendon's wide eyes said he regretted his words as soon as they left his mouth. "I mean, it's just policy and . . ."

Daddy surprised me again by smiling and pulling out his wallet. "I'm glad you take your job seriously, Brendon." Something in the way Daddy said his name made me flinch. He flashed him his driver's license. "That's an important skill to have. Remember that."

"Yes, sir." Brendon fumbled to put his pad and pen back in his apron pocket before he hurried away, tripping a little over his feet.

Daddy's smile disappeared, and his hand landed on my knee under the table. He squeezed my kneecap with his thumb and pointer finger. "How well do you know him?"

It took everything in me not to flinch. Daddy always strongly grasped my knee when he wanted the truth from me. "Not well. We have French together. That's it."

"Do you talk in class?"

"No, Daddy. This is the first time I've ever spoken to him, I swear." He squeezed harder, and I held in a cry. He hated that word. "I promise. I meant to say, I promise."

"Are you going to talk to him at school?" The storm in his eyes hadn't calmed.

I shook my head. "No, Daddy. I promise."

He released my knee. "That's my good girl."

Brendon cautiously approached the table, setting down an ice water in front of me. He placed a straw next to the cup. "The bartender will be bringing your beer, Mr. Snow. I'm not allowed to handle alcohol."

Daddy's smile was back. "Your parents run a fine establishment here, young man."

A smile slowly landed on Brendon's lips. "I'll be sure to tell them that." He left again, not daring to look my way.

If Daddy was this mad about a guy from my school knowing my name, I needed to find my journal soon, or I'd end up with more than a sore kneecap. Daddy couldn't find out what I had done.

CHAPTER 4

I hardly slept. Fear and shame attacked my dreams all through the night, practically strangling me. Drawing the encounter of Brendon and Daddy hadn't shook the image from my mind like I'd hoped. Brendon had been killed in a few of my dreams, with Daddy making me watch the entire ordeal.

My dreams always ended with everyone finding out our secret and Daddy being thrown in jail, leaving me all alone in the cold world. A couple dreams, though, left me six feet under – a fate I dreaded.

When Daddy dropped me off at school in the morning, I had to do my best to keep my eyes open and alert. He had his hand on the steering wheel, gripping a little too tight. "Remember all our rules."

I ran my fingers over Husky's soft fur. "Of course, Daddy."

He kissed my forehead, and my fist engulfed Husky. "Have a great day."

"You, too." The anxiety from my missing journal ate away at me. My shaking hands swung my backpack over my shoulder, smacking the bag into Daddy's coffee. It fell from the cup holder, smashing onto the floor of the van, the black liquid creating a river of deceit.

His whole body tightened in anger. "Watch what you're doing." He picked up the cup and shook out his hand, grimacing in pain. He pointed to the glove compartment. "Napkins. Now."

I scanned Husky, making sure he hadn't been caught in the crossfire. "What?"

His hand wrapped tightly around my arm. "Napkins."

I needed to remain calm. Nerves got me in trouble. With a deep breath, I opened the compartment, pulled out some napkins he kept stacked neatly in the corner, and placed them over the stream of coffee going under Daddy's seat. "I apologize, Daddy. It was terribly foolish of me to be so clumsy."

A car behind the van honked, wanting us to get out of the way. I kept my focus on Daddy. He acted like he hadn't heard a thing. He took some napkins from me and wiped off his hands, making sure to get every crevice. Each movement was deliberate and controlled. His deep breaths slowed until the anger had been washed from his face. He folded the napkins into fourths and then placed them in the trash bag that hung from the dashboard. "It's okay, angel. We all have these moments. Please be more careful in the future."

"I will, Daddy. I promise."

I waited for him to smile, to let me know everything was okay. If I hurried out, he'd know I was nervous about something. So, I smiled patiently until his eyes locked with mine and the storms retreated.

"Get to class," he said. "We wouldn't want you to be late."

With another smile, I got out of the van like our secret remained safely locked away. Daddy couldn't be suspicious. Most of my life had been spent acting, so it was easier than I thought.

In first and second period, I glanced around the room. There weren't any students who looked like they knew my secret or had read my journal. They all ignored me as usual.

During break, I walked over to the library. I checked the spot where I'd been the day before, all the shelves and even underneath them, but my journal was nowhere to be seen. I hated what I had to do next, but it needed to be done. Every possibility needed to be ruled out.

Licking my lips, I slowly approached the counter where the librarian sat comfortably in her chair, reading a travel book on perfect destination spots for single ladies.

Before I could talk myself out of it, I cleared my throat. "Excuse me."

The librarian set down her book, rested her reading glasses in her gray, curly hair, and joined me at the counter. Her soft eyes sent a small wave of calm through me. "Yes, dear?"

I clasped my hands on top of the counter, fiddling with my fingers. "Did someone happen to find a book in here yesterday?"

Her smile reached all the way up to her eyes. "Why, sweetie, we have lots of books in here."

I silently scolded myself for the stupid question. "You know, a book kind of like a journal."

"*Like* a journal, or an actual journal?" The laughter behind her eyes distracted from the wrinkles on her face.

"An actual journal."

She patted my hand, the cold surprising. "Sorry, dear, but nothing has been turned in. If you'd like, I could take down your name, and I can send word if we find it."

That was the last thing I wanted. "That's okay. It's probably at home. Thanks for your help." I hurried away before she could ask any other questions, and then hid behind a bookshelf so I could collect myself.

The library was my favorite place at school. I loved the peace and quiet, and the smell of books. In my solitude, I read every book Daddy brought home for me. All the characters were my friends. Sometimes I'd stand in front of a row of books at the library and breathe in the scent. It calmed my nerves and wrapped a blanket of security around me, reminding me of my bedroom.

"Hey, did you see Cora walk in here?" Brendon's smooth voice came from around the corner. He said my name so different than Daddy did. It didn't have an edge attached to it.

"Who?" It was a girl's voice I didn't recognize.

As quietly as I could, I tiptoed down the aisle and peered around the corner. Brendon stood there with his hands stuffed in his jeans' pockets. He wore a T-shirt that appeared to have some logo, but I wasn't familiar with it. Daddy didn't like me listening to music or watching TV.

"Cora," Brendon said to the girl. "She's a little shorter than me, hair is always in a braid, blue eyes, beautiful smile."

Warmth spread through my body causing sweat to form on my palms. He thought I had a beautiful smile?

The girl shrugged. "Didn't see anyone like that."

Brendon thanked her and then walked in my direction. I quickly went down the aisle and hid behind a book cart. I had hoped Daddy had scared him off the night before. We couldn't talk or become friends. Daddy wouldn't allow it.

I stayed in my position until the bell rang to go to class. Keeping my eyes on my watch, I waited until I had one minute before the tardy bell would ring and then bolted out of the library.

My lab partner's eyes didn't waver from me when I arrived in Earth Science. The bell rang the second I sat down.

"Why do you look so out of breath?" Kendra asked. She

had her pink hair in a messy ponytail. Daddy would never allow me to dye my hair – not that I wanted to. Not really.

My fingers drummed along my backpack that sat in my lap. We never talked about anything other than our class assignments. Why was she suddenly curious about me?

"Hello?" Kendra waved her hand in front of my face, all her rings clinking together. Her blue nail polish had started to chip.

I focused on Husky. "I ran so I wouldn't be late."

She gave a little huff. "You know, it wouldn't kill you to be late to class."

No. But then I'd be splattered on my teacher's radar, and that couldn't happen.

"What is that you're playing with?" She reached over and almost touched Husky.

I snapped him away and lowered my backpack to the ground, far away from her. "Nothing."

She held up her hand. "Wow. It was just a question. No need to be all testy. Are you on your period are something?"

Heat climbed up my neck to my cheeks. Daddy said I couldn't talk about my body or any of its functions with anyone other than him.

The teacher passed out a quiz, so I pulled out a pencil and ignored Kendra. All through the test, I couldn't help but wonder if she had taken my journal. She'd never shown any interest in me and suddenly – the day after my journal disappeared – she started asking questions. Personal ones. Maybe it was just a coincidence, but I added it to my list of possibilities.

When I arrived in fourth period, Julien was already in his seat at our table. He tapped my arm. Why were guys touching me all of a sudden? "You look flushed. Rough day?"

I nodded.

He had his shirt buttoned all the way to the top like me,

but it was stylish on him and suited his persona. His cologne wafted toward me. I had no idea what kind it was, but it always reminded me of one of Daddy's clients, an ex-football player who constantly wanted his piano tuned and would give me a stick of gum every time I went with Daddy to his appointment.

Julien had knocked over my backpack the day before when we started our assignment, but he put it back up right away and apologized. My eyes had never left my backpack during the scuffle, so I wasn't sure if Julien saw the journal or not. If he had, why would he want it?

"So, I forgot to do my portion last night." Sydney plopped down in her seat on the other side of me. Her fingers flew across her phone, completely unaware of what was happening around her. No way she knew I had a journal or would be interested in reading it.

"No surprise there," Dalton said, sitting down. Since he rarely spoke or made eye contact with anyone in class, he didn't strike me as the type who would steal something from my backpack. Or maybe it was all an act.

Sydney continued to text with one hand while twirling her long hair with her other. "I hate going to the library. It's full of weird people and the homeless."

Julien laughed. "Have you even been inside a library before?"

"They're nice," I said. "For people who know how to read." It had left my mouth before I could think it through.

"Oh!" Julien held up his hand for me to high-five. "Nice one!"

Daddy didn't like me touching anyone, especially boys. But he wasn't there to stop me, and Julien was just being nice. So, I slapped his hand.

He shook it out. "Not so hard, Cora."

"Sorry." I straightened my cuffs. "First time."

Sydney stopped texting long enough to look up at me. "That was the first time you've high-fived someone?" Her twisted hair stayed frozen in the air.

They couldn't know I was truly different from most teenagers. I smiled at her. "Yeah, seeing as it went out of style in the nineties." Thank goodness I read the newspaper that Daddy had delivered to our front porch every day. I could keep up with what was happening in the world. At least in the sections Daddy allowed me to read.

"She's on fire today!" Julien shoved me playfully on the arm. For a split second, I forgot about my worries.

Then Dalton spoke up. "How have you never high-fived someone?" He brushed some of his shaggy hair out of his face.

My smile faded from my lips. I reached down for Husky and stroked him under the table, willing myself to stay calm and answer rationally. "Why do you care?"

"It's just weird." Dalton twirled his pen around his fingers, his intense glare on me.

"Dalt, you're the president of the weirdos," Julien said. "You shouldn't be talking."

The pen dropped from Dalton's hand, and he flushed. "Whatever."

The rest of class, Dalton kept glancing over at me. He normally kept to himself with his eyes unfocused on his desk. Had he taken my journal? Had he read any of it? If he knew the truth, wouldn't he have said something by now? But he probably couldn't have read the entire journal that fast.

Everyone looked suspicious to me.

During P.E., I faked a sickness and told the gym teacher I needed to go to the nurse's office. Instead, I stayed in the locker room, out of sight, but still in visual range of my locker. Maybe the person who had stolen it would put it back. Or maybe I'd find someone wandering around, breaking into other people's lockers.

None of that happened.

That left only one more class. The one with Jenna and Brendon.

CHAPTER 5

A pink envelope sat on my desk. *Cora* was scrolled in blue glitter ink on the outside. I didn't recognize the handwriting. With a thud, my backpack dropped to the ground next to my desk. My hands trembled toward the envelope, afraid to open it. The paper in my journal had been pink. Daddy bought me a bunch of glitter gel pens so I could color for him, and I had been using the blue one in my current journal.

Someone had read it. Someone knew my secret. What was inside the envelope? A page torn from the journal? A note saying the truth had been revealed and Daddy would be locked away in prison?

Breathing became hard. Dizziness overcame my body, and I swayed where I stood.

"Cora, are you okay?" Jenna's voice sounded beside me. My gaze went to her. "You look like you're about to pass out. Maybe you should sit down."

I lowered myself into my seat and gripped the sides of my desk. I couldn't tear my eyes away from the envelope. Did I dare open it now? Or wait until I was alone in my room?

"It's too much, isn't it?" Jenna sighed and sat down in her seat. "I was going for fun, but maybe it's too little-girl-cute."

"What?" I turned my attention to Jenna.

She pointed to the envelope, her eyes dancing. "I just love glitter. It's a weird obsession, I know." She leaned toward me and whispered. "I even use glitter pens to write in my journal."

I took the envelope into my quivering hands. "This is from you?" Jenna had taken my journal? I didn't want to believe it. She knew how private they were.

Her glossy lips parted in a smile, revealing her braces. "Yep. Open it!"

With my hands shaking, I tore open the envelope with too much force and sliced my finger. Blood pooled on my finger tip.

"Looks like you could use a Band-Aid." Brendon's voice came from the right of me. I glanced up to see him pull one out of his pocket and hand it to me.

"You keep Band-Aid's in your pocket?" Jenna asked. She did her best to make sure her braces didn't show as she talked. She was obsessed with keeping her braces hidden and minimal. Well, only from boys. I didn't understand why.

"Professional hazard." He held up his hand, showing off two bandaged fingers. "I cut myself a lot at work folding pizza boxes."

I stared at his shirt. It had two red circles and a star in the middle.

He glanced down at it. "Fan of the Cap?"

"What?" I asked, my eyebrows furrowed in confusion.

"Captain America." He pointed to his shirt. "He's my favorite of all the Marvel gang." He smirked, a slight smolder in his eyes. "Well, I love Black Widow as well."

I had no idea what he was talking about, so I turned my

attention to the Band-Aid. My hands wouldn't stay still long enough for me to open the packaging on the bandage.

"Uh, why don't I get that for you?" Brendon took the bandage from my hand, his fingers grazing mine. Heat erupted on the spot he'd touched, and I had to hold in a shiver. So that was what it felt like to have his skin touch mine. It was . . . nice.

Jenna snatched the envelope from my hand, the light reflecting off her perfectly manicured nails. The neon pink matched with her wardrobe for the day: pink skinny jeans and tennis shoes, a green argyle top, and dangly pink earrings. She had so much jewelry and layers with her clothing that she could switch it up every day and it looked like a brand new outfit. I just alternated between my five button-down shirts and three pairs of pants. Daddy said I didn't need more than that.

"Since you're obviously in a weird mood, I'll show you." She held up the card that had been inside the envelope. "I'm having a party for my sixteenth birthday!" She rolled her eyes. "Finally. I swear I'm the only fifteen-year-old left in the tenth grade."

I wanted to let her know I was still fifteen as well, but I couldn't speak. A party invitation? That's what it was? My nerves subsided, but then started back up again. I'd never been invited to a party before. I shouldn't have gotten so close to Jenna. We couldn't be friends.

Brendon's warm hand wrapped around mine and he placed the bandage over my cut finger. "All better."

My hand tingled from his touch, and suddenly it was hard to breathe again. I gripped onto my desk for additional support.

Jenna slid the card onto my desk. "Keep next Friday open. It's going to be awesome! Music, movies, goodies, and the best part." She pointed to the bottom of the invite. "My parents are letting me do a slumber party! I had to beg and beg and could only invite five friends, but it was worth it."

Brendon snatched the invite from my desk. "Wow, Jenna. I didn't think I'd make it in the top five of your friends, but alright. I'm game."

Jenna reached over me and yanked back the invite. "Very funny, Brendon. No boys allowed." She wiggled her eyebrows at me. "But we can talk about them."

"Just make sure I'm one of them." Brendon winked at me, and my neck and cheeks ignited. The smile left his face. "It was just a joke, Cora. I'm not that bad, am I?"

"I've seen better," Jenna said. She could only keep a straight face for a few seconds before she busted out laughing, covering her mouth with her hand.

Brendon threw the empty bandage packaging at Jenna's head. "You dig me." He knelt next to me. "You doing okay? You're looking real pale."

Words wouldn't form. My mouth went dry. I wrapped my hands tightly around my braid hanging over my right shoulder.

"Listen, if this is about last night," he said, "I didn't mean to get you in trouble with your dad."

Daddy wouldn't want me talking to Brendon, but he'd also want me to make sure no one suspected Daddy's mean side. I worked moisture back into my mouth. "You didn't get me in trouble."

Brendon's eyes landed on my legs. I tensed, realizing he was staring at my knee. Had he noticed Daddy squeeze my knee under the table? Brendon opened his mouth to say something, but the teacher told him to sit down so we could start class.

"You can come, right?" Jenna whispered.

There was no way Daddy would let me. I shook my head and kept my voice low. "I'm sorry, Jenna, but I'll be out of town next weekend. Visiting family." It was the first lie that came to my mind. I didn't have any family aside from Daddy.

Jenna's whole happy demeanor drifted away, replaced by a pout. "What horrible timing." She tapped her lips. "Maybe I can change the date. We can do it the weekend after that."

I quickly shook my head. "Don't change your birthday party for me. That's silly. Look on the bright side. Now you have an open spot and can invite Brendon."

A smile worked its way back onto Jenna. "My parents would kill me." She leaned back so she could look over at Brendon. "He is pretty cute. I can't believe we haven't talked about him before. What do you think? A six? Seven? If I knew his personality better, I could narrow down the number."

I couldn't think anything. No friends. No boys. No fun. That was my life. But Jenna looked at me so expectantly. She'd be sad if I disagreed with her. I'd already let her down once and in a big way. Really, Brendon was cute. Hot even. Probably a ten in my book. If I had been allowed to have a book. "He has nice eyes."

"They almost match yours," Jenna said.

A pang of guilt and excitement struck me. Daddy had set very specific ground rules in allowing me to finally go to public school starting in tenth grade. I'd tried to keep to myself and make no friends. But then I met Jenna. She had such a loving, bubbly personality. She was a firm believer in getting to know someone before making judgments. She saw the good in people even when others couldn't.

I never knew it could be so nice to have a friend. Someone to confide in and laugh with. I almost felt normal. Having her as a friend would be dangerous. Daddy would be livid if he found out. He'd lock me up in the basement and take me out of school.

I thought Jenna and I could just be friends at school. I

didn't think about the fact that she might invite me to her birthday party. She said she could only invite five friends and I was one of them. Something rippled inside me. I didn't know what it was or how to describe it. I'd never experienced it before.

Things had shifted. If I intended to keep my secret hidden, I needed to do a few things. One, find out who took my journal. Two, learn what they planned to do with it and how I could get them to stay quiet. Three, not make anyone suspicious that something was wrong. Brendon already asked too many questions. If I could pretend I was Daddy's little girl at home, talk how he wanted, act how he wanted, then I could act at school.

It would take breaking a lot of rules, but I had to work my way into every suspect's life if I wanted to uncover the truth of the theft.

"Cora?"

I shook out of my trance and turned my attention to the teacher.

She smiled at me. "You're wanted in the front office."

My insides coiled into a tight ball. Had someone found my journal?

CHAPTER 6

I'd never been called to the front office. I'd never been on the school's radar. So, it couldn't be good.

With one hand tightly wrapped around the strap of my backpack, I strode in the door, doing my best to keep calm. I took long, steady breaths – something I did whenever Daddy was mad at me. My fingers brushed along Husky, his fur soothing my soul.

It was quiet in the front office. No one sat behind the desk, so I didn't know what to do. There wasn't a bell on the counter, or anything to signal I was there. What did students usually do? Panic tried to rise, but I pushed it down before it could take over.

A man stepped out of a back office. He was tall and wide, with jet black hair and dark brown eyes. Instinctively, I took a step back. Intimidating was an understatement when it came to the man now before me.

"Cora Snow?" he asked in a low, gruff voice. It didn't help the wariness that surrounded me.

"Yes," I managed to get out. My eyes continued to scan the front office, searching for solace, but no one was in sight.

The man held out his large hand. "Mr. Mendoza. I'm the new guidance counselor here."

Guidance counselor? I had no idea what he'd want with me. I shook his hand. His grip was strong and firm. Confident. Opposed to my weak, soft handshake.

"Why don't we speak in my office?" Mr. Mendoza turned and went into his office, expecting me to follow.

A part of me wanted to bolt. I had no idea what he wanted, but it could lead to problems. It meant someone poking into my personal life. I'd never met with a guidance counselor, but he wasn't what I'd expected. I assumed the counselor would be personable; someone who could put students at ease. The man waiting for me to enter his private office projected the complete opposite.

I couldn't run, though. Running raised suspicion. With a deep breath and a silent prayer, I stepped into the room.

"Close the door, please," Mr. Mendoza said from his chair. He adjusted his tie that didn't seem natural around his neck.

I did as asked and then sat down in the chair on the other side of the desk. I held my backpack against my chest and wrapped my hand around Husky. It would keep me from yanking on my braid.

Aside from the school provided clock, Mr. Mendoza had nothing hanging up in his office. Only a computer, a pad of paper, and a pen were on the desk. He had said he was new. Maybe he hadn't had time to decorate. Or maybe guidance counselors didn't hang up personal things. I thought there'd at least be a filing cabinet for student records.

What I *did* know? Mr. Mendoza, sitting uncomfortably in the chair across from me, looked completely out of place. A tiny spark of a connection ignited inside me. I could relate.

"How do you like high school?" He fiddled with the handles underneath his seat until he lifted higher in the air, adding to his larger than life persona.

"It's great," I said. A panic attack wanted to barge in and intrude on our meeting, but I held on tightly to Husky and the fact that Mr. Mendoza was, like me, out of his element. I wondered what had happened in his life to land him in the front seat of a guidance counselor's office.

He leaned forward and stared at his computer screen with squinty eyes. "You didn't start public school until this year."

So all the student files were electronic, which made sense. I shook my head. "No, sir. I did home school until then." The clock on the wall ticked with every second that passed. My fingers drummed along Husky, following the beat.

"Who taught you?" Mr. Mendoza asked. "Your mom? Dad?"

"My dad." It was partly true. He'd bought all the books and given them to me. I mostly taught myself. But Daddy would help me when I had questions.

Tick, tick, tick.

He sat back in his chair. "Does your mom work?"

"I don't know my mom." Another truth. Being as honest as I could without divulging the entire story was always the best option. "It's just me and dad."

Tick, tick, tick.

"So, he works during the day?" He yanked at his collar. He definitely didn't wear ties often.

"Yes," I said.

Tick.

"You were by yourself during the day, then?" He furrowed his eyebrows, the sternness radiating from him unsettling.

Was that bad? Wrong? Concern sat in his eyes, so I needed to be careful how I answered. "He's a repairman. He'd come home in-between appointments. He'd take me along with him when I was younger."

Tick, tick, tick, tick, tick, tick, tick.

Too many seconds were passing by. Had I answered wrong?

He scratched his goatee. He calmed, but wasn't completely satisfied. He glanced back at the screen. "You're getting good grades. Almost perfect. So whatever your dad did, it went well."

I smiled, a small breath of relief escaping my lips. "Yes, Daddy is very smart. He taught me all he knows and helped me learn more."

Mr. Mendoza had frowned when I used the word Daddy. I'd recently learned that children stopped saying Daddy when they grew out of the toddler phase. But I'd called him that since he'd first brought me home. It was what he had wanted. What he still wanted.

Tick, tick, tick, tick, tick.

"I found something interesting as I was scrolling through student records," he said. *Tick, tick.* The dark look in his eyes made me squirm in fear. "There seems to be no trace of you before you started public school. No birth records. You have no doctor or dentist records. Nothing that marked your existence. It's like you magically appeared this year."

The clock's ticks faded away into the background, replaced by a dull thud in my ears. Mr. Mendoza stared at me, waiting for a response. I didn't have one. Telling him the complete truth was out of the question. But how did I explain it all? Daddy had said he'd take care of it. That I'd be safe in public school and wouldn't raise any flags.

The flags were up in full force, viciously whipping in the wind.

"I really need to get back to class," I finally said, my hand tight around Husky.

"Your teacher won't mind." He pulled at his collar again, and I instinctively did the same with mine. "You have nothing to tell me?"

Heat ignited in my ears as they throbbed with my heart-beat. I wanted to unfasten my top button and let some air circulate underneath.

"Or maybe you can't tell me?" he offered.

I shook my head. Lies were a trap. They created a web, small lies all tangled together, weaving in and out, until the web grew. If one truth slithered in and smacked against the web, every lie would scatter away, broken and messy.

I would not let that happen.

"I'm well taken care of, Mr. Mendoza. Daddy . . . Dad, he looks after me. Gives me everything I need and makes sure I get good grades. I'm lucky to have him for a father. Not every parent cares like he does. He's had to do it all on his own. No help." My hands shook, but not in fear – in intensity. Because I meant every word.

Daddy could be rough and overpowering, but everything he did was out of love. He just wanted the best for me.

"That's good," Mr. Mendoza said.

Every muscle in me relaxed, the tension falling away. I released Husky from my iron grip and smoothed out his fur. The throb in my ears slowly subsided.

"While you have excellent grades," he said, "you should also sign up for some extracurricular activities. They look great on college applications."

The tension flooded back. Afraid of destroying Husky, I gripped the bottom of the chair tightly instead. "I don't have time."

"What keeps you so busy?" Mr. Mendoza asked.

Tick, tick, tick.

"Getting good grades doesn't come easy for me, sir. I spend a lot of my time studying. The rest of my time is spent with family." Daddy being my only family.

He made a note on the pad of paper in front of him. "Well,

I still think you should investigate it. Joining one club won't take too much of your time."

"I'll think about it." *No.* There. I thought about it.

"I'd like to keep seeing you, Cora. The transition from homeschool to public school can be overwhelming." He loosened his tie. "I never could stand these things, but the principal insists I wear them. Thinks they're professional. I think they make me look stiff and unrelatable. Don't you think?"

I shrugged, trying to hide my agreement. "I've never thought about it before."

A small, throaty laugh escaped his mouth. "I'm sure you haven't." He tapped his fingers on the pad of paper. "How are you fitting in here?"

"Fine. I've made a couple friends in my classes." Sort of true. And if somehow Mr. Mendoza told Daddy I said that, I'd just tell Daddy it was to make Mr. Mendoza happy. Which was true.

Tick, tick.

"Do you hang out with these friends outside of school?"

Tick, tick, tick, tick.

I had no idea if these were typical questions from a guidance counselor. I'd never met with one before. "Like I said, I'm busy."

He scribbled something on his pad. "Right. Well, let's plan to meet next week. If that's okay with you."

It wasn't. Mr. Mendoza digging into my life was a bad thing. Terrible. I couldn't have him finding out the truth. Uncovering my secret. Daddy's secret.

"Okay." If I said no, it would only make him suspicious. I was very good at bending the truth. Forcing a smile. I'd stick to that and hopefully appease Mr. Mendoza without causing alarm.

"Good." He stood, smoothing out his tie. "It was nice to meet you, Cora. I'll call for you again next week."

"Thanks." I hurried out before he could ask any other questions.

My main worry as I left was why Mr. Mendoza had called me in. Out of all the students in the school, had he really come across my file and decided to search? Or had the person who had my journal tipped him off?

Or, had Mr. Mendoza found the journal himself?

CHAPTER 7

*E*verything sat in its proper spot on the kitchen table. The polished silver gleamed under the light. Both glasses were filled with water, with two ice cubes for me and none for Daddy. He liked his water at room temperature. Easier to digest, he'd say.

I'd made sure to remove the Band-Aid Brendon had placed on my finger from the paper cut. Daddy would be furious if I got hurt at school, and completely livid if he found out Brendon had held my hand while gently bandaging it. My cheeks flushed at the very thought of his skin brushing mine.

I'd chosen my mid-calf, light pink cotton dress and white cardigan for dinner wear that evening. I stared down at the exposed part of my legs, grateful no one could see me. I'd never thought about shaving until I saw girls at my school with no hair on their legs, or even in their armpits. Daddy had never given me the option. My dresses were the only times my legs showed, so I hadn't cared until recently. Thankfully, I wasn't allowed to wear my dresses to school.

We were to dress nice for weekend dinners. It was the

only time Daddy smelled like aftershave instead of sweat, grease, or shampoo. He allowed me to do a fishtail braid on the weekends instead of the usual three-strand braid, so I'd opted for that. It was the fanciest I'd ever get.

The smell of garlic wafted from the kitchen. I'd prepared penne with alfredo sauce, broccoli, Caesar salad, and garlic bread for dinner. I wasn't a fan of alfredo, but it was one of Daddy's favorite meals. On the weekends, he wouldn't lock me in my room if he went on short errands. That way I could cook dinner. He'd installed a silent alarm on the front and sliding glass doors that would alert him if I left the house. Most of the windows had an alarm that would trigger if it opened wide enough for a person to fit through – that way we could still open it to let in a breeze, but I couldn't escape.

Outside, Daddy's van rumbled into the driveway. He'd gone to run an errand at the home improvement store. He wouldn't tell me what he was getting or planning on doing. He never did. It was always a need-to-know basis for him.

I'd cracked open the family room window so I'd be able to hear when he arrived. Rushing to the room, I quickly shut and locked the window before heading back into the kitchen. I removed the foil covering the serving bowl of penne, set a piece of garlic bread on a separate plate next to the glasses, and placed the bowl of broccoli perfectly in-between us.

"Smells delicious, angel," Daddy said from the doorway. He kept the door hinges greased so I'd never know when he was coming or going. The only times I dared open the window to hear his arrival were when I'd be close enough to shut it before he came in the house.

I waited patiently while he went and changed into his dinner attire. My hands stayed clasped in front of me so I wouldn't fiddle with them. To Daddy, fidgeting was a sign of anxiety, which meant you were lying about something.

When his footsteps sounded down the hall, I spoke in the sweetest tone I could muster. "It's all ready."

As I smoothed out my dress, I noticed a small, straight line running down Daddy's knife. Fear wove through my body, almost choking me. I had no idea how it could've gotten scratched. I hand-washed all the dishes and handled them with care.

Daddy came around the corner and smiled at me. He wore a nice, button down shirt that had been perfectly pressed. His tie was a plain green – he didn't like anything flashy. "See, I wasn't gone long, now was I?"

I swallowed, forcing my eyes to stay on Daddy and not wander to the ruined knife. "Nope. Barely noticed you were gone."

"I always miss you when I'm away." His icy hand landed on my cheek. "You mean the world to me, angel. I wish my dad had been as nice to me as I am to you." He kissed me on the forehead, the coldness sending a chill down my spine. "I'm starving. Let's eat."

"There's a message for you on the counter." The words tumbled out of my mouth. Gripping the sides of my dress, I took a breath to calm myself. "Mr. Anderson called while you were gone." I'd only answered the phone because I saw on the caller ID that it was a client I knew and Daddy had preapproved me answering calls from them. Otherwise, I wasn't allowed to answer the phone without his permission.

He had been about to sit down in his seat but stood and went to the kitchen at my declaration. "Never a day off, right?"

"Uh huh." I made sure Daddy's eyes were focused on the message before I quickly traded our knives, putting the scratched side down. All I had to do was make sure not to use it and discard of it after dinner.

"I'll call him back after we eat." He joined me at the table.

50

"We wouldn't want this meal you've prepared to get cold, now would we?"

"No, Daddy." I forced a smile and sat down a second after he did. Since he was the authority figure at the table, he sat and left first.

Daddy reached his hand out toward his plate, and his smile quickly vanished. The gray in his eyes turned dark, drowning out the blue. "Where are the napkins, Cora?"

Heat rushed to my face. How did I forget them? "I left them in the dryer. So sorry, Daddy. I'll go get them right now, if that's okay with you." My body itched to leave the table, but I had to wait until I was excused.

After an excruciating minute, my fingers drumming the seconds under the table, he gave a slight nod of approval. I calmly walked into the laundry room, took the cloth napkins out of the dryer, and folded them nicely. When they were arranged how Daddy liked them, I brought them back and placed Daddy's on the center of his plate.

The storms in his eyes had died down. He took the napkin, unfolded it, and tucked it in the top of his shirt.

"All better, Daddy?" I asked, grateful for the calm in my voice.

"Yes, Cora." He opened and closed his fists a few times. His tone dropped. "Don't let it happen again."

I swallowed, trying to quell the fear. Too many mistakes and I'd end up in the basement. "I won't." I moved toward my seat, but Daddy stopped me.

"Aren't you forgetting something?" He pointed to his cheek.

I gave it a kiss and then went to my seat, tucking my own napkin into the top of my dress.

We ate in silence for a good five minutes. Daddy was so focused on his plate that I didn't want to interrupt his thoughts. I didn't want to anger him again. I hated making him mad. It was never intentional. Seeing him smile gave me joy. Peace. Something I never had before I came to live with him.

He patted his lips with his napkin when he finished off his penne. "How would you feel about piano lessons?"

I almost dropped my fork but thank the stars it stayed in my hand. "Like, go somewhere, or someone would come to our home?"

Only Daddy and I were allowed in the house. Not even a delivery man had crossed the threshold.

"I repaired a clock for a lady the other day," he said. "She played the piano. It got me thinking how nice it would be to have my angel girl playing melodies in our home."

I carefully set my fork down next to my plate, making sure not to clink it against anything. "We don't have a piano."

His chin jutted out. "Not yet. I was going to go look for one tomorrow." His cloudy eyes stared at me, waiting, hoping for an excited reaction.

"I'd love that, Daddy," I finally said. "Thank you for giving me this opportunity to learn something new."

He tugged on his cuffs. "I'll let Ms. Simms know of your desire to have lessons, and we'll get something set up." He stood and reached out to grab my plate.

I placed my hands on it. "I'll clean up, Daddy. You've had a long week. You should relax."

Before he could respond in the negative, I took his plate and mine, plus the silverware, to the kitchen.

Daddy's eyes lingered on me, so I hummed a Beethoven song as I cleaned, one I knew he loved. His shoulders relaxed, and he wandered into the front room and turned on the TV, settling on the news like he always did.

I shoved the scratched knife into the bottom of the trashcan and covered it so it couldn't be seen. It seemed rather silly to have to throw a perfectly good knife away over a small scratch, but Daddy didn't like his things ruined. I was to treat them with the utmost care and respect. To him, destroying something he owned was a personal attack. Unfortunately, there were too many things in life I couldn't control, no matter how careful I had been.

Stealing a peek at Daddy to make sure he was still occupied, I let out a deep breath and went about cleaning the kitchen. Everything inside me shook with nerves and excitement. Having someone come into the house was new territory. I'd have to make sure I was on my best behavior. If I said or did anything out of line, Daddy would terminate my lessons.

Learning the piano didn't really pique my interest – I'd rather learn the guitar. A neighbor at one of my foster homes would sit out on his porch and play. He'd let me sit there and listen to him. It always spread a peace through my heart that I'd never received anywhere else.

But the thought of making a new friend and having someone else to talk to in Daddy's home intrigued me more than anything, so I'd learn the piano.

It took me forever to fall asleep that night. I shook in anticipation of what the following weeks would bring.

CHAPTER 8

"Cora!" Daddy's gravelly voice bellowed down the hall, waking me from my restless sleep. The thud of his boots thundered toward my door. I'd barely pulled back my canopy when the latch on the outside of my door was forced open, and Daddy burst into the room.

"What's wrong, Daddy?" I rubbed the sleep from my eyes and held back a yawn. Noah fell from my arms and landed softly next to me on the bed. My shirt was saturated with sweat from another nightmare.

Daddy held up his hand, and I shrunk back in fear. The scratched silver knife. My nightmare had become a reality. His body shook, eyes and jaw tight, and his fists clenched. "I found this in the trash as I was taking it out." He crossed over to the bed in moments, wrapped his callused hand around my arm, and yanked me out of bed. "First I tried to figure out why you would throw away something so valuable. Then I saw the scratch." His hand squeezed tight as he shook my body. "How could you let this happen?"

Tears formed at the corner of my eyes, but I fought them

back. I wasn't allowed to cry. "It was an accident. I'm not sure how it got there."

He held the knife in front of my face, the small nick taunting me. "Well, the scratch didn't magically appear on its own, did it? You must have been careless." His voice was deep and rough, making me shiver.

"It won't happen again, I promise." I forced the words through gritted teeth. His hold on me burned.

"Do you think I'm made of money, Cora? That I can just replace valuable silverware any time I want?"

I hated the quiver in my tone, but I couldn't stop it. "No, sir."

His raspy voice grew louder. "Should we just switch to plastic knives like we're poor so you can be as reckless as you want?" Fury seeped out of every pore. His whole face turned crimson, veins bursting from his forehead and neck. "Do you *want* a childhood like mine?"

A yelp escaped my mouth when his grip on my arm twisted, causing the pain to grow. If it hadn't been for my long sleeve shirt, it probably would have burned as well.

"You want to live like that, Cora? After everything I've done for you? I've provided you a home, a nice room, clothes, and food – all the things I never had." He pushed the scratched side of the knife into my cheek, the cold making me shudder. "This is how you repay me?"

"I'm sorry!" The words flew from my mouth.

"Sorry?" He dragged me out of the room and down the hall. "Forget the piano. Forget lessons."

My fingers slid along the walls as I tried to grab onto something firm. The tips of my fingers finally settled against the door frame to Daddy's room. My arms stretched as far as they could go. He yanked me away like a ragdoll, my arms falling from my last resort. I fought from his grip, but he held on firm. "Daddy, please don't do this."

When we got to the stairs leading to the basement, I wrapped both my hands around the banister. The wood burned against my skin as Daddy threw his arms around my waist and pulled my body farther down. Both hands slid along the banister, the shrill sound of my palms on the wood filling the air.

"Let go, Cora," he growled. Spit sprayed onto my neck. He hadn't been that furious in a long time. I knew he'd get mad about the silverware, but not this mad.

"I don't want to go down there." The basement was chilly and lonelier than the solitude of my room. At least I had Noah in my room. Plus, with my sweat-dampened shirt, it would only make it colder.

Daddy tugged at my body until he pried me away from the railing. "I don't want to make this longer than I have to, but if you don't stop, you'll be in timeout for a long time."

Letting my body go limp, I allowed him to drag me into the cold basement. He tossed me on the ground near the thin, lumpy mattress – the one that had been his as a child. He liked to remind me that I was lucky to have a real bed in a real room.

"Cora, you need to learn to respect my property." He had his hands on his hips, his eyes in a full-on storm. The dark gray whipped around, any trace of blue nowhere to be found. "You can't take for granted what I give you. Show me gratitude, that's all I ask."

If I fought back, he would extend the time. To be set free, I had to confess to being wrong, truth or not. "I'm sorry, Daddy. I shouldn't have ruined the silverware you bought for our family with your hard-earned money. I will treat your things with respect."

His tension slightly released. "Good." He started toward the stairs. "Three days."

"I'll miss school." I said it out loud because I was used to talking to Noah. It wasn't meant to be rude or whiney.

"Make it five." Daddy stomped up the old, wooden stairs, slammed the door, and locked me in the dark basement. He'd taken out the only light bulb years before so I could "soak in my sins." A part of me had appreciated the darkness so I couldn't see the filth or unwanted insects around me at night.

In the top corner of the room, the only window let in a fraction of light. I crawled over to the mattress and lay down. The smell of sweat and urine immediately filled my nose.

I gripped the side of the mattress tight, remembering when I'd first come to Daddy's house. He kept me locked in the basement until I made the adjustment and promised not to run. Or scream.

It had taken over a year. Almost four hundred days of living in the basement with minimal food and a litter box to go to the bathroom. He made me clean it myself. Once a week he'd let me have a sponge bath.

I finally let the stubbornness go. Gave in to his demands. Acted how he wanted. Said what he wanted to hear. Did everything he wanted me to do.

It beat the alternative of being homeless. I had no family and no one looking for me. I probably wasn't registered on any missing children list.

At least I had food and a roof over my head. For the most part, Daddy could be nice. Every now and then his temper would flare. But the storm always ended, replaced by a nice summer breeze. I needed to do a better job at keeping him happy.

The only problem with being locked in the basement was that I couldn't investigate my stolen journal. It would have to be put on hold, and I'd have to hope that no one would come forward during my timeout. If they did, the basement could become my permanent home.

Five days. I curled into a ball and fought the tears. I was strong. I was smart. I would live to see another day.

The night of my transfer haunted my dreams. Most of my life before that night was fuzzy. Apparently my parents abandoned me. Left me at a hospital in the middle of the night. I was thrown into the foster system since they had no record of who I was. I bounced around from house to house.

Warmth had filled the air the night he took me. The heat in the house was stifling, so I had snuck out to sleep under the stars. I had on a pink nightgown and floral underwear. No shoes. The backyard held two large dogs, so I slept up front.

As I lay on the grass, I heard a muffled noise come closer. A rusty door opened, then loud footfalls. Suddenly a man towered over me. He had bent down and placed his hand over my mouth.

"Don't scream, angel," he'd said in a soothing voice. He'd stroked my hair with his other hand. "Daddy has come to take you home where you belong." He'd picked me up in his strong arms. The overwhelming heat had made me weak and drowsy. Even if I'd wanted to scream, I probably couldn't have.

Something about Daddy had made me feel safe at the time. He'd gently placed me in the back of the van and put a blindfold over my eyes.

"Why are you doing that?" I'd whispered.

Daddy had rubbed my arm. "Because where I'm taking you, it's a surprise. You'd love a surprise, wouldn't you?" He'd tied the blindfold around my head. I lay down, my eyes fluttering, wanting to sleep. I could vaguely feel him tying up my legs and arms. Before he had started the engine and left, I was sound asleep on the floor of his old van.

CHAPTER 9

*E*very muscle on my body ached when I woke in the basement the morning after Daddy found the silverware in the trash. The thin mattress did nothing. I was practically sleeping on the cement floor.

Being without a blanket, and only wearing thin pajama pants and a wet shirt had left me cold all night long. It led to a fitful sleep. My mind dragged me into horrid nightmares of Daddy beating me, being torn from me, and losing the only family I'd ever had.

Rubbing my arms, I stood and went over to the window, peering up at the morning sun. The first time Daddy let me go outside after he first brought me to his house was magical. The warmth on my skin caused a smile to explode across my face. I never knew I could miss something so much until then. I'd forgotten how much I liked to be outside – running, playing, and chasing butterflies.

I'd taken it all for granted before then. If I earned Daddy's trust, then I could go outside more. So I did everything he asked of me. Those fleeting moments outside since then, I wrapped up and held close to my heart. Each one was poured out into a journal.

When Daddy let me move to a bedroom, he kept me locked in the room when he wasn't home or while I slept. A year or so ago, he started letting me stay out of my room on the weekends if he went to run short errands. He'd turn on the alarms so they would trigger if I tried to escape. Those were the times I got to cook. Those were the times I cherished.

But when I first made the move to the bedroom and I was locked up tight, I needed an outlet. I never had one when I was locked in the basement.

So I started snatching up pieces of papers that I found lying around the house. In the middle of the night, I'd draw my feelings using the moonlight to see the pages. If I sat in the perfect spot, I'd see my shadow aligned with the shadow of the bars from the window, trapping me in.

Every hiding spot I could find was used to stash the papers, but I knew eventually I'd run out of places to store my life. Every single piece of paper was a piece of my heart. They were the only things that were truly mine. Something I never wanted Daddy to find or be able to take away from me.

After a while, random pages weren't enough. I grew older and learned to write. It was easier to fill up a few pages every night. With drawings added to the end of each entry, I needed something else. So I learned how to steal.

Once a month, Daddy would let me go with him to get groceries. He always went to different stores to not draw attention to us. They were long trips since we got all our groceries for the whole month in that one outing, so I used the excuse of having to use the bathroom every time. My route was mapped out. Down the candy aisle to snatch a chocolate bar. Then over to the stationary to take a pen and journal. I stuffed them anywhere I could. My pants, shirt, and jacket. I became a master at camouflage and diverting Daddy's gaze to anywhere but me at the store. I didn't relish the thought of stealing, but I needed to release my emotions. It was for the benefit of our family staying together.

With all the journals, I needed a better hiding place. On one trip to the store, I stole a utility knife. At night, when Daddy was sound asleep, I went into my closet and cut a journal size opening in the drywall. I'd been shoving them in there ever since. If someone were to tear down the wall in my room, dozens of journals would pour out. My life would be at their feet.

If I could become a master at stealing, I could become a master of espionage. All it took was practice and a lot of patience.

Out of the corner of my eye, I saw a red piece of fabric stuffed behind one of the metal shelves against the wall. I went to it, pulling it out. A smile spread on my face.

"Sally."

My year of solitude in the basement had been lonely. So I'd created a friend. I had torn a piece of a shirt Daddy had given me and used it for the dress. A search of the basement had landed me some duct tape, an old rusted wrench, and some green and yellow electrical wiring. Using the duct tape, I stuck the red dress to the wrench. Then I'd created hair with the wiring and duct taped it on as well.

For being so old, Sally was still in decent condition. I stroked her yellow and green hair. I kept my voice low so Daddy wouldn't hear me. "Hey, Sally." I went back to my mattress and sat down. "So, I have a bit of a problem." I held her so she faced me. "Someone took one of my journals."

"Oh dear," Sally said, her voice hoarse from lack of use. I was grateful that, just like Noah, Daddy couldn't hear her. But Sally did a better job of staying quiet when Daddy was around. He also didn't know about her.

"Oh dear, indeed." I shivered from the chill in the basement, and my shirt that was still damp.

Sally's non-existent eyes stared at me. "Do you know who took it?"

Shaking my head, I continued to stroke her wire hair. "I'm trying to figure it out. There are a few options."

"You need to find the thief and the journal."

"I know. I've made a list of suspects."

"If your father finds out, one of two things will happen."

I tilted my head to the side. "What?"

Her metal body felt cold against my skin. "You'll become my permanent roommate down here, or he'll kill you."

I sucked in a sharp breath. "You don't really think he'd kill me, do you?" The thought had crossed my mind a few times over the years, but I didn't think Daddy capable of going through with it. He loved me too much.

She chuckled, the sound almost strained. "Of course he would. He can't have the truth revealed. He'd need to hide all the evidence."

"Including me," I whispered.

"Including you."

Coldness surrounded me, causing my entire body to tremble. "I don't think I'm ready to die." Death had been a tempting option in the past, as a way out, but I'd come to love my life in a twisted way.

"Then fix your problem."

I frowned at her. "How? I'm stuck here in the basement. I can't even follow any of the suspects." Closing my eyes, I leaned my head against the cement wall. "Even if I were out of the basement, I couldn't follow them. Daddy keeps me locked up."

"School."

"I'm not sure that will be enough." A single tear slid down

my cheek and instead of wiping it away like I normally did, I left it. Daddy wasn't there to stop me.

"You need an ally. Someone who can look into it for you outside of school."

My eyes shot open. "Sally! Are you crazy? I can't tell anyone my secret. That's the whole point of getting the journal back; so *no one* ever finds out." The thought of confiding my abduction to another human being downright terrified me. They would turn me in. They would call the police. Daddy would go to jail. My safety would be unraveled, and I would be thrown out into the cold, cruel world. People left you out there. Abandoned you. Broke your heart into a million little pieces and scattered them through the air so everyone could blow them farther away.

Her tone held a hint of annoyance. "Cora, you don't have to tell them what's inside the journal, only that it means a lot to you and you need it back."

"They'll ask why I can't do it myself. I have no excuse. I can't tell them it's because Daddy locks me up when he's not home." How could she not understand that?

Sally began to hum while she thought. I hummed along with her. Who would I even ask? The only plausible answer was Jenna. She knew I kept a journal and knew how important it was to me. Jenna would want me to get it back – unless she had been the one who'd stolen it.

Sally broke the silence. "Tell them that you're afraid people won't open up to you. They might be more honest with someone else."

"That's good," I said, tapping my fingers along her side. "I can start with that."

The lock on the basement door grinded open. Taking Sally, I stuffed her under the horrid excuse of a mattress, glad that she wouldn't be able to smell all the stale sweat and urine. "Sorry, Sally, nothing personal," I whispered.

She sighed. "I'm used to it."

Daddy's boots clomped down the basement stairs. He held a bowl and water bottle. Dark folds of skin were under his eyes. He hadn't slept. "Here's your meal for the day." Daddy set the bowl next to my feet. Oatmeal.

"There's no spoon," I whispered.

The thunderstorms began in his eyes. "You obviously don't know how to treat utensils. How could I trust you not to ruin it?" He threw the water bottle into my lap. "I hope you've had time to think about your grave mistake."

My hands gripped the bottle. "I have." A little fraction of me hoped he would reduce my sentence, but he'd never done it before.

"Good. I'll see you tomorrow. Same time." Daddy remained in front of me. My eyes slowly raised from his old, brown workman boots. His breathing sped up, raspy and broken. His shaking, callused hands landed on his belt – his favorite weapon to use against me.

Setting the water bottle next to me, I stood, wanting to get the lashings over and done. I turned my back to him and rested my hands against the cement wall. The heat flaring inside me dulled the chill of the wall against my palms.

The belt flapped against his waist as he drew it out. My body tensed at the sound and for a moment I couldn't breathe.

I am strong. I am brave.

The sting of the first lashing against my back pushed bile up my throat. My fingernails dug into the cement, creating a small layer of dust on my fingers. I put my hands in the same spot every time. The wall had slowly broken over the years, creating little divots for me to hold onto. A very small comfort during the horrendous ordeal.

"You need to be obedient!" Daddy roared.

Each strike burned hotter on my back.

I am strong. I am brave.

A cry from the pain left my mouth after the fourth lashing. I'd held it in for as long as I could.

"Little girls need to show their parents respect!"

My tears gave way at the fifth. Daddy's labored breathing grew intense. His belt went into the air, ready for another strike.

I am strong. I am brave.

The strike never came. He lowered his arm and left me alone in the basement.

Dropping to my knees, I covered my face with my hands and held in my screams. Some tiny miracle stopped him after only five lashings. It was the smallest amount of gratitude I'd had in years.

CHAPTER 10

*W*hen Daddy finally released me, there was only one day of school left for the week. He hadn't struck me again. Just the once for the punishment. My back stung a little, but it wasn't anything I couldn't manage. I'd been through it before. Having my shirt between the belt and my skin helped. Besides, Daddy always ended up feeling bad and would rub cream on my back to soothe the pain.

I'd told everyone at school I'd caught a nasty bug and needed to stay quarantined at home. They immediately dropped the subject after that.

I paused in the doorway of my French class. Jenna was already in her seat, talking to the girl in front of her. Her color for the day was yellow, and I couldn't help but smile. She even had a yellow ribbon intertwined with her fancy braid. The fact that she had skinny jeans and tennis shoes in every color imaginable blew my mind. Her parents probably had a hard time saying no to her and her contagious smile.

With a deep breath, I finally went into the classroom and took my seat.

"I thought you were going out of town?" Jenna asked. Her

eyes held a decent amount of hurt, which contrasted with her vibrant yellow eye shadow.

"We leave after school." I hated to see her sad, so I quickly placed a present on her desk.

Her eyes lit up, all the sadness drifting away. "You didn't have to get me anything!" She placed her hand on the package. "Oh, who am I kidding? I love presents!" Her fingers trailed the wrapping. "This is so cool! You must have put so much work into it."

I didn't have access to wrapping paper at home. Daddy kept it hidden. Every year he gave me one gift for my birthday. Santa brought me one for Christmas. Daddy didn't know it, but I saved all the scraps I could. For Jenna's present, I taped all the pieces together, creating a patchwork of paper.

The huge smile on her face made one equally as big break out on mine. "It fit you. A bunch of little, beautiful moments put together to create a masterpiece."

Happy tears pooled in her eyes as she got up from her desk and hugged me. "You're the best, Cora. I'm so lucky to have you as a friend."

"I'm the lucky one." I'd tried not to squirm under the pain from her hug. She was a tight hugger, squeezing the life out of people.

"A little over the top, don't you think?" Brendon suddenly appeared at my side. He had on a shirt with what looked to be a black bat inside a yellow oval. Did it belong with the gang he'd been talking about? Marvel or something?

Jenna waggled her finger at him, the oversized butterfly ring making it hard to take her seriously. She sat back down in her seat. "Don't ruin this for me." Her bold, brown eyes pleaded with me. "Can I open it now?"

"Of course." I sat up straight, not wanting to press my back against the seat. It still stung from my lashings.

Her freshly manicured yellow nails almost dug into the

wrapping, but she stopped herself. "I just can't get myself to ruin this paper." She slid her finger under the tape and slowly lifted it, creating only a slight tear. "I used to be so much better at this. I knew where my parents hid the Christmas presents, so I would sneak in, open them, and seal them all back shut without them ever knowing."

Brendon laughed. "Doesn't that take all the fun out of it?" He sat on the edge of my desk, facing Jenna.

She pursed her lips. "That was more of a thrill than waiting for Christmas day to see what the presents were."

"Your parents give you presents in addition to what Santa brings you?" I asked. That hardly seemed fair.

Jenna's hands froze around her present, and her jaw dropped.

Brendon chuckled but stopped when he saw the confusion on my face. He stole a glance at Jenna before he spoke. "You're joking right?"

"Your parents give you stuff, too?" I asked him. Why didn't Daddy get me a present for Christmas? Or more than one present?

"Don't yours?" Jenna asked, her hands still frozen in place.

I shook my head, trying to hide my disappointment. "Only Santa brings me a present."

The present I'd given Jenna, a cell phone holder, fell from her hands and onto the desk. "Hold up. You only get one present?"

At the same time, Brendon asked, "Do you still think Santa is real?"

Fire burned in my cheeks. I'd said something wrong. They were both looking at me like I was crazy. Fear overtook me to the point no thoughts or words would form so I could speak.

Santa wasn't real? Why would Daddy lie about that? I tried to stop a frown from forming on my lips.

Jenna's gaze landed on the cell phone holder I'd made for her. She turned it over in her hand, examining it. "This is so cool!" She slid it on her arm, and it fit perfectly.

"It's to hold your cell phone," I forced out. What had I said wrong? Why couldn't I be normal?

"Where did you get that?" Brendon asked. "I think I might want one for myself."

I stared at the band on Jenna's arm. "I made it." I'd used plastic bottles and pieces of fabric from old clothes in the basement. On the last trip to the grocery store, I'd stolen Velcro, and also some paint so I could decorate the band with butterflies. Jenna loved them.

They both turned their attention to me. Jenna smiled broadly. "That. Is. So. Cool!"

"Will you make me one?" Brendon asked, staring at the band around Jenna's arm.

Jenna slipped her cell phone into the holder. "You're going to be famous, and I'll get to tell everyone I was friends with you *before* you made it big."

My smile faltered. Being famous was the last thing I wanted. I didn't need any added attention to my strange life and family.

"Back to Santa," Brendon said, tapping me on the arm. "You know he isn't real, right?"

I forced myself to roll my eyes. "Of course I know that. It's just sometimes I forget how spoiled other kids are."

Jenna fingered the yellow hoop dangling from her ear. "Hey, I'm not spoiled. Just well taken care of."

The teacher broke up the moment and started class. I couldn't focus. Daddy had lied to me about something. Granted, it wasn't all that big, but it meant he was capable of lying. To *me*. Was Daddy lying about other things?

Someone flicked my arm, taking me from my trance.

"Earth to Cora," Jenna said.

"What?" I asked.

She pulled off a yellow fuzzy stuck to her nail. "Were you even listening? We have to do a project."

My eyes skittered to the teacher. The past thirty minutes were a complete blur. What project?

"I'm joining your team." Brendon knelt between me and Jenna. He pointed his thumb at me. "She's fluent and I don't want to flunk."

"You're fluent?" Jenna smacked her forehead with her palm causing all her bracelets to clink together. "It all makes sense now. You never miss anything. You speak like you were born in France."

"I wasn't born in France." The words tumbled out of my mouth, falling all over each other.

Jenna scooted away from me. "Are you still sick? I don't want to catch it. Your brain obviously hasn't healed."

Brendon reached up to touch my arm, but I snapped it away from him. He sighed and ran his hand over his fohawk. "We need you focused, Cora. What's going on?"

My eyes darted between the two of them. I had only planned on telling Jenna about the journal. Brendon was still a suspect. Really, so was Jenna. But I needed help.

"Someone stole my journal," I whispered.

Jenna gasped. "What? That's awful! I can't believe someone would do that!"

"What's the big deal?" Brendon asked. "I'm sure it's just a bunch of squiggly hearts and lame poems about her crushes." When I glared at him, he smiled. "Which obviously isn't me."

Jenna smacked him on the arm. "This is serious, Brendon. It's her *journal*. Her deepest, most private, thoughts."

Brendon's red eyebrows shot up. "Whoa. What do you write about in your journal? Now I want to find it."

By both of their reactions, it didn't seem like either of

them had taken it. I slid out a piece of paper from my note-book and handed it to Jenna. "That's a list of the suspects."

Jenna's eyes scanned the page until they got wide. She pointed a finger into her chest. "You think I'm a suspect?"

"Everyone is," I said.

"Sweet." Brendon rubbed his hands together, showing off yet another new bandage from a pizza box cut. "I made the list."

I handed her a pen. "I'm fairly certain it's neither of you, so you can cross your name off the list."

"Obviously." Jenna snatched the pen and scribbled over her name to the point you couldn't read it anymore. She moved her pen to cross out Brendon's name, but he stopped her.

"Leave it there." His lips twisted in a smile. "It makes me more mysterious."

Keeping her glaring eyes on Brendon, Jenna drew a line over his name. But it was still obvious his name had been on the list.

Brendon motioned to the bat on his shirt. "You're right – Bruce Wayne wouldn't want people to even suspect him."

Jenna turned the paper over and saw the empty page. "That's it? This is your list?"

"They're all the people I interact with during the day."

"What about your friends?" Brendon picked at his Band-Aid. "People you hang out with outside of school. I know you want to trust them, but you need to consider every possibility."

Jenna scanned the list again. "Who do you hang out with, anyway?"

When I didn't respond, they both stared at me. I kept my voice low. "I'm really busy outside of school. I don't have time for friends."

"Doing what?" Jenna asked. "Do you play a bunch of different sports or instruments or something?"

My finger trailed Husky. "Family stuff." I took a deep breath. "Can you help me or not? I don't have time after school, but I really need the journal back. It's extremely important that I get it back. Very, very, important."

Jenna shook the list in her hand. "Yeah, sure, I'll help. I'll interrogate the crap out of these people."

"Thanks." I breathed a sigh of relief. Then I noticed the time. "When did the final bell ring?"

"Uh, when it always does," Brendon said.

I was already out of my chair, trying to stuff my notebook into my backpack. I couldn't be late. Especially not after finally being released from timeout. I didn't want to be thrown back in. My sanity couldn't manage it.

"Slow down," Jenna said.

"I can't. If I'm late..." Daddy would punish me. "Thanks. Bye." I took off running, going as fast as I could. Jenna shouted my name, but I kept on sprinting, pushing past all the students in the hall until I reached the front of the school.

"Cora."

I came to a complete stop, whipping around, my shoes squeaking against the linoleum floor.

Mr. Mendoza stood there with his hands in his pockets. "Where have you been? You've missed four days of school." His eyes managed to look uninterested and interrogating at the same time.

"Sick." Sick of being locked in the basement. Sick to my stomach of my secret being exposed.

"Better now?"

No. I nodded. "Yes, but I'm running late."

His eyebrows furrowed and then released. "Busy life."

"Yes, sir," I said.

He glanced around at the students passing by before

turning his attention back to me. "I'd like to see you on Monday. Since we didn't get to talk this week."

"We're talking right now." I fiddled with my backpack straps, itching to leave.

He took a few steps toward me. "A real conversation, Cora. Monday."

I wanted to say no and tell him to stay away from me, but he worked for the school. I couldn't raise suspicion. "Monday."

Someone bumped into me, but when I turned around, there were students everywhere. Anyone could have done it. It was probably just an accident.

Looking down, I went to straighten my shirt so I would look good for Daddy. A note sticking out of my pocket caught my eye. I scanned the area, but no one was paying any attention to me. With shaking hands, I pulled the note out of my pocket.

I know your secret.

The piece of paper crumpled in my death grip. I frantically searched around, but all I saw was student after student leaving the school. No one paid me any mind.

Even though fear consumed me, I had to leave. I'd made Daddy wait too long. He'd be upset with how late I was running.

Daddy's van caught my eye in the line of vehicles. I didn't have to see his face to know he was mad. I could feel it radiating from him. The air had shifted. There was a high possibility of going back into timeout for the weekend, making my heart sink.

His hands were wrapped tightly around the steering wheel. His chest rose and fell with his deep breathing. "Where. Were. You?" Daddy asked the second I sat down in the passenger seat. When he'd already cranked the volume on his angry tone, it was never a good sign.

"Sorry." I panted and wiped sweat from my brow. I wanted to unfasten the top button of my shirt to let some air in, but he wouldn't like that. "We were assigned a project at the end of French. We had to decide groups before we left." *Weave a lie.* "I don't know anyone in the class, so I waited until everyone had picked and then had the teacher put me in a group."

Daddy fumed next to me. His fingers drummed along the steering wheel. He slowly moved forward in the line, trying to make his way out of the chaos. "Smart thinking."

Inside, the fear melted. At least I wouldn't make it into timeout again. My hand gripped the seat, clinging on for life. My heart needed to calm before Daddy suspected anything – before he figured out I was lying.

"Anything else happen at school?" he asked.

My eyes wandered to the sea of students pouring out the front door of the school. I spotted Jenna and Brendon both standing near a large ash tree, watching me and Daddy. They both wore frowns, their faces masks of confusion. What must they have thought of me?

Mr. Mendoza stood near the top of the stairs, also staring at the van. His eyes locked with mine. All I could see was concern with maybe a slight hint of uncertainty mixed in.

Sweat formed on my palms, soaking the crushed note. It would probably shred into a million pieces when I finally pried it from my hand.

"No, Daddy," I said. "The day was perfectly free of excitement."

CHAPTER 11

Sunlight radiated through the kitchen window, warming up the air near the sink. Sunday afternoons were my favorite. Daddy would mow the front and back lawns, giving me some free time. He'd also been working on a new project. For years he talked about building me a swing set in the backyard. Somehow my latest trip to timeout caused him to finally want to start.

Spring was coming to an end and summer was well on its way. Sweat glistened down Daddy's head as he worked. He lifted his cap, wiped his forehead with the back of his hand, and put the cap back on. When he glanced over at the kitchen window, I gave him a little wave, which he returned.

On the outside, I was calm and happy, appearing to be the perfect child. Inside, I writhed. Someone out there knew my secret. Mine and Daddy's secret. If they told anyone, my life would fall apart. I'd be torn away from Daddy, never to see him again. How would I survive that?

I needed to focus on something else before I broke. It was too early to start dinner, so I decided to bake cookies. Oatmeal raisin. Daddy's favorite. I preferred chocolate chip, but he didn't like chocolate. The preheated oven warmed the kitchen, so I turned on a fan standing in the archway, the breeze cooling my skin.

I had just put a cookie tray in the oven when someone knocked on the front door. Hurrying over to the window, I peered outside to see if Daddy had heard the noise. Over the sound of his saw, he hadn't heard.

Normally I didn't answer the door. Daddy didn't allow it. But he had been waiting for a delivery, so I went to the sliding glass door and yelled out to him. He didn't hear me. My foot only made it an inch outside when I noticed I wasn't wearing shoes. I couldn't go outside without them. Daddy took that rule very seriously after finding me with no shoes on the day he'd taken me.

The person knocked again, louder. Daddy didn't flinch. I hesitated a few seconds before I finally shut the backdoor and went to the front, peeking out of the peephole.

My breath caught in my throat. Turning around, I slammed my back into the door and wiped my cookie dough covered hands on my apron. Why were they at my house? How did they know where I lived?

With a deep breath, I placed my shaking hand on the doorknob and opened the front door just a crack.

"Good, you're back." Jenna smiled brightly at me. Her color of the day was red, and it looked amazing on her. "Aren't you going to open the door all the way?"

"What are you doing here?" I hissed.

The smile on Brendon's face dissolved. "We have a project to work on, remember?"

"You left so fast on Friday." Jenna tried to push her way inside, but I held the door firm. "What's with you?"

"You need to leave." I tried to shut the door. Brendon used his foot to block me from closing it. "Please. Leave."

"It won't take long." Brendon shoved the door open and came inside. "Do I smell cookies?"

He started for the kitchen, so I took hold of his arm to stop him, which made me turn my back to Jenna.

Her fingers ran along my fishtail braid. "Oh, going fancy today. I like."

I ignored her, terror the only thing on my mind. "Please, Brendon, I'm begging you. Leave." If Daddy saw them, timeout would be the least of my worries. The thought of them being locked in the basement flashed through my mind, but I pushed the image aside. I couldn't dwell on the unknowns. They drove me insane.

"Cora, why are you so afraid?" Brendon asked me. His eyes wandered over my body, searching for something. "Is he here?"

"Is who here?" Jenna asked. She came into view with her hands on her hips and a frown on her mouth. "I thought we were friends, Cora. First you bail on my birthday party, which was *so* much fun by the way."

"Yes, it was." Brendon wiggled his eyebrows at Jenna, who returned the gesture with a slap on the arm.

"He wasn't there," Jenna said. "Cora, now you're bailing on our project? That's so not like you."

"I'm not allowed to have friends over on Sunday," I said. The back door opened, and a cold, nauseating fear swept over me. "Hide. Now." I shoved them down the hall and went into the kitchen, forcing a smile onto my face and hoping my friends obeyed my orders. "Hey, Daddy. Do you need a drink?"

Daddy used a kitchen towel to wipe off his face and neck. "Where were you?" His eyes flickered toward the entryway. Some people looked more youthful and fun when they wore baseball hats. For Daddy, it made him appear more suspicious and stern than he normally was.

"Had to use the bathroom." I peeked inside the oven. "First batch of cookies are almost done." My hand froze on the oven door handle as Daddy walked to the hall and stared down it. "What are you doing?" *Please let them be hidden.*

"I thought I heard something." His eyes grilled mine, trying to find the truth. He needed to stay in the kitchen. He couldn't know Brendon and Jenna were in the house.

I released the oven from my death grip. "Oh, I opened the window in my bedroom. Wanted to get a small breeze going. You probably heard the blinds being ruffled by the wind." After wiping the sweat from my palms onto the apron, I rolled the dough into balls and placed them on a clean cookie sheet. "How's it going outside?"

He took a step down the hallway. A hurricane of anger raged in his eyes. He'd just taken another step when the timer buzzed. A breath of relief escaped over my dry lips.

"Daddy, can you get the cookies out of the oven?" I wiggled my doughy fingers. "I'm a mess."

He hesitated before he tromped into the kitchen, grabbed an oven mitt, and removed the cookie tray, setting it on the counter. "Not too much longer out there." He took a glass from the cupboard and filled it up with water from the sink.

I set another ball of dough on the sheet. "Good. I'll start dinner after I finish with the cookies. Is chicken and rice okay?" It was one meal I loved that he didn't mind.

"As long as there are brussels sprouts." Daddy downed his cup of water and then set the cup in the sink. "Wash that when you have a moment." He eyed my hair. "Why is your braid in back?"

I'd been so distracted that I hadn't thought to put my braid in its place up front. "I like to keep it back there while I bake so I don't end up with dough in my hair."

Grabbing it with his fist, he lifted my braid and rested it over my right shoulder. "Just be careful and you'll be fine." He gave me a kiss on the forehead, for once his lips warm from the sun, and then returned to the backyard.

I made sure he was fully engaged in his work before I ran down the hall and into my room. The horror pounding in my heart multiplied when I walked in and saw Jenna and Brendon standing there, gazing over all the pink. What had I done?

"Daddy likes it this way," I whispered.

Jenna jumped at my voice. "Cora!" She cleared her throat. "Your room is very . . . I mean, it's, you know . . ."

"Pink." Brendon peered into the dollhouse in the corner of the room and pulled out a miniature poodle.

I hurried over and took it from his hands, putting it back where it belonged. "How did you know where I lived?" Had I put my address in my journal? Some of them had it, but I couldn't remember if it was in my latest one.

Jenna smirked. "I aide in the front office. I may have snuck into the student files."

My tension relieved the slightest bit. There was still a chance neither of them had taken my journal. "You can't be here. You both need to leave."

"What about the project?" Jenna sat down on my bed. "I kind of like this canopy." She closed it around her.

"Excuse me, Cora Bora." Noah grunted. "Who is this strange creature on our bed? She's so bright it's blinding me. And what on earth is on her teeth?"

Noah had never seen braces before. Daddy didn't want me to have them. He said society put too much pressure on appearances and we should be proud of our natural look. It was why I couldn't wear make-up, dye my hair, or paint my nails.

I wanted to glare at Noah, tell him to butt out, but Brendon came close to me and ran his fingers along my fish-tail braid. He almost looked mesmerized by it. I took a step back, knocking into the dollhouse and rattling everything inside. I hated that my life caused me to act this way. I couldn't even have someone in my room without freaking out. Maybe Noah had been right. Was this how I wanted to live my life?

Brendon kept his voice low so only I could hear. "Why can't we be here? And don't give me the 'it's Sunday' excuse."

"I can't," I murmured. "I can't talk about it. Please, Brendon, leave. For me. I don't want to get in trouble." I couldn't believe how close he was standing.

"Will he hurt you?" Brendon asked. His breath smelled like spearmint from the mint in his mouth. It rattled against his teeth as he moved it around.

My head nodded on its own accord, and I desperately wished Brendon hadn't thought to ask that question. He sensed too much.

"What are you and that guy talking about?" Noah asked rather loudly, making me cringe.

Jenna hopped off the bed and appeared at our side. "What are you two whispering about? Should I leave you alone?"

"No!" Heat rushed to my cheeks. "I'll see you both Monday, okay? We can work on our project during lunch or something." I took a moment to put the dollhouse in its proper order and then left the room, hoping they would follow. When I got to the entryway, I peered around the wall and looked outside. Daddy was still busy working.

Brendon opened the front door and ushered Jenna out. Before he closed the door, he slipped a piece of paper into my pocket, which reminded me of the blackmailer. "Call me if you ever need help. Any time of day or night."

"Okay." I'd never call him. Daddy checked the phone records.

"Promise me." His eyes pleaded with me.

So I lied, which I hated to do. "I promise." I only made promises to Daddy. Well, only promises I kept.

Brendon gently squeezed my hand before he closed the door and left. Warmth lingered on my skin from his touch. I stared at my hand thinking I'd see a glow that matched what I felt inside, but it remained the same.

My hand tightened into a fist. That had been too close of a call. Why had they gone so far as to break into the school files to get my address? Maybe going to public school had been a mistake. Too much was unraveling and I couldn't control any of it.

The oven buzzer went off, and I jumped. I hurried into the kitchen and retrieved the cookies, trying to push Brendon and Jenna from my mind.

CHAPTER 12

J'd wanted to compare Brendon's note to the one the blackmailer had given me, but my sweat had obliterated it. Even if I hadn't ruined it, Brendon's note was mostly numbers, so there was a chance I couldn't tell anyway.

Monday during lunch, I found an empty table in the library and sat down. A part of me held some hope that Brendon and Jenna would forget about working on the French project. Maybe they'd just want to get it over with so they would do it without me. I also hoped Mr. Mendoza would forget about meeting with me, but I wasn't about to hold my breath.

"There you are." Jenna plopped down in the seat next to me. Using her finger, she wiped some pink lip gloss from her braces and then ran her tongue along them. "I can't wait to get these things off. They're seriously ruining my life." She'd clipped a strip of pink in her hair that brought her entire spunk-slash-pink outfit together.

Brendon sat down in the chair on my other side and placed a blue floral gift bag on the table in front of me. He was wearing a red shirt with a black spider on it. It was the first shirt I didn't really care for. I hated spiders. They reminded me of the basement.

"Happy birthday!" he said.

"It's not my birthday," I said, looking at the bag. He'd gotten me a present? The only person who'd ever given me a present was Daddy. At least, that I could remember.

Brendon laughed, running his hand over his fohawk. "Okay, so I have no idea when your birthday is. I just saw this at the store and thought of you."

Something inside of me stirred. He'd been thinking of me outside of school?

"Open it!" Jenna clapped her hands in excitement.

The librarian held up a finger to her lips. "Shhh!"

Jenna's cheeks flared. Her voice dropped to a whisper and she mimed clapping. "Open your present or I will."

Normally fear would flash its sinister smile in these situations. Worry and dread of Daddy finding out would eat at me, clawing at my poise. But I couldn't stop the smile that inched its way onto my face. Taking hold of the bag, I put it on my lap and peered inside. A journal and gel pens. The urge to kiss Brendon on the cheek traveled through me, taking me by complete surprise. No guy had ever caused that reaction. Heat rushed to my neck and cheeks. I pulled out the journal and used my finger to trace the purple floral design on the cover. "Thank you."

"It's so beautiful!" Jenna covered her mouth and smiled sheepishly at the glaring librarian. She mouthed, *sorry*, before the librarian could scold her again.

"I know it's not your missing one," Brendon said, "but I thought this could replace it in the meantime." He pointed to the combination lock on the outside. "Small protection, in case someone tries to take it."

My eyes wandered over his arms. I'd seen girls give guys

hugs at school. It seemed common among friends. Was Brendon my friend? Would hugging him be a normal reaction to a present? The thought of touching someone else, especially a guy, riled up too much panic in me. What if I made him angry? He probably didn't want me touching him. Or he'd get the wrong idea.

"Speaking of your missing journal," Jenna whispered, "I've ruled out Kendra. She has absolutely zero interest in you." She blushed. "Sorry."

I held the journal close to my chest. My first, real journal. One I hadn't stolen. Someone had bought it and given it to me. My eyes went to Brendon.

He scooted his chair a little closer to me in a casual manner. "I don't think it's Julien, but I'm not one hundred percent positive. I talked to him last period." His finger tapped the top of the table. "Dalton's next on my list. He seems more likely than any of the others."

Jenna held up her palm. "My money is on Sydney. She's done stuff like this before."

My fingers curled around the journal. "What? When?"

"In elementary and middle school," Jenna said. "She has a history of taking things that don't belong to her." She sat back in her chair and folded her arms. "Like my Shawn Mendes binder."

Brendon chuckled. "She probably took it so she could light the thing on fire."

Jenna rolled her eyes. "Why are guys so jealous of Shawn?"

"Who's Shawn Mendes?" I asked. "Does he go to our school?"

By their reactions, I'd said something wrong. Again. Jenna's jaw was practically on the ground. "Please tell me you're joking."

Brendon wiped the shock off his face and replaced it with

a smile. "You don't need to know who he is. This makes me like you even more."

Even more than what? He liked me? As a friend? I needed to talk to Noah or Sally. Sally was a better listener, but I had to go to timeout to talk to her. Noah always gave me attitude. We'd hardly spoken since I'd lost my journal.

"I'll send you some of his songs." Jenna pulled out her phone. "What's your phone number?"

I fiddled with the numbers on the lock of the journal. "I don't have one."

"Okay, your email address." Jenna's fingers moved across the screen on her phone, but I couldn't see what she was doing.

My voice was low. "Don't have one."

Jenna's wide eyes went to mine. "Do you have anything? Snapchat? Twitter? Instagram?"

Both my legs bounced, and I pressed the journal tight to my chest.

Brendon's hand landed on my leg, and I quickly pulled it away. He held up his hand. "It's okay, Cora. I'm not going to hurt you."

"Why would she think you're going to hurt her?" Jenna asked, her eyebrows furrowed. "You seriously think the weirdest things, Brendon. Have you been binge watching Bates Motel or something?"

Brendon and I locked eyes, and I swore he could see into my soul and all the dark things I kept buried way below the surface. Normally people didn't pick up on my fear and anxiety. They just took it as a social problem and left me alone. Somehow Brendon saw past all of that and knew what was inside of me.

He slowly moved his hand toward my leg. My eyes stared as his hand inched closer and then landed right above my knee. My leg immediately stopped bouncing and tensed.

"I'm your friend," Brendon whispered. His volume turned back up. "It's okay if you don't use all these social sites and know lame singers."

Jenna held up her hand. "Shawn Mendes is *so* not lame." She threw a rolled-up piece of paper at Brendon. "You're lame." The bell to end lunch rang overhead. Jenna groaned. "We didn't even get to work on our project. We'll have to get together after school."

Despite Brendon's hand being on my knee, my leg began to bounce again. "I can't."

"Another *family* thing?" Jenna used air quotes.

Brendon shot her a dirty glare. "It's okay. Jenna and I will work on the project, and then we'll show you what we came up with tomorrow during lunch. You can help fix all our mistakes."

"What?" Jenna crossed her arms. "Why do we have to do all the work? That's not fair."

"I'll do it." I shoved the journal, bag, and pens into my backpack. "I'll do the project tonight at home. You two won't have to do a thing." I stood, stepping away from the table.

Jenna's anger melted, her arms loosening. "That's not what I meant. I don't want you to do all of it. I just want us to do it as a group. Equal participation and all that."

"Is there any way your father will let us meet at the library after school?" Brendon asked.

I shrugged. "Not sure. I can ask."

Brendon stood and came close, pulling me away from Jenna. "Will that get you in trouble?"

Licking my lips, I folded my arms and hugged them close. "I don't know. Maybe. It all depends on his mood."

"Okay." Brendon twisted his lips in thought. "If he seems happy, tell him you have a school project that's very important and is due soon." How did he understand so well? Was his father like mine? He hadn't talked about his family much, so I didn't know.

"When is it due?" I asked. My mind had been so scattered, I hadn't been paying much attention in any of my classes.

"Friday," Brendon said.

Jenna came up to us. "Sorry to interrupt, but I have to get to class. See you in French." She sauntered out the library doors.

Brendon began walking, pulling me with him. We stepped outside into the afternoon sun. The warmth made some of my anxiety flutter away.

"Jenna and I will be at the library at four," Brendon said. I headed toward my class, and he followed alongside me. The concern and understanding hadn't left his eyes. "Only ask him if he's happy. Tell him it will only be for an hour." He grimaced. "Tell him he can come if he wants."

"Don't sound so excited." I tried not to smile, but one came anyway. Brendon somehow made me smile even in the darkest times.

He bumped my shoulder. "Can you blame me?"

"Nope. It's how I feel every day." My feet stumbled. I shouldn't have said that out loud. How did Brendon keep getting me to drop my guard – say and feel things I shouldn't?

We stopped outside the locker room. Brendon placed his hands on my arms, causing me to flinch. My bruises from Daddy's tirade hadn't healed. But Brendon took my motion as fear of him touching me, not of me being hurt.

"Cora, we can get you out of this and away from him."

I wasn't ready for that. I couldn't be alone. "I don't want out." Tears welled up in my eyes, and I fought them back. "I love him. He loves me. We're usually very happy."

Brendon dropped his arms. "That makes me feel a little better." His tone wasn't convincing. The tardy bell rang. "I'll see you next period." He waited for me to nod before he left, a hint of doubt lingering in his eyes.

I hoped that Daddy would be in a good mood when he picked me up from school. Otherwise, I had no idea how we'd complete our project. Keeping Daddy happy was my number one priority. But feelings had developed for Jenna and Brendon. Friendly, warm ones. I wanted to be around them and get to know them – which broke every survival rule I'd created.

If anything happened to either of them, I'd never forgive myself.

CHAPTER 13

*M*r. Mendoza called me into his office during P.E., which relieved me somewhat. My athletic abilities were non-existent. I never played sports with Daddy, so starting P.E. in public school was my first introduction to softball, basketball, and volleyball. So far, it hadn't gone well.

"Feeling any better?" Mr. Mendoza asked, sitting tall in his chair.

I clung to my backpack and Husky. "Yes." Sticking to one-word answers would be my best bet when it came to the guidance counselor. Short sentences and thoughts were so much easier to manage and gave me a smaller chance of making a grave error. It was why I used them a lot.

"Good," he said. He wasn't wearing a tie. He'd opted for a sweater over his button-down shirt, which still didn't fit him and his wide frame. It looked wrong on him. Out of character. "Have you thought more about signing up for a club?"

"Yes."

He raised his thick eyebrows. "Yes, you've thought about it, or yes, you want to join a club?"

I rubbed Husky. "Considered."

"And?" He stared at me, hope in his eyes.

I hated letting people down, especially authority figures. But I couldn't join a club. Daddy would never agree to it. He'd been on edge lately and getting upset at everything. I couldn't afford to anger him. My body couldn't handle it. "No."

He sighed and sat back in his chair. "Why not?"

One-word answers were harder than I thought they would be. Almost impossible. "Time."

"Time," Mr. Mendoza repeated. "I think this is worth making time for." He drummed his fingers along the table. "I'd like to meet your father."

"No!" My fist tightened around Husky.

His eyes widened. "Why not?"

I couldn't lose control. It added suspicion. Exactly what I didn't need or want. One-word answers were stashed aside until further notice. "He's busy and I don't want to worry him."

"Why would that worry him?" He leaned forward, clasping his hands and resting them on the desk.

I stroked Husky. "Getting called into school to meet with you? He'll think I'm in trouble or something. He has a lot on his mind. I don't want to add unnecessary worry."

"Cora, meeting with parents to talk about their child's future is common. If anything, he'll be happy that we're investing time into your future."

My future involved living with Daddy. Taking care of him. College was not in my future. Having a career, getting married, having kids, owning a home – none of that would ever happen for me.

Daddy was my future.

"I don't want to join a club, sir. I'll keep getting good

grades, focus my time on graduating high school, but that's it. It's all I want."

Mr. Mendoza studied me for a minute. My answer had upset him. I could see it in his eyes. But I wouldn't change my mind. Not everyone had to be in a club or organization.

He finally sighed and sat back in his chair. "Okay, then. Classes going well?"

"Yes," I said.

"Friendships?"

"Great." I was so happy and relieved to be back to one-word answers. I could handle those.

"Boyfriend?"

Heat flared on my cheeks. The smirk on Mr. Mendoza's face told me he'd noticed.

"No." My thumb grazed across Husky. It wasn't a lie. The thought of being with someone, being close or physical, had caused me to blush. I'd never had a boyfriend, nor did I think I ever would. I thought Brendon was cute with his red hair, freckles, fun shirts, and endearing smile, but that didn't mean anything. He'd never look at me that way, and he couldn't. Relationships were out of the question. Daddy would never allow it. People couldn't get close to me.

"You still with me?" Mr. Mendoza asked.

"What?" I hugged my backpack tighter. "Yes."

He pointed to my bag. "You can put that on the floor."

"No, thanks," I said, stroking Husky.

"Something valuable in there?" he asked.

My eyebrows furrowed and my heart fluttered for a moment. "Why would you ask that?"

He smiled. "You're gripping onto it like you never want to let go. So, you're nervous, have something valuable, or have something you don't want anyone to find." He sat back in his chair. "Which is it?"

Nothing important was in my backpack. I'd hand it over

if he asked. I had nothing to hide since my treasure had already been stolen. But if I admitted I was nervous, he'd want to know why. *Spin the truth.* "Nervous. Sitting alone in a room with a man scares me."

Mr. Mendoza pulled back in surprise. "Has something happened to make you feel that way?"

I stared at my lap. "It just makes me uncomfortable." I shrugged. "Maybe I read too many books."

"That's usually not a bad thing." He folded his arms, closing himself off from me. "I'm here to be an aide for you, nothing more. We can always have the secretary sit in on our meetings if it would make you more comfortable."

"That won't be necessary." Because I wanted nothing more than to end my meetings with him.

He leaned forward, clasping his hands together. "Cora, how is everything at home?"

I swallowed the thick lump in my throat. "Why?"

"I saw you get in your father's van the other day," Mr. Mendoza said. "He looked angry."

I rubbed Husky. "Dads get upset. It happens."

He shook his head and sighed. "It was beyond anger. It was more like fury. And you . . . you were scared."

How did I respond to that? I'd hoped Mr. Mendoza hadn't noticed. But there were some things that were hard to hide. I was lucky he couldn't see my back. My scars, both inside and out.

"He had an appointment, and I made him late. One of his top clients." Partially true.

"Why did that scare you so bad?" He had his pen in his hand, ready to write down anything I said.

"I, uh." I licked my lips. Lies created too big of a hole. Daddy always found out when I lied. I had no doubt Mr. Mendoza would do the same. The bell rang, and I jumped from my seat. "I have to get to French."

I bolted out of there before Mr. Mendoza could stop me.

I'd never talked to a guidance counselor before Mr. Mendoza. I wondered if I was obligated to see him. Just because he called me into his office, did I have to go? Maybe I'd say no next time. Refuse to go. But I wasn't sure if I was brave enough to do that.

CHAPTER 14

addy's van drove up along the curb, falling into line with all the other vehicles. As I approached the van, I saw his fingers drumming along the steering wheel, and he was singing along with an oldies song that drifted out the rolled down window. A good sign.

"Hi, Daddy." I hopped in the seat and shut the door. "How was your day?"

He leaned over and kissed me on the forehead. "Wonderful. You?"

I did my best to ignore my wildly beating heart. "It was good. Aced a test in history."

"That's my girl." He checked both directions of traffic before he slowly pulled out of the parking lot and headed home.

"Daddy, remember that project I told you about for my French class?"

He stopped at a red light and looked over at me. "Yes."

Swallowing, I worked moisture into my mouth. "It's due on Friday, and we can't work on it in class."

"When does your teacher expect you to do it then?" His good mood was slipping away.

"After school." My hand itched to reach up and yank on my braid, but I refrained. "At the library."

The light turned green, so Daddy accelerated, but after a noticeable pause. "I see. Will all the groups be there?"

I shrugged. "Maybe some. I didn't talk to anyone else, so I don't know when they are meeting. My group said they could only meet today at four. Will that work for me?"

He remained quiet for a while. His fingers wrapped tightly around the steering wheel.

"You could come with me." I'd hate for him to come, but it would ease his worry.

"I have an appointment at four. I don't want to cancel with my client. They're a regular."

He couldn't know how much I wanted to go and spend time with Jenna and Brendon. I pulled my backpack into my lap so I could run my fingers along Husky. "Maybe they could just do it without me."

"You really want to rely on others for your grade?"

I shook my head and made sure there was hesitation in my tone. "Not really. But what choice do I have?"

He took a few deep breaths. "I'll drop you off at the library on the way to my appointment and pick you up as soon as it is done."

Inside, excitement bubbled, but I kept the uncertainty in my voice. "Are you sure, Daddy?"

He briefly smiled. "You'll be fine. Just stay in car and eye shot of a librarian. If you feel unsafe or scared at any time, go stand by them and wait for me to come get you."

"Okay, Daddy." My fingers tightened around Husky. "I can do that."

He pulled into the driveway and turned off the van. "I'm

sure your group partners will be very happy to have you. You'll be the smartest one there."

"I hope so," I whispered, trying to conceal my enthusiasm. "I don't want to let them down or hurt their grades."

Daddy rubbed my cheek, his fingers rough against my skin. "You'll do great, sweetheart." He opened his door, jumped out, and came around to my side to open the door. "Let's get you a snack before you have to go. We want your brain ready to work." He poked my nose, and I forced a giggle.

"Thanks, Daddy." I gave him a kiss on the cheek before we went inside. That went a lot better than I had anticipated. Usually, I was good at reading him. I'd know how much to say or how far to push things. But lately, his anger had magnified, which I hadn't thought was possible. There had to be something going on, but there was no way I could ask him.

Daddy dropped me off at the library ten minutes before four. I found a table near the front desk, smiling at the librarian as I sat down.

I'd just put my French textbook on the table when Brendon sat down next to me. "He let you come."

"He let me come."

Brendon smiled. "I had a feeling he'd drop you off early, so I waited outside, out of sight."

My eyes widened. "He didn't see you, did he?"

He picked at one of the Band-Aids on his fingers. "Nope. I made sure to wait until he was gone before I ran inside. I had a friend in elementary school who had an angry father like yours. I know the drill."

"What happened to them?" I asked, not sure if I wanted to know the answer.

Brendon took a deep breath and continued to pick at his

Band-Aid. He wouldn't make eye contact with me. "They moved. I never heard from him again."

The pack of gel pens that Brendon had given me fell out of my backpack, so I stooped over to pick them up.

"Cora!" His fingers grazed my bare skin along my lower back. My shirt had ridden up from me bending over.

I quickly pulled down my shirt, covering up my scars. "It's nothing. It's from an accident long ago."

He lifted my shirt in the back and swore under his breath. "Did he do this to you?"

I slapped his hand away. "It's none of your business."

He leaned toward me. "He can't do that to you. If he did, you need to report him."

My hand landed on Brendon's. "The scars aren't from him. They're from an accident. Long ago. Like I said."

He placed his other hand on top of mine. "It's not safe being with him. I know you love him, but the way he treats you is wrong."

"I didn't know loving me was wrong." I stared at him, forcing myself to stay calm and steady. Trembling would be a sign of weakness.

"I'm not saying he doesn't love you." Brendon paused, staring at our clasped hands. "He just rubs me the wrong way."

I tried to pull my hand away, but he held on tight. "Forget I said anything. I'm okay. I'm safe. You have nothing to worry about."

"I have to hand it to you, Cora." He let go of my hand and finally looked me in the eye. "You're a good liar."

"I've had years of practice," I whispered. I had a feeling that no matter what I said, he wouldn't believe me. Had his friend fed him the same lies?

Brendon's worried eyes stared into mine. His hand reached for my braid, and he slowly trailed his finger along it. It was so much different than when Daddy did it. Then he moved his hand like he was going to place it on my cheek. Would it be rough like Daddy's? Or soft to the touch? He was so close I could smell the spearmint in his mouth.

Jenna sauntered up at the perfectly wrong moment and sat down across from us. Brendon quickly dropped his hand and sat back in his chair.

"You're here," she said.

I put on a smile. "I'm here."

She plopped her French textbook on the table. "Good. Let's get this over with. There's a guy who works at the coffee shop across the street, and I want to leave plenty of time to flirt with him." She tapped her fingers on top of her book. "What's going on between you two? You're always leaned in close and whispering. Listen, I'm totally cool with the two of you hooking up. You don't need to be all secretive about it." She held up a hand. "Just don't make-out in front of me, okay? Unless you can find someone to make-out with me at the same time."

Before I could say anything, someone else sat down at our table, his green eyes narrowed on me. Dalton from my history class. High up on Brendon's list of suspects. And mine. What he'd want with my journal, I couldn't figure out.

"Hey, Cora," Dalton said. He had his hair pulled back in a ponytail.

Jenna's eyes flickered between me, Dalton, and Brendon. "Oh, a love triangle." She rubbed her hands together. "This just got so much more interesting."

Dalton glared at Jenna. "I'm not interested in Cora – I just want to talk to her." His eyes went to mine. "You have a minute?"

I shook my head. "We're working on a school project, and we only have a limited amount of time." How had he known I was at the library? Had he been following me?

"It'll be quick," Dalton said. "Two minutes." He stood and motioned for me to join him. What would he want with me? Had he found my journal?

"Why can't you talk to her in front of us?" Brendon asked, sitting up tall.

Dalton frowned. "Because it's none of your business."

Nerves crept in, settling into my stomach. It had to be the journal. What else would he want to talk about in secret?

"It's okay," I said to Brendon. "I'll be right back."

I followed Dalton into the reference section. He'd pulled me out of sight of Jenna and Brendon, making me wary.

Dalton had his hands stuffed in his pockets. "I heard you wanted to learn to play the guitar."

"What?" I leaned against the bookshelf. "Where did you hear that?" I couldn't remember telling anyone that. I did, however, write it in my journal. Either Dalton read it, or the person who stole it had told him.

He shrugged. "Can't remember. Listen, I need to earn some money. I thought maybe I could give you some lessons for a small cost." He scratched behind his ears. "Maybe a couple times a week after school?"

I held up my hand to cut him off. "Who told you I wanted to learn guitar?"

"I can't remember."

In the heat of the moment, fear and anger overtook me. I grabbed him by the shirt and pulled him close. "Dalton. How did you know I wanted to learn to play the guitar?" I didn't know exactly what I'd do if I found out Dalton had my journal. All I knew was that I needed it back.

He peeled my hands off his shirt. "What's your problem? I already told you twice I can't remember who said it. I just remember hearing it. But if you're going to act like this, never mind."

"I . . ." I sucked in a sharp breath and stared at my hands.

Where had *that* come from? The person who stole my journal was turning me into a crazy person. Or maybe I was turning into Daddy, which terrified me more. Dalton's tone had been genuine. He couldn't remember where he'd heard I wanted to play the guitar.

I did want to learn, but there were too many problems with me taking lessons from him. "I don't have money." Also, Daddy would never let me take lessons, especially from a guy.

He leaned his head back, staring at the ceiling. "Of course. Just my luck."

"What do you need money for?"

"A trip to New York." He put his back against the shelf, his arm brushing against mine. He didn't even notice.

I took a step away, creating a larger distance between us.

"What if you sold your cell phone holders?" Jenna appeared next to us, her arms folded, sizing up Dalton. She turned her attention to me. "Everyone has been asking me where I got mine. You could make some money off that."

"Do you have it with you?" Dalton asked.

Jenna held up her arm, showing him the band. "Isn't it amazing? This girl has skills."

"You still haven't made one for me." Brendon stood right next to me, resting his arm on the shelf behind me. He smiled brightly when I looked at him.

I returned the smile. "I'm almost done with it. Be patient." I'd been slowly working on it at night, but I only had so much time from when Daddy locked me up and went to bed, and needing to get some sleep myself.

Jenna slapped Brendon's arm. "Pretty sure Brendon has no idea what patience is."

Dalton pointed to the arm band. "Do you have materials to make more?"

"I have lots of paint." I stole it often. "Getting the plastic bottles and cloth shouldn't be too hard. Velcro might be difficult to get my hands on."

Brendon bumped my arm. "I can help you with the bottles. We have tons at the restaurant. I'll tell everyone to save them instead of trashing them."

"My mom went through this crazy sewing phase," Jenna said. "Pretty much bought out every fabric store in town. Once she actually bought a sewing machine and tried to use it, she gave up. So now we have boxes of fabric in the garage. Pretty sure there's Velcro in there as well. I can bring it by your house."

"That won't work," I said. My brain tried to think of a logical reason why she couldn't bring boxes to my house, but nothing came to mind.

Jenna scrunched her eyebrows. "Why not?" Her tongue ran along her braces under her closed mouth.

"Uh . . ." A blank void filled my head.

"Her dad is a total neat freak," Brendon said. "He doesn't like clutter. You can bring the boxes to my place, and I'll sneak her some fabric every day." He looked at me. "Will that work?"

My natural smile spread across my face. "That'll be perfect." I turned to Dalton. "I couldn't do lessons after school, though. Maybe during lunch?"

Dalton sighed. "I guess that'll have to work." His eyes travelled over me, pausing on my braid. "As long as we do it somewhere we won't have a lot of interruptions or an audience or anything."

He didn't want to be seen with me. Typical, but it still stung. It shouldn't have bothered me. I should've been glad. I was supposed to stay off everyone's radar. I nodded. "That'll work. I'll start making the bands tonight. Spread the word that I'm selling them."

"Finish mine tonight so I can show it off." Brendon pulled

a ten from his wallet and handed it to me. "I'll even pay in advance."

My wide eyes took in the bill in my palm. I'd never had money before. Daddy said I didn't need it. He provided me with everything I needed. The high didn't last long, though. Dalton snatched the ten from my hand.

"This will cover our first lesson." Dalton tucked the money into his pocket. "I'll see you tomorrow during lunch. Meet me behind the gym." After I nodded, he took off.

Jenna looked at her phone. "We're running out of time. Let's get started." She turned around and hurried toward the table, the usual sass in her walk gone.

"I'm coming with you," Brendon said, giving my braid a little yank. I loved when he did that.

My eyes narrowed. "With me where?"

Brendon folded his arms. "To the guitar lessons. I'm not leaving you alone with the guy. I still think it's possible he's the one who took your journal."

"He did know I wanted to learn how to play the guitar." I blushed. "I'd never told anyone that before."

"You wrote it in your journal?"

I nodded. My eyes kept wandering to his lips. He had a small freckle in the corner on his bottom lip. I'd never noticed it before.

"I knew it." He swore under his breath. "I knew it was him."

"We don't know it was him," I said, peeling my gaze from his lips. "He denied it."

He smirked. "Of course he did. He's not going to own up to it."

"For all we know, the person who stole it could have told him."

"That's true." He took my hand and guided me back to the table.

The warmth from his hand terrified me. To him, the gesture seemed so natural and easy. No big deal. He probably didn't even realize what he was doing. To me, it sent my heart into overdrive. If Daddy came into the library and saw us holding hands, he'd kill Brendon and maybe me.

Even though the fear overwhelmed me, I didn't want him to let go. I hadn't felt that safe in the longest time, and I never wanted it to end.

CHAPTER 15

I'd stayed up late making the cell phone bands. I could only use what materials we had in the house so I couldn't make many. Brendon's was the first one done. Then I made one for Dalton, plus two others.

Brendon had been waiting for me inside the front doors of the school in the morning. He had on a shirt that said, 'Black Widow,' and had an illustration of a beautiful, strong lady with red hair.

He caught me staring. "Don't be jealous. She's fictional. Nothing can happen between me and her." He sighed. "Unfortunately."

Hoping my cheeks weren't flaring, I handed him his band. "Here you go."

"This is amazing." He put the band on his arm and tucked his cell phone inside. His had swirls of red and blue, the tone vibrant and inviting. I'd tried to match his personality to the design. "Seriously, Cora, you're a talented genius. It's so . . . me." He surprised me by taking me into his arms and hugging me.

Daddy had been the only guy to ever hug me that I could

remember. Having someone else touch me so intimately created a bubble of anxiety in the pit of my stomach. My normal reaction would have been to run and hide, but the warmth overtook me and pushed the fear aside. If a hug could do that to me, what would a kiss do?

When Brendon pulled back, his eyes were on the band. He had no idea what he did to me. All the feelings he stirred inside. It was wrong, yet wonderful.

"Do you have any others?" he asked. "I have a couple friends who might be interested."

"I could only make two others." My fist wrapped around Husky. My nerves wouldn't settle. I'd never felt this way around a guy before. "Aside one for Dalton."

He frowned. "You made one for Dalton? I don't remember him asking for one."

The warmth of Brendon still lingered on my body, bouncing around. I soaked it all in. "I figured if he wore one during his performances, maybe people would ask about them and want to buy them."

"That's a good idea," he said, but a faint frown remained on his lips.

"Thank you. For saying you'll come with me to the lessons. I don't want to be alone with him." My finger twirled around Husky's fur.

His frown evaporated, replaced by a smile. "Of course. I'm happy to help."

Letting go of Husky, I swallowed and decided to push Brendon lightly on the arm – something I'd seen Jenna do. His smile grew, expanding the warmth inside me. Was this how it felt to have a crush on someone? To like someone more than a friend? It was all so new to me. Uncharted territory that I didn't know how to navigate and certainly didn't have the tools to do so. The terrain was dangerous and could cause me serious injury. It could only remain a crush, if that's what it was. Maybe I could talk to Jenna during class. She would know. If I had the courage to bring it up.

~

*B*etween 3rd and 4th period, I sold another cell phone band to one of Brendon's friends, Jake. He turned the band over in his hands, his brown eyes wide in awe before he strapped the Velcro around his arm. A smirk suddenly landed on his thin lips. "So, this is the girl Brendon can't stop talking about."

Brendon punched his friend on the arm. "Shut up." The flare on his neck had to have matched mine. It practically scorched my skin.

Jake rubbed his arm, laughing. "What? It's true." He grinned at me. "We should all hang out sometime. I gotta see what the fuss is all about."

Brendon shoved him in the chest, his face almost as red as his hair. "Seriously, man, stop." He turned apologetic eyes to me. "Sorry. Jake just says whatever's on his mind. You can ignore him."

Sweat broke out on my forehead from the heat wave inside. I fumbled to put my backpack back on. "I'll see you later, Brendon." I hurried away before Jake could say anything else. My quick feet screeched across the linoleum as I stumbled, but I kept on going, not looking back until I arrived in history. I took a minute to calm down, hoping the red would fade from my skin.

Brendon talked about me to his friends. The thought was exhilarating and terrifying. I needed to think about something else before I broke out in another sweat.

I glanced over at Dalton next to me and handed him a band.

"It'll only cost you a lesson," I said. I smiled as his eyes lit up in excitement. It was the most emotion I'd ever seen from him.

Dalton slid the band on his arm. I'd used yellow, black, and orange for him. The band emoted a mysterious vibe, slightly arrogant, yet quiet.

"These are pretty cool." He took his cell phone out of his pocket and tucked it inside.

"What is that?" Julien asked, taking a seat. "That design is freaking awesome."

"It's a band to hold your cell phone." I pulled one out of my backpack.

Julien took it from my hand and put it on his arm. "Not sure if I'm digging all the pink and purple. Love it, though. You have any others like Dalton's?"

"I'll be making more soon." I motioned to the band, and Julien handed it back. "I'll let you know when they're available to buy."

He pointed to the lightning design shaved into the sides of his hair. "Can you do something like this?"

"Sure."

Sydney snatched the band out of my hand. "This is adorable. What's it for?"

I pointed at her phone that she had permanently glued to her hands. "A safe place to tuck your cell during class. Easy access, but harder for someone else to take it from you." I got a blank piece of paper from my backpack and drew Julien's design so I could remember it.

Sydney placed the band on her arm, still holding her cell in her hand. "How much?"

"Ten."

Sydney reached into her backpack and fished around for a minute. She pulled out a five and set it on my desk. "Hold on." A search of her pockets resulted in three more dollars. "I'll bring the rest tomorrow. Is that cool?"

"Sure." I put the money into my backpack. I knew the money would be going to Dalton for the lessons, but it was a treasure to me if only for a fleeting moment.

Sydney took a picture of the band on her arm, and then typed furiously on her phone. She slid her phone into the band and smiled, flexing her hand as she did. She placed her empty hands on the desk, then set them on her lap under the table. She had no idea what to do with her hands without a phone in them. I held in an eye roll. I found it odd that so many students at my school were attached to a small, material item.

During lunch, Brendon and I went behind the gym and found Dalton waiting for us. I'd hoped Brendon would hold my hand again, but he kept his hands in his pockets on the walk over.

Dalton strummed a song I didn't know, which wasn't difficult. Daddy listened to classical music, and sometimes sixties music when he was in a particularly good mood. "I forgot to ask you what artists you like." Dalton rested his arm on his black acoustic guitar. The dark blue strap hung loosely around his back. "It might be easier to start with something you know."

I tried to think of a song. Anything. Closing my eyes for a moment, I thought back to my childhood and my neighbor who played the guitar. He loved Journey and would play their songs for me all the time.

"Do you know Don't Stop Believing?" I asked, opening my eyes.

Dalton raised his eyebrows. "The Journey song?"

Brendon smiled at me. "That's a great song. A classic."

"It's old," Dalton said.

Folding my arms, I leaned toward him. "So, you're basically saying you don't know how to play it, right?"

"That's not what I said." Dalton played a few chords, trying to find the melody.

Brendon winked at me, and I couldn't fight back the blush.

Dalton showed me how to hold the guitar. Excitement swept over me. I had a real guitar in my hands. I never thought it would happen. Good things didn't happen to me.

Dalton took my hands and put them in place. "Let's start with A."

I waited for his touch to warm my body like Brendon's did, but nothing happened. I noticed Brendon turned a little stiff when Dalton's hand landed on mine. Was he worried about my safety? I didn't think Dalton would try anything with Brendon there. Daddy always beat me in the confines of our basement where no one could see or interrupt.

Playing the guitar was a lot harder than I thought it would be, but I really enjoyed it. Dalton would get frustrated anytime I got a key wrong and Brendon, and I would have to calm him down.

"I said E minor!" Dalton pulled a little at his shaggy hair. The bell rang, and he took his guitar from me. "I'm not doing this every day. You'll drive me crazy. Let's do Monday, Wednesday, and Friday." He put his guitar in its bag and stood, slinging the bag around his back.

"Deal." I smiled at him as he walked away. I couldn't be mad at him for getting so upset. I'd just had my first guitar lesson, something I never thought would happen. Warmth spread inside, and I was tempted to squeal like Jenna always did when she got real excited. But Daddy didn't like outbursts like that. I clenched my hands. I hated that no matter where I was, Daddy snuck into my mind and took control.

I turned to Brendon. "If he'd taken my journal, don't you think he would've brought something up by now?"

Brendon twirled an apple core in his hand. "He has. The whole guitar thing."

But he hadn't mentioned anything else or been hesitant around me. Whoever stole it, if they read the entire thing, they'd do something about it. Threaten me or call the cops. The stories in there, all the truths . . . they were dark and torturous. The high I'd just had quickly vanished, and I fought back a shiver.

"I'm scared, Brendon."

He put his arm around me. "Why?"

I quickly stood up, removing myself from his embrace. I enjoyed it too much. "I need my journal back."

Brendon stood. "We'll find it. Don't worry."

"I better get to gym class." Wrapping my arms around my backpack, I hurried to the locker room. Being near Brendon threw too many emotions at me. I didn't know how to handle them, let alone know what they all were.

There was a small part of me that thought Brendon might *like* me, especially after everything Jake had said. The happiness came back. Could we ever be more than friends? Would he hold my hand again? Or kiss me?

With a smile, I opened my locker. There was a piece of paper sitting in the back corner. My smile slowly faded as I glanced around at the other girls, but none were looking at me. I slowly picked up the paper and opened it.

The fun is about to begin.

That was all it said. But my world came crashing down. All the sounds around me drowned out. Panic burst through my veins, exploding like tiny pinpricks covering my body. Crushing the paper in my hand, I held it close to my chest and thought of all the things Daddy would do to me if he found out we'd been exposed.

CHAPTER 16

*D*addy locked me in my room after he'd dropped me off after school. I threw my backpack on my bed and paced the length of the room. My hands fumbled as I undid the top button of my shirt. I usually kept my sleeves down, but I threw caution aside and rolled them up. It put me in thinking mode.

"Rough day?" Noah asked.

My head snapped to the bed, but he wasn't there. "Noah?" I went around the side of my bed and saw him lying on the floor. "What are you doing down here?" Picking him up, I set him on the bed in his proper spot between the two flower pillows.

"It's about time. It's boring being on the floor all day."

"And being on the bed is thrilling?"

He chuckled. "Touché." He sighed. "It would be so much easier if I was stuffed with muscles instead of cotton. Then I could actually move."

I thought of him wandering around my room, playing with everything. If he could move, he'd get me in trouble one day. He'd probably break something or make a complete mess out of boredom.

"So, still no journal." I began pacing again. "It could be Dalton. He knew I wanted to learn how to play the guitar. Although, he said he couldn't remember how he found out I wanted to learn."

"The person who stole the journal could have told him," Noah said.

I smiled at him, pointing my finger into my chest. "That's what I said. If that's true, then he knows who it is. Maybe I'll need to pry that information out of him."

"Who else could have taken it?"

Pausing for a second, I kicked off my tennis shoes before I went back to pacing. "Brendon and Jenna have already ruled out Kendra, and maybe Julien as well."

"We can trust them, right?" Noah asked. "This Brendon and Jenna." Their names sounded so strange on his tongue.

I turned to him. "You met them. Kind of. They were the ones here in the room."

"How can I forget? They were very nosy. Snooping where they don't belong." His tone held a twinge of annoyance.

"You didn't give them a chance." I had really wanted Noah to like my friends. They were my only friends aside from him and Sally. But with the way Noah had reacted to them being in my room, he hadn't been fond of them, and I'd been too chicken to bring them up since then.

Sally was the one I needed to talk to, but she was stuck in the basement, and I was locked in my room.

Noah grunted. "They were okay, I guess. Did I mention they were smelly?"

I sat down on the bed next to him. "You know they can't replace you, right?"

"That's nice to hear. I was beginning to worry."

I took him into my arms, squeezing gently around the middle. He smelled like vanilla. I hadn't been able to talk Daddy into getting a pine air freshener like Noah had wanted. Daddy said that little girls shouldn't like the smells of the outdoors. We were meant to be inside the house.

"You'll always be my best friend." I'd never told Noah about Sally. He'd be too jealous. "We can trust Brendon and Jenna. That leaves Sydney, Dalton, and maybe Julien. Unless it's someone else from my classes. Really, it could be anyone at the school. It doesn't have to necessarily be someone *I* know. They could just know *me*." There was also Mr. Mendoza, but I hadn't told Noah about him yet. I wasn't sure how to bring it up. As much as I loved Noah, he could be judgy. With Sally, I could tell her anything.

"Well, that's comforting," Noah said.

I kissed the top of his fuzzy head. "I love your sarcasm."

"You seem awfully calm about this," he said. I put him down next to me.

"I'm good at faking, remember?" I leaned against the headboard and paused to make sure there weren't any noises in the house before I continued. I always kept my voice low, but it was good to be extra cautious living with Daddy. "I found another note. It was in my locker." I'd hoped I could avoid the subject. I'd smashed my fears almost as quickly as they had come – I couldn't have a meltdown at school. But now I had to face reality.

"What did it say?"

I pulled the letter out of my pocket and showed Noah.

He sighed. "Well, Cora Flora, it was nice knowing you."

I slapped his trunk. "Not helping."

"If you could donate me to a nice young boy, that would be great. Not too rowdy, though."

Taking the note, I analyzed the writing, trying to see if I

recognized it. If I remembered correctly, it matched the first note.

I'd never paid attention to anyone's writing before. I'd have to take the letter to school and compare it to Sydney, Dalton, Julien, and Mr. Mendoza's handwriting. But would Dalton, Julien, or Mr. Mendoza have gone into the girl's room to put the note in my locker? I guess they could have asked someone else to do it.

"The invitation." Reaching over, I grabbed my backpack from the floor and set it on the bed. I'd kept Jenna's party invitation. It could be the only invitation I received in my lifetime, so I couldn't part with it.

I didn't want to believe Jenna would take my journal – just the thought of her betraying me broke my heart. But I couldn't afford to rule out anyone without solid proof. Holding the invitation and note side by side, I compared them. Jenna's writing was just as bubbly as her personality. Lots of squiggles, too. The note from the locker room was slanted with straight lines. They were nothing alike.

I tucked the invitation and note into my backpack, relieved.

Then I checked the note against Brendon's phone number, but with just numbers and his name to go off of, I couldn't tell. I needed something more substantial.

Noah kept quiet while I studied. I'd been so focused on my Algebra II assignment that I didn't hear Daddy pull into the driveway. All of a sudden my door swung open and Daddy barged in.

"Hi Daddy!" The smile on my face melted away.

Fury burst from every inch of his body. Storms raged in his gray eyes, thick and heavy, and I had no way to shield myself.

I pushed myself into the headboard and yanked Noah into my arms. "Daddy, what's wrong?"

"I ran into a *friend* of yours at the store today." Daddy picked up a pink snow globe he'd given me for my tenth birthday. It had a smiley teddy bear inside wearing a pink bow around its ear. He tossed the globe in his hands a few times. "I told you that you couldn't have friends." Wrapping his hand tightly around it, he chucked the snow globe with everything he had, and it smashed into the wall above me. Water and glass shards rained down, showering me with sparkles.

The terror in my body made me freeze. Nothing would move no matter how hard I tried. Why was he so upset? I'd never seen him destroy something like that.

"She knew who I was." With a growl, Daddy yanked a fabric doll from the dollhouse. "She asked me how our trip was."

"Daddy please calm down." My voice quivered.

"Calm down?" Veins bulged from his neck as he took the doll by the head and pulled, the cloth tearing away until the head had fully come off.

I watched in horror as the pieces fell to the floor, the cotton leaking from the head and body. Would he ever do the same to me?

"I had no idea what she was talking about. I looked like a fool." Taking a wooden chair from inside the dollhouse, he smashed it in his shaking hands. "She said you couldn't go to her sleepover because we were going out of town to visit family."

A warm sensation slid down my skin. Peeling my gaze from Daddy, I pulled a quarter-sized glass shard out of my arm. I'd forgotten to roll my sleeves back down. The cut wasn't too deep, but a small amount of blood trickled out. I worked moisture into my mouth. "I had to make an excuse of why I couldn't go."

Daddy stomped over and wrapped his fist around my

arm, yanking me off the bed. Noah fell from my arms and onto the floor.

"You didn't tell me about her inviting you." Daddy threw me against the wall, so my back was to him. "She shouldn't have invited you in the first place." His belt paddled his pants as he yanked it off, the sound turning my blood to ice. "No friends, Cora."

The belt whipped hard against my back and I screamed in agony. He'd never beat me like this in my room before, so the smooth walls left me with nothing to grip.

"No keeping things from me." Pain rippled through my back on the next strike. "No making me look like a fool."

The belt slapped along the middle of my back, tearing open the skin under my shirt, the sting unbearable. A distorted cry fled my mouth. Why was he doing this to me? I didn't deserve it. Not this bad.

"No disobeying your father."

I focused on the sparkles left on my arm as his leather belt slashed open another section of skin and blood dripped down my back. The warmness contrasted with the cold swirling inside of me. The blows kept coming. I lost track after twelve. My legs finally buckled and I fell to the ground, my fingers digging into the carpet. He continued to strike me with the belt. My hand begged to reach out for Noah, but pain and fear paralyzed me.

I could hear the spittle on Daddy's lips. "Boy, you're a pathetic excuse of a man!"

Surprise snaked through me, dulling the pain for a brief second. Had he called me a boy?

The doorbell rang, and Daddy paused, his heavy, ragged breaths replacing the sound of the belt. His tone was animal-istic, almost feral. "Now look at what you've done. A neighbor probably heard your crying."

He dropped the belt on the floor and left me alone in the

room, his footsteps thunderous down the hall. I curled into a ball, wrapping my trembling arms around my legs, and sobbed. My back screamed out in pain with each shudder of my body.

Something had changed within Daddy. In all the years I'd lived with him, he'd never been *this* violent. He'd whipped me, but it wasn't hard enough to rip open my skin.

Had Daddy stopped loving me? Was I not safe with him anymore? I had nowhere else to go and no one to take care of me.

After a few minutes, Daddy stormed back into the room. I tried to cower into the corner, but he was too quick. His hand gripped my arm tight, and he pulled me off the ground so hard I worried my shoulder would come out of its socket.

"I had to lie." His voice held a dangerous edge. "That was Mrs. Roberts. She wanted to know what was happening." He dragged me down the hall, my heels sliding across the carpet. "I told her we were watching a horror flick and we'd turn down the volume." He unlocked the basement door and forced me down the stairs, my feet thumping against the wood. With a grunt, he tossed me on the stained mattress. "You'll stay down here until I'm ready to see your face again." I didn't need a light to see a tornado had overtaken his eyes. His whole body heaved in a stiff way that made goosebumps break out on my skin.

Finally – after several excruciating moments of me fearing he'd start hitting me again – his boots pounded against the steps as he walked back up, leaving me alone in the dark, cold basement.

I lay there on the cement, crying uncontrollably. Any way I turned, my back stung. I finally lay on my stomach, clutching my hands against my chest and grinding my teeth in pain.

For the first time in years, I wanted out – away from him

and his controlling ways. The thought terrified me. I had no idea who I was without him, and I had no way to take care of myself. I wish I knew how to make him happy, but nothing satisfied him anymore. Maybe he'd forever be angry, and I'd just ruined everything.

CHAPTER 17

*I*n the middle of the night, I woke to the sound of spraying water. My eyes scanned the dark basement, trying to find the source. Water burst from a pipe near the water heater. Knowing I needed to turn off the water, I stumbled around in the pitch blackness, searching for the valve. Daddy didn't allow lights in the basements, so all I had was a strip of moonlight slipping through the window.

I searched in vain. There were too many pipes and objects and with no light, I couldn't tell the difference between any of them.

Cold water slapped against my feet. That was when the panic really sunk in – the basement was flooding. Daddy would be furious when he found out. Somehow, he'd blame it on me and my carelessness.

I sloshed to the basement steps, falling a few times. Water soaked my pants, shirt, and hair by the time I reached the bottom step. I crawled up, sucking in sharp breaths at the pain in my back. The water stung against all the lashings.

When I reached the top of the stairs, I knocked on the door, softly at first. I wanted to wake Daddy but didn't want to alert the neighbors. After a few minutes, I pounded harder, hoping and praying that Daddy would finally come.

As the lock grinded and the door opened, I fell onto the ground, tired and sore.

"Cora?" Daddy grabbed a flashlight he kept in the hallway near the basement door, hopped over me, and ran into the flooding basement, his thuds shaking the stairs.

Holding in screams from the pain, I crawled to the bathroom, my wet and bloody body dragging along the carpet. Inside, I slid over the tile and reached into the shower, turning the valve to hot. I wanted to wash off as much as I could in case the water upstairs turned off.

Water rained down as I peeled off my clothes, took out my braid, and climbed into the tub. I sat on the bottom, letting the water fall onto my skin. The burn overwhelmed me. Blood slithered through the water, creating a pool of red all around me. I closed my eyes and focused on my breathing, trying to not pass out.

My tears blended in with the water. Pulling my legs into my chest, I rocked back and forth, humming a soft melody while trying to wash away all my sins.

The water turned off before I had finished. Daddy must have shut off the water through the whole house. It took every ounce of energy I could muster to crawl out of the tub and wrap a towel around my damaged body. I leaned against the cupboards and continued to rock and hum.

After a few minutes, Daddy appeared in the doorway. His pants were soaked to his calves. He stood there, panting, staring at me on the floor, his eyes softer than they had been in a while.

"A pipe burst," I whispered.

"I saw," he mumbled.

I wrapped my arms tight around myself. "I tried to find the valve to turn off the water, but it was too dark."

With a deep sigh, he fell down beside me and pulled me into his arms. "I know you tried, angel. I should have trusted you with a light so you could see down there." He kissed the top of my head, his lips lingering on my wet hair. "I'll put the bulb back tomorrow morning." He rocked with me, the motion soothing. "I've been thinking about my encounter with the girl at your school." He stayed quiet for a moment – like he was trying to collect his thoughts – before he spoke. "Maybe I was too rash. She seems like the type of girl who would make friends with anyone, even if they weren't trying." Again with the dramatic shift in moods.

"I wasn't trying to be her friend, Daddy," I said. Being friends with Jenna had just come naturally. We had stuff in common.

He ran his hand down my hair. "I know. You did the right thing by saying you couldn't go to her party. I just wished you would have told me so I wouldn't have looked so stupid in front of her."

I buried my head into his neck, pushing past the stench of sweat. "I thought you'd be mad at me. I don't like to make you angry."

"You're a good girl, Cora," he said, so soft and caring, like I was the only thing that mattered to him. "You're my little angel. I love you."

"I love you, too, Daddy." I sniffed and wiped my nose with the side of my hand. "Why did you call me 'boy' earlier?"

His body stiffened. "I did?"

"Yes," I whispered. I pulled back in time to see him close his eyes and purse his lips in a way that it looked like he was scolding himself.

His demeanor finally loosened and his eyes opened, the composed blue relaxing me. "Must have been a slip of the tongue." He poked my nose. "I know you're a girl."

He removed some cream and bandages from under the

sink and cleaned up my back. Every press against my back burned. I clenched the muscles in my body and held in the tears. Would the pain ever end? Or would my life always hurt?

When he finally finished with my back, he put a bandage on the cut on my arm. It had been small and not very deep. Hopefully it wouldn't take long to heal. My long sleeves would cover it up, though, so no one would see.

He helped me stand. "Go get dressed in something warm and try to get some sleep."

I stared at my water-wrinkled toes. "Do I have to go back downstairs?"

He lifted my chin so he could look in my eyes. They were calm and breezy, like a warm summer's day. "No, angel. You can sleep in your own bed. You'll need energy for tomorrow."

"What's tomorrow?" Would he really let me go back to school after what had happened? I wasn't sure if I could. With the injuries on my back, there was no way I could conceal the pain.

He guided me into the hallway and pointed to the carpet. My blood stained the entire hallway. He put his arm around my shoulder. "You need to rip up the carpet. I've been wanting wood flooring for a while now, and this just gives me a good excuse." He rubbed my arm. "I'll put some buckets near the top of the basement stairs. You can use them to get the water out."

"Where should I dump the water?" My muscles ached from the thought of all the work that lay ahead of me. It would take me hours to empty the water from the basement, especially in the state I was in.

"The backyard."

No one would see me that way. "Can't I dump it in the bathtub?" It would be so much easier – and closer.

His cold finger ran the length of my cheek. "No, angel.

There may be random objects in with the water. We don't want that going down the pipes. It would create an even bigger mess than we already have on our hands."

With a nod, I forced myself to move toward my room, using the wall and door frame for support.

The lock outside my door clicked into place, trapping me in the room for the rest of the night. I slowly shuffled to my dresser, fighting through the pain. I wished I could take some sort of pain reliever, but Daddy didn't believe in them.

"Are you back in here?" Noah asked.

I'd almost forgotten he'd fallen to the floor when Daddy had taken me to the basement. I picked up Noah, biting my tongue from the sting, and placed him on the bed. At least he had dried from the broken snow globe water.

"You're back early," Noah said. I turned him so he couldn't see me.

Dropping the towel, I opened my dresser drawer and pulled out fresh clothes. The motion from putting my top on pulled at my lashings, and I clenched my teeth so I wouldn't scream out.

"Something needs to change," Noah said.

"What do you mean?"

"I can't watch him do that to you again." He cleared his throat like he was trying to hold back tears. "It's too much."

With stiff arms, I slowly lowered myself to the bed and sat down. "I'm sorry you had to see that."

"Me, too," he whispered.

After closing the canopy, I lay down on my stomach and took him into my arms. "How did everything get so out of control?"

"That's life. An uncontrollable mess."

I kissed his trunk. "Going to public school ruined everything."

"Will he let you go back?" Noah asked.

I closed my eyes, pulling him closer. "I have to. At least to figure out who knows my secret."

"Then what? Kill them?"

"I can't do that. Murder is wrong. I'd go to jail. I just need to talk the person out of reporting anything. Maybe I can convince them the journal isn't real. Tell them I like to make up stories and want to be a crime writer one day."

Noah laughed, the sound strained. "They'll never believe you."

"They have to," I mumbled, exhaustion taking over my body.

If I could get the journal back, I could quit public school. Daddy's anger had increased when I started high school. Maybe going back to homeschool would make him happy again. Maybe he'd start loving me again, and then I wouldn't have to worry about being alone.

But with Daddy, wouldn't I always be alone? Was that what I wanted? There was no positive outcome. I was either alone and under Daddy's control, or alone and under the foster system's control.

I'd always thought the latter was worse, but maybe that wasn't entirely true.

CHAPTER 18

*A*s soon as Daddy left for work, I got down on my knees, gritting through the pain on my back, and slowly removed all the carpet and padding in the hallway. I rolled them up and hobbled into the garage. Daddy would have to use his van to dispose of it later.

All day I sloshed up and down the stairs, using the railing and walls for support, removing buckets of water from the basement and tossing it in the backyard. It didn't take long for my legs to wobble during each ascent and descent. Daddy would have to change my bandages when he got home.

Each flight brought an overwhelming fear of what was to come. I'd made a mess of things. Not just in the basement. I'd made friends – something I wasn't supposed to do. I'd wrote all my deepest, darkest secrets in a journal, risking exposure of me and Daddy.

The fun is about to begin. That was what the second letter had said. What did they mean?

The worst part? I didn't have the slightest clue what to do. I had no one I could go to for help. Noah and Sally were just outlets, not people to go to for actual advice. They had no clue what lay beyond the front doors – Sally didn't know what lay beyond the basement.

There were moments I wished I didn't know what was out there either. If I'd kept in my bubble – didn't have a never-ending need to learn new things – I would have been safe in my room, locked away from the world and all it had to offer. Away from friends and knowledge and a chance at life.

At the end of the day, I wanted to take a long, hot shower, but Daddy had only been able to temporarily fix the pipe. He'd shown me how to turn the water back on but said I needed to keep all water usage to a minimum.

So after I turned it on, I hurried upstairs and took a quick shower. I needed to wash away all the regret, the grime from the basement water, and the dirt my life had to offer. I was filth – disgusting waste that no one wanted.

If someone were to uncover the truth, I'd be thrown back in the system. I still had two years until I was a legal adult. That would be two years of being bounced around by a bunch of random strangers who didn't want or love me. I'd be on my own.

Daddy had hurt me, but I'd been the source of the anger. If I hadn't wrote in the journals, been careless and taken it to school, I wouldn't be injured. I wouldn't be covered in gross basement water. I'd be safe in my room with Noah, completely unharmed by the world.

Daddy wanted me when no one else had, and I'd betrayed him by keeping the journals. Somehow I had to dispose of all of them without him finding out.

I hated that I was trapped. Why had I ever been born? If there was a purpose to me being alive, I had no idea what it was.

After turning the water back off, I curled up on the pink rug in my room and hummed a lullaby.

~

*S*ince I wasn't locked up, I shuffled into the kitchen, staying close to the walls so I wouldn't fall, and prepared dinner for Daddy. Meatloaf. It wasn't my favorite, but he loved it, especially when I used his mom's recipe. She'd died years before Daddy took me and I'd only ever seen pictures. I wondered what it would be like to have a grandparent – someone else to love and care for me.

Going through the cupboards, I removed everything I'd need to cook and arranged it neatly on the counter, in the order I'd use it. I did the same with the ingredients, setting them in front of the bowl or measuring cup they'd be used with. Organization always helped the process go smoothly and calmed the butterflies in my stomach. If I followed a structured method, nothing could go wrong.

When I finished preparing it, I opened the preheated oven and set the pan smack in the center. Smiling, I closed the door and leaned up against the counter. Before I cleaned up the mess, I always liked to take a moment to focus on my breathing. Closing my eyes, I inhaled through the nose, counted to three, and then exhaled from my mouth.

Stick to a process that was guaranteed to work. Daddy taught me that.

The phone on the wall rang, startling me. It listed *unknown* on the caller ID. We didn't get many phone calls, especially at the house.

Daddy didn't like me to answer the phone unless it was one of his clients or him. But a small part of me tingled in anticipation. Ignoring my shaking hand, I lifted the receiver.

"Hello?"

"Is this Cora?" The voice on the other end was deep and rumbly, like it was automated – not a real human voice.

"Who's this?"

"Someone who knows your secret."

I froze in shock. Every part of me wanted to panic, but I had to find out what they knew first. "What secret?"

The voice laughed, the raspy tone making my skin crawl. "The question isn't what secret, it's which one? I know many of yours, perfect angel." They'd used Daddy's nickname for me.

My fist clutched tightly around the phone. "If you give me back my property now, I won't turn you into the police." It was a weak argument, which we both knew.

They laughed harder. "Yes, please, let's go to the police and turn in your precious Daddy."

A wave of fear crashed over me as spots appeared in my vision. I swayed where I stood, so I reached out and gripped the counter, trying to stay standing. Everything in the room closed in on me until I felt trapped. Breathing. Oh, how it hurt to breathe. My lungs were on fire, threatening to burn me down to ash.

"You still there, *angel?*"

So many questions raced through my mind. Who were they? How did they get my journal? Why had they taken it? How did they get my phone number?

But, really, there was only one question that completely outweighed all the others, and I knew this person wouldn't be answering any of the other ones any time soon. I licked my lips, trying to work moisture back into my mouth. "What do you want?"

"Finally, the correct question." Their deep breath broke through the phone, crinkling like thick plastic in the wind. "I need you to steal something for me."

"What?" Of all the things they could ask of me, that hadn't even crossed my mind. "Why?"

"From what I've read, you're an expert at stealing." Even

through the automated voice, their smile was apparent. It turned my fear into anger. Bad move on their part.

Placing my hand on my forehead, I shook my head. "Small things."

"This is small."

"What is it?"

"Test answers," they said. I desperately wished I could tell whether it was a male or female voice. It would narrow down my suspect list. "I need all the test answers for every single biology class."

My hand balled into a fist. "You can't possibly expect me to do that. Why not just one teacher?"

They laughed. "But where's the fun in that?"

Maybe Jenna could let me know who took biology since she TA'd in the front office. It could possibly point me toward the blackmailer.

"And before you think of asking Jenna for help, you should know that these answers may not be for me."

I shouldn't have been surprised that this person knew my friends and what their classes were. I had to go off the assumption that they knew everything about me, which made finding out who they were so much harder. "Wow, what a noble student. Stealing answers for someone else."

They laughed. "Or maybe I just want to test you to see if you'll do as you're told." They hadn't commented on my usage of *student*, but that didn't really mean anything.

"If I do this . . ."

"*When* you do it," they cut in. "Your other option is to have me call the police."

"Where do I put the answers?" I hated that this was happening to me.

"Leave them in a bag near the flagpole tomorrow after school."

The phone almost fell from my hand. "That's too soon. I may not even be at school tomorrow."

"Not my problem. Tomorrow after school." They hung up.

My hand shook as I placed the phone back on the receiver. How would I possibly steal all the test answers before school ended? What if Daddy didn't allow me to go back to school?

The oven timer went off, reminding me of the meatloaf. I'd have to come up with a plan later. Now, I had to prepare the rest of dinner for Daddy. He needed to be happy if I intended on going back to school.

~

I double checked every piece of dinnerware, looking closely for scratches or nicks of any kind. Every piece was put in its proper place – the plates, the utensils, and the cups – and the napkins were folded precisely. I'd opened the front window so I could hear when Daddy pulled into the driveway. The second his van rumbled into its spot, I closed the front window and dished the food onto the plate, wiping away any drops that splattered.

As the front door opened, I pressed the tip of my finger into his meatloaf, making sure it was the perfect temperature. Smoothing out my dress, I stood tall next to his seat and plastered on my smile.

Daddy rounded the corner, back straight and chin held up, his tired eyes lighting up when he saw me. I lifted onto my tiptoes just barely and smiled wider.

"Hi, Daddy." I gestured to his seat. "Welcome home."

He pointed to the kitchen. "I need to wash my hands."

I picked a warm towel up from the counter and held it out. "Let me."

With a smile, he held out his hands, and I wiped them

clean, making sure to get every spec of dirt and every crevice. When I finished, he kissed me on the forehead, the coldness lingering, and sat down in his seat. His eyes wandered over my dress.

"But I'm not dressed the part today."

I sat down and slid my chair closer to the table. "You look handsome, Daddy."

I tucked my napkin into the collar of my dress. Daddy did the same, putting his into his shirt.

"How was your day?" I asked, waiting patiently for him to take his first bite before I took mine.

"My day was just okay until I came home." He moaned. With his fork, he pointed to the meatloaf. "This is perfect, angel."

Warmth burst inside me, and I smiled. He was in a good mood. "I'm so glad."

He took a few more bites, slowly chewing, and then wiped at his mouth. "And how was your day?"

"I finished cleaning up the basement. No serious damage. Aside from the busted pipe."

His shoulders stooped, surprising me. He rarely showed his vulnerability. "I repaired it best I could. I stopped on the way home from my last appointment and got everything I need to replace the pipe."

"Good," I said. He always checked the caller ID, so he'd know someone called. "A telemarketer called."

He lifted an eyebrow. "You answered the phone?"

"I thought it might be one of your clients." I took a bite of meatloaf, forcing it down my throat. "They were trying to get us to switch cable providers. I did as you taught me. I was polite, yet firm, and let them know we weren't interested. It took a while to end the conversation, but I finally did."

"That's my girl." He took another bite of meatloaf, his mouth working slow and deliberate. His blue-gray eyes bore

131

into mine, and I did my best to stay calm. With a deep breath, he tore his gaze from mine and drove his fork through another piece of meatloaf. "Saturday, I'll go down to the store and buy some hardwood. Then we can install it."

I set my fork down next to my plate, careful not to clink them together. "You want me to help you? I'm not sure how good I'll be...."

He patted my hand, his skin rough against mine. "I'll show you how to do it. My father never let me help around the house – he was always worried I'd screw things up. I had to figure everything out on my own." He winked at me. "I'm sure you'll be a natural like me."

Smiling, I took a drink of water and set the cup back in its correct position on the table. "Daddy, may I go back to school tomorrow?"

He clenched his hand in and out of a fist. "I'm not sure if you've earned that privilege back."

I finished off my meatloaf and then folded my hands into my lap. "You make an excellent point, Daddy. I guess I'm just eager to learn. But if you don't think it's time ..."

He wiped his mouth with a napkin. "You did work hard today." He put his shoulders back. "And I love the fact that you like to learn so much. You remind me so much of myself. Diligent and eager." His eyes focused on the pan of meatloaf. He drummed his fingers on the table, keeping a rhythm with the second hand on the clock hanging in the kitchen.

Both my fists clutched onto my dress under the table. Each second that passed added to my agony. I wanted to shout, *just let me go!* but that would ruin my chances of ever going back to school. All I wanted was to get my journal back and destroy all the evidence of mine and Daddy's secret. Then I could figure out what to do from there.

"Fine," he finally said. "You may go back to school tomorrow."

My fists released their death grip on my dress and my muscles relaxed. "Thank you, Daddy."

Before I got my journal back, I had to figure out how to carry out the culprit's wishes: steal test answers.

There was this small part of me that hoped I'd get caught and arrested. Then the truth would be revealed, and I'd be thrown into a juvenile detention center. I wouldn't have to worry about Daddy hurting me again or being in the foster system.

I'd finally have a place where I belonged.

CHAPTER 19

I pressed an ear against my bedroom door, listening and waiting patiently for Daddy to finally go to bed. His boots paced along the hall on the floorboard. Mumbles drifted through the cracks of the door, but I couldn't make any of it out – until he got loud.

"I'm doing better than you ever did!" Daddy roared.

Who was he talking to? There was no way he'd let someone else in the house, and he normally wouldn't be on the phone that late.

His fist pounded against the wall, the sound of cracking drywall filling the air. "I'm the best father she'll ever have, no thanks to you."

A sneeze slithered up my nose, and I tried to hold it in, but it exploded out of me. Dead silence rang on the other side of the door. A minute passed before his footfalls faded toward his room, and just a few minutes later, his snores drifted down the hallway.

As much as I wanted to figure out what was going on with Daddy, I didn't have time. Standing, I thought through my plan. I would sneak out my window, walk to the school, break in, take the answers, and come back home.

When Daddy finally let me have a room, he installed iron bars outside my window to keep the bad guys from being able to get in. Almost every night, I'd opened the window and stared out at the moon and stars. One evening when I was thirteen, my elbow banged against one of the bars, and it wobbled. I shook the bar, twisting it back and forth until it came loose.

At that moment, panic had flooded my body, practically drowning me. I didn't want Daddy to find out I'd broken something of his – he got so angry whenever I did. I'd searched all over my room trying to find something – *anything* I could use to put the bar back in place, if only temporarily. In my backpack, I'd found a pack of gum I'd taken from the store. I'd peeled back the wrapper, shoved a piece into my mouth, and worked it into a moldable consistency so I could use it on the bar. It wasn't ideal, but it held for the night until I could get some sticky putty from the garage the next day.

I'd never snuck out of the house, but I liked knowing I had the option. It gave me some comfort I desperately needed and a way out.

I was small enough that I should've been able to squeeze through the bars. I'd thrown everything I would need, plus a couple journals I'd retrieved from the walls, into my back-pack. I picked it up, threw it on my shoulder, and went to the window. I was about to lift the pane when someone rapped on the glass.

I jumped into the air, my hand landing on my chest. Who was outside my window in the middle of the night? Maybe the blackmailer had come.

They tapped on the glass again, and I looked over my shoulder, hoping Daddy was too deep in his sleep to have heard anything. I waited a few seconds before I pushed the panic down inside and opened the window.

Brendon stood on the other side, his hands on two of the bars. I stumbled back a few steps, adrenaline rushing through my body. What was he doing at my house?

He had on a blue shirt with a red triangle with an S in the middle. "How did I not notice these bars before?" He frowned. "Sorry. I should have. . . . Are you okay?"

Forcing my trembling legs, I stepped forward, closing the distance between us so I could see his eyes. Worry was etched all the way around. His fingers extended and I did something I'd never thought I'd do: I linked my fingers through his. Heat ignited inside.

"I'm fine," I whispered, my shaky tone betraying me.

He leaned his forehead against the bars. "You're imprisoned inside a room. I wouldn't qualify that as fine."

Taking hold of the loose bar, I removed it from the putty and quietly set it down on the floor of my room. "See? I'm not imprisoned. They were here when we bought the place. Dad's never gotten around to removing all of them."

The tension in his body slightly released and he linked his fingers back with mine. "Where have you been? We've missed you at school."

I couldn't meet his eyes, so I stared at the fraying Band-Aids on his fingers. "I've been sick."

His fingers squeezed mine. "You don't have to lie to me."

"I'm not lying." I licked my lips. "I tend to get sick a lot."

His voice turned sad. "My friend was the same way. And I always believed him and never did anything about it. Now I'm wondering if I made the wrong decision."

I wanted to ask him about his friend but didn't want to give him the wrong idea that I was in the same situation. I forced myself to look into his eyes. "Brendon, I'm fine. I promise. I have everything under control."

He sighed. "You don't have to hide everything from the world and go it alone."

"It's easier that way," I said, casting my eyes downward at the S on his shirt.

"Easier for you or me?" he asked, his tone filled with frustration.

I raised my eyes to his. "Both."

We remained quiet as we stared at each other, both silently shouting and begging each other; me, to be helped, and Brendon wanting to help me. But neither of us knew the answer. We were both powerless.

I absolutely hated the feeling.

Maybe if I told him about the blackmailer, it would move his focus off my home situation and make him feel like he was doing something to help.

"I need your help," I whispered, slicing through the silence. I needed to leave as soon as possible. Daddy could walk in at any moment.

"Anything. Name it, and I'll do it."

I'd never met anyone like Brendon. So completely selfless and kind, and putting his neck on the line for someone he hardly knew. Jenna cared about me, but she wasn't the one standing outside my window in the middle of the night, knowing she'd have to come late so Daddy wouldn't know she was here.

"I have to break into the school tonight."

Brendon's eyebrows rose in surprise. "That's not what I was expecting." A smile broke out onto his face. "Why are we breaking into the school?"

I unlinked our fingers and lowered my hands. "You aren't going to like it."

He gestured to my current situation of being locked in my room. My own personal prison that I couldn't tell him about. "I don't like *any* of this."

"I have to steal some test answers." I stared at him, waiting for his reaction.

He just stared at me, face blank. "Test answers? You're smart, Cora. Why would you need that?" He arched an eyebrow. "Unless you're just one of those people who do things for the thrills."

I rolled my eyes. "Yep. That definitely sounds like me."

"Why?"

"The person who stole my journal. They called today. If I don't deliver what they want by tomorrow after school, they're calling the police." I wanted the words back as soon as they left my mouth.

He took a step back and folded his arms. "I like that plan. Let's call the police."

Being gentle, yet urgent, I reached my arms between the space where I'd removed the bar, took hold of his shirt, and pulled him toward me. "No police, Brendon. Ever. Promise me."

His hands squeezed between the bars and landed on my waist, making me tense. But I held firm. "Why?" he asked.

"I know you're worried, but I know what I'm doing. You must trust me. No police. Please."

He shook his head. "I could never promise you that. But if it's what you want for now, then fine. But I swear, if something happens to you, I'm calling the police."

"Why do you care so much?" I let go of his shirt and smoothed it out, my hands running over his chest. I traced the S on his shirt.

"Because no one should be treated like you are," Brendon whispered, a tenderness in his voice I'd never heard before. "You don't deserve this." A fraction of a smile appeared on his lips, making me look at his freckle. "It also helps that you're pretty."

Heat erupted on my neck and cheeks. I was grateful for the dark so Brendon couldn't see.

Noah suddenly cleared his throat. "Could you shut the window, please? You're letting in a draft."

His declaration snapped me back into reality. We needed to leave before Daddy caught us. Picking up my backpack, I handed it to Brendon.

"What's in here? A rock?" he asked, setting my backpack on the ground. "It's freaking heavy."

"Just a few things we might need."

He pointed to the opening. "You really think you can fit through there? I mean, you're tiny, but this isn't very wide."

I shrugged. "Won't know until I try."

I lifted my leg and pushed it through the opening. It was a tighter fit than I thought. Brendon wrapped his arms around me and helped me out. Being so close to him helped distract from my back, which burned from where Daddy had struck me. Thank goodness Daddy had replaced the bandages before he went to bed.

When my feet landed on the grass, I looked up at Brendon, our faces inches from each other. He held me, staring down into my eyes, and running his hand over my braid. A new sort of fear worked its way into my blood.

Brendon was the first guy I'd ever been physically close to. Most guys scared me and wove alarm deep into my bones, strangling me tight. I didn't trust them. They were bad.

Something was different with Brendon. His eyes held concern, so sincere it pained me, but also warmed me. It gave me the smallest ounce of hope that maybe there were decent people in the world. Maybe it wasn't as bad as Daddy said it was.

Daddy.

He'd hurt me if he saw me in Brendon's arms. He'd definitely hurt Brendon – maybe even kill him.

Brendon must have seen the fear in my eyes, because he immediately dropped his arms and stepped back. "I'm so sorry, Cora. I'm not trying to take advantage of you or anything. If I ever get too close, tell me. The last thing I want to do is scare you."

How could he know me so well? How did he know my fears that I kept locked away inside?

Unless he'd seen my journal. Then he'd know everything.

CHAPTER 20

*T*he night was a tad chilly. I hadn't thought to bring a jacket, but at least I had on long sleeves as usual. We passed all the brick homes in silence. Brendon was probably thinking as much as I was. Would my plan work? Could we possibly get the test answers, or would we just get caught?

When we got to the grassy park halfway to school, I turned down the sidewalk and headed toward it. Ash trees were scattered through the area. What would it be like to sit under one during the day and read a book?

"What are you doing?" Brendon asked, glancing around. So late at night, there was no one around. Only a few street-lamps illuminated the area.

"I need to burn my journals."

He laughed but stopped at my frown. "You're serious? They took one journal. You don't need to destroy all your others."

I moved my backpack to the front of me and held it tight. "You don't understand. No one can see what's in these journals. No one." They weren't just damaging to Daddy. They were damaging to me. All my sins were in there as well. I'd never worried about people judging me if they read my journals, but I never had anyone like Brendon and Jenna where I cared what they thought of me.

Brendon tried to take one from my hand, but I yanked it away from him.

"What's in there?" he asked. "Evidence?"

"It doesn't matter." Because if he knew, he'd never let me burn them. He'd find out the entire truth and probably hate me for it. He'd look at me differently. He was the only one who'd shown concern for me. Once he read the journals, he'd see the weak, damaged version of me and run.

We stopped near a pavilion, and I set my backpack on a metal table. I unfastened my cuffs and rolled up my sleeves.

Brendon took hold of my arm, looking at the bandage covering it. "What happened?"

I sighed in frustration. He questioned everything. "Accidents can happen to me, you know. I cut myself when I was making dinner." I'd done that in the past. It was rare since I always tried to be careful, but occasionally, I lost focus.

He raised his eyebrows. "You cook?"

I stood tall. "Yes, and I'm good at it."

I took a journal, ripped out a few pages, and set them in a fire pit near the pavilion. I stared at the papers lying there. My words. The only things that had ever truly been mine were about to be burned. Maybe it would be therapeutic and help me start over. I could stop holding onto the past and focus on a future with Daddy. Without my journals, I could quit school, and everything could go back to how it was.

I looked over at Brendon. He watched me in a contemplative silence, like he was trying to read my thoughts. I'd pulled him into this entire mess. He knew too much. I never wanted him to get hurt. I took a step closer to him, looking up into his eyes, seeing the concern and compassion.

He gave my braid a little yank. "You sure you want to do this?"

Licking my dry lips, I nodded. "I have to."

My attention went back to the papers in the fire pit. Destroying my journals would help Brendon as well. It would end our friendship, and he would be safe from Daddy and his wrath. We'd all be safe.

I pulled a matchbook from my pocket. I'd taken it from a restaurant Daddy had taken me to for my twelfth birthday. It was one of the few times we'd gone somewhere nice. I wanted to remember it, but I also liked the thought of having the matches just in case I ever needed protection.

Before I could talk myself out of it, I took a deep breath and with a shaking hand, I lit a match, and touched the flame to a page, watching it ignite. I threw page after page into the fire, until every single piece from both journals was destroyed. The smell of ash taunted me, reminding me I could never undo the damage. I'd never get those pieces of my life back. A few tears slid down my cheek.

Brendon watched, not saying anything. He may have thought I was crazy, but I was doing what I had to do to protect my family. And him.

A part of me died with the burning pages. My whole life was in those journals. Every truth, every fear, everything I had been through faded away with each destroyed page like it had never happened. My life was being erased in the blink of an eye. Inside, I screamed and writhed in agony. I hated that I had to erase my life.

But the journals had to be destroyed. All of them. Including the one that had been stolen. I had to get it back and burn it like the rest.

The last embers faded, releasing some of my tension. I still had a few dozen to burn. A couple at a time wasn't going to be enough. I'd have to figure out another way. But I didn't trust anyone else to burn them for me. Not even Brendon or Jenna. The only person I'd ever be able to fully trust was myself.

Or maybe not. Could I trust myself? Would I really be able to burn the rest of my journals and wipe out my entire life? After the mistakes I'd made and all the emotions I'd let control me, I wasn't so sure.

"We should get to the school," Brendon said, his voice soft like he knew the pain I was feeling. He gently took my hand in his. It was soft and warm. "Before your dad notices you're gone."

He was right, but the impact of what I'd just done slammed into me. Turning around, I wrapped my arms around his middle and buried my head into his chest.

He held me close, being gentle. When I began to sway - the motion soothing - he moved with me. He kept his cheek pressed against the top of my head and I soaked in his warmth. Closing my eyes, I hummed a calming melody in my head until the tears stopped.

I pulled back just enough to look up at him. I placed my hand on his cheek, wanting to thank him, but I couldn't find the words. He put his hand over mine. With his other hand, he wiped away my tears.

My gaze fluttered to his lips and the freckle in the corner.

Brendon took my hand on his cheek and pressed a soft, warm kiss against my palm. "We really need to go."

If a real kiss felt as good as that, I hoped I got a chance to experience it before I never saw him again. I sighed. "I know."

With clasped hands, we headed toward the school.

*I*t took longer than I hoped to get to the school. We'd gone slow, taking lots of turns and hiding in the shadows. The last thing we wanted was to be spotted. We also wanted to make sure we weren't followed.

I stared up at the large, two-story brick building and sighed. They locked the school up tight at night. None of the doors or windows were options.

"Know how to jimmy a lock?" Brendon asked.

Pursing my lips, I shook my head. "It's not on my list of skills." The locks were on the outside of my door, so I could never attempt to break free.

"Then how do you expect to get in?"

"Follow me."

We crept around to the back of the school. Luckily, the science classes were on the first floor. I stopped near a large window, cupped my hands, and peered inside. The sight of flasks and beakers made a small smile spread across my face. A science class.

Shadows covered the area behind the school, leaving a creepy feeling. But I was grateful for the darkness. I pulled out a rock and towel from my backpack.

Brendon scratched his forehead. "You know, I was kidding about the whole rock thing."

I smiled at him. "You have a better plan of how to get in?"

He rubbed his hands together. "Well, seeing as breaking and entering weren't on my original to-do list tonight, nope."

Wrapping the towel around the rock, I made sure every spot was covered and then bunched the remaining part of the towel to use as a hold.

"You might want to step back," I said.

He took a couple of steps away from me. I swung the rock

into a window, shattering the glass. The motion tugged at the cuts on my back, and I cringed in pain. Brendon kept looking around, seeing if anyone had heard the ruckus. It had been louder than I had expected. I smashed the rock against all the glass still stuck to the frame until there was plenty of room to get in without cutting myself.

I placed the rock in my backpack.

"You're going to carry that all the way back home?"

"I'm not leaving evidence behind."

He smiled, shaking his head. "You're full of surprises, Cora."

Holding in my smile, I draped the towel over the window pane, pulled myself through the window, and set my feet quietly on the floor of the classroom. I glanced around as Brendon crawled through next. A chemistry lab. One class I had been looking forward to taking in the future. But I knew deep down in the pit of my stomach that my school days were limited.

My backpack jerked as Brendon stuffed the towel back inside and zipped it closed.

"So, where we headed?" he asked.

"We're in the right area, but the wrong classroom," I said, weaving through the desks until I arrived at the door. Turning the handle softly, I pulled the door slowly open and peered out into the hall. Lockers lined the walls. I wasn't used to seeing them without students in front of them. "Coast is clear."

In the middle of the night, the school was eerily quiet. My tennis shoes squeaked against the freshly washed floors.

"It sounds like you have on those noisy shoes kids wear so their parents won't lose them," Brendon said with a warm laugh. He was behind me, but I could hear the smile in his voice. Goosebumps crawled across my skin, and my stomach fluttered in a way I couldn't explain. It was stronger than I'd ever felt. I loved his laugh and practically everything about him.

I hurried into a classroom to distract myself from all the feelings I didn't want to navigate.

"This isn't a biology room," Brendon said right behind me. The heat from his body radiated to mine, and I wanted to stay right there and feel it forever.

But I'd already wasted too much time. I pushed past him and out the door, checking another room. A sigh of relief escaped my lips when I saw 'Biology' on the marker board. "Finally." Going over to the teacher's desk, I tried to open a drawer, but it was locked. I sat down in the chair and opened my backpack.

Brendon knelt at my side, leaving a noticeable distance from me. "Have a special rock for opening a drawer?"

"Yep," I said, rifling through my bag.

"Really?"

Pausing, I looked up at him. "Of course not."

He quietly chuckled, and I couldn't hold back my smile. I wished I could record the sound so I could listen to it whenever I was in timeout. I think Sally would have enjoyed it as much as I did.

"I have a pen," I said, pulling it out.

He shook his head and reached across the desk. His warm smell jolted me back to a memory I'd pushed down and forgotten. It reminded me of summers at the beach when I'd lived with a foster family. They'd been the first set of parents that were extremely kind and treated me like one of their own. Unfortunately, they moved and I got thrown back into the system.

He pulled back and held up a paper clip. "Maybe we could do something with this." He lowered the clip when I just stared at him. "What?"

The warm sensation spread throughout my body. He'd

brought me back to the safest place I'd ever been. An urge overtook my body that terrified me. Yet I suddenly found myself leaning in and pressing my lips to his.

I'd never kissed anyone before – I'd never *wanted* to kiss anyone. Until that very moment, alone, in the dark, in a classroom we'd broken into, about to commit another crime. And I wanted to kiss Brendon. The list of things wrong with me were piling up.

His lips were warm, soft, and slightly wet. I'd caught him off guard. I'd caught myself off guard. I slowly pulled back, our lips breaking apart.

I stared at him, not sure what to do next.

Brendon stared back, surprise in his eyes, and a faint smile on his lips. That cute freckle stared up at me, and I wanted to kiss it.

He tapped the paper clip against the table. "I'll take that as a yes." He unfolded the clip and stuck it in the lock in the drawer. "I've never done this before." He wiggled the paper clip around.

His body was unbelievably close to mine. Warmth. Ocean. Comfort. Three things I hadn't felt in the longest time, yet Brendon contained them all.

"It worked!" He pulled the drawer open and glanced inside, frowning. "No test answers. We'll have to keep looking."

I'd frozen on the chair, trying to process all the emotions that had overtaken my body. He tried another drawer. How could one person make me feel that way? Was it just because he'd paid attention to me, or was it something beyond that? I couldn't trust my emotions. I had zero experience in the guy department.

Could I trust Brendon?

Papers shook in front of my face, taking me from my trance.

"Cora?" He lowered the papers. "Test answers. In my hand."

"Oh." I took the papers and shuffled through them before I stuffed them in my backpack.

"Shouldn't we make copies and put the originals back?" he asked. "That way the teacher doesn't know."

"Uh, yeah."

Brendon smiled. "I had no idea I was that good of a kisser. I've left you speechless."

A smile broke out on my face. I playfully shoved him in the chest and stood. "I've had better."

His smile disappeared, replaced by a pout. "You bring all the boys with you on criminal runs, don't you?" He stood, shaking his head. "And here I thought I was special."

We broke into two other desks to retrieve all the biology test answers and then snuck to the front office to make copies.

"So you have no idea who's doing this to you?" Brendon asked.

I watched the light go back and forth on the copy machine. "Nope."

He leaned against the counter near the copier. He slapped the palm of his hand against the side of the counter. "I wish I knew. I'd love to beat the crap out of them for doing this to you."

"I wish I knew, too," I whispered.

He pushed away from the counter and approached me with caution. "We'll figure this out. It's just driving me crazy." He set his hand on my arm, so much warmer and kinder than Daddy. "I hate seeing you so upset." He lowered his hand. "I mean, the criminal thing is kinda hot, but I'm not sure how well you'd look in orange."

"Oh, it's definitely not my color." Not that I'd ever worn it. Daddy would never buy me a color so bold. I pulled the finished copies from the tray and straightened them out against the counter.

"At least we know you'd be able to take care of yourself," Brendon said. "You could smuggle stuff in for people. They'd love you."

A light bounced along the wall outside in the hall.

"Someone's here," I whispered.

Brendon took me by the arm and pulled me down. The cuts on my back screamed in protest, but I ignored it as we squeezed into a small spot under the counter.

Someone whistled on the other side of the wall. They opened the office door and stepped inside. Two, large black boots walked by as the guy continued to whistle.

I did my best to keep my breathing as quiet as I could, but my anxiety made it difficult. The copies of the test answers were clutched in my fists. The originals were still in the copier. Closing my eyes, I mouthed *please don't find the tests.* Over and over again. I squeezed my arms tight around my legs, still mouthing the words. I so desperately wanted Sally with me. Even Noah would do, despite his constant sarcasm.

Brendon's arm wrapped around my waist, and he pulled me into him. I rested my head on his shoulder, shaking in his arms.

If we were caught, Daddy would put me in timeout forever. He'd kill Brendon. It would be *my* fault.

"Cora?" Brendon's words cut through the silence.

I pulled back and stared into his eyes.

"Are you okay?"

I pressed my finger to my lips, telling him to be quiet.

He smiled, but it didn't touch his eyes. "He's gone. He's been gone for a while. It was just the janitor."

I hated the look in his eyes – the look that pitied me and felt sorry for me and my situation. It sends me on edge.

I pushed away from him, crawled out from under the table, and stood. "We should get going." I grabbed the papers from the copier and left without looking back.

I didn't need pity. I needed to solve my problem before someone got seriously injured.

CHAPTER 21

Don't forget. Test answers. After school. Flagpole.

Taking the note I'd found in my P.E. locker, I bunched it up and stuffed it in my pocket. I had kept reading it over and over, but it didn't change what was there. Deep in my gut, I knew it was just the beginning of the blackmail. What other laws would they make me break?

My fingers wrapped around Husky. I desperately wished I could tuck Sally in my backpack, carrying her with me everywhere I went, but Daddy would never allow it. Sally was my creation, not his. But, oh, how she'd comfort me. Husky would have to do for the moment, even though Daddy had given him to me.

I stole a sideways glance at Brendon. I had him, too. My own comfort Daddy knew nothing about and had nothing to do with . . . if I could trust him.

"Where's the exchange?" Brendon asked. His shirt had a symbol with a yellow W on top of another. The sides of it almost looked like wings. It was my favorite I'd seen of all his shirts. There was something about it that made me feel strong – like I could do anything.

We were walking out of our French class, heading down the hall toward the front of the school. Other students passed by us in a blur, stopping at their lockers, talking and laughing, but I stayed close to Brendon, wanting his warmth.

"Near the flagpole," I whispered.

He was silent for a moment before he busted out laughing.

"What?" My fist gripped Husky so tightly that I worried he would break off the chain. Was he making fun of me? I stopped walking, my palm rubbing back and forth on Husky.

It took Brendon a few seconds to figure out I wasn't walking with him. He turned around, the laughter falling off his lips. He back tracked to me, confusion on his face.

"What's wrong?"

I took two steps away from him. "You were laughing at me."

He shook his head. "What? I was laughing about the flagpole." When I just stared at him, my strained body showing no signs of releasing, he continued. "You know? *I'll meet you at the flagpole after school.*"

"Is that a pun for something?" Flames erupted across my face.

Laughter pulled at his eyes and cheeks, but he held it in. He closed the distance between us and gently put his hand on my fist that threatened to rip Husky to shreds.

Slowly, ever so slowly, my grip loosened.

"It's what kids say when they're going to meet after school for a fight."

The confusion stayed on my face. I worried it might never come off. There were so many things I just didn't understand. So much I had missed out on by being locked up. But did knowing that make life better? It just added to all the confusion and all the weirdness out in the world.

Brendon lifted my chin so our eyes could meet. "It's nothing. Don't worry about it. Let's get the bag dropped off and this whole thing over and done."

"What if it's not done?" I whispered. "What if they threaten me with new things?"

Brendon pulled me into a hug, and I let him. I let him wrap his arms around me and hold me close. I was breaking so many rules. I didn't even care that it hurt my back so badly.

"We'll worry about that if it happens," he said. "Right now, let's focus on finishing this one thing."

"Will one of you please finally admit you're together?" Jenna appeared in my vision, her neon green theme sticking out among the sea of students leaving the school. How did she find skinny jeans in every color imaginable?

I quickly wiggled myself from Brendon's embrace, heat radiating on my skin. "We're not together."

Jenna put her hand on her hip. "I'm your *friend*, Cora. *Friends* don't lie to each other."

"Cora's having a rough day," Brendon said with a shrug. "Just trying to console her. It's what *friends* do."

Jenna threw her arms around me. "You're having a bad day? Why didn't you tell me?" She rubbed my back and I sucked in a sharp breath. "How about I come over and we can hang out?"

I shook my head, taking the opportunity to push away from her. The pain from her tight hug was unbearable. "I can't today." Or any day, really.

Dalton slowly approached, one hand stuffed in his pocket, and his focus on Jenna. His shaggy hair hung over his eyes enough that it was hard to detect his mood, which was common for him. He slipped something into her hand without saying anything.

"Hi, Dalton," I said.

He was about to walk away, but his eyes landed on Brendon's shirt. Dalton scoffed. "You're wearing a Wonder Woman shirt."

"What!" Brendon glanced down and tugged at his shirt in shock, but his tone was rich with mockery. He rolled his eyes. "Yeah, I know."

"Why?" Dalton asked. He'd stuffed both hands in his pockets. He seemed to be forcing his gaze to stay on either Brendon or Jenna. Not me.

"Uh, because she's awesome," Brendon said. "What? Because I'm a guy, I can't wear a Wonder Woman shirt?" He crossed his wrists together like an X.

I wanted to ask who Wonder Woman was, but by their conversation, I had a feeling I should've known. But if Brendon liked her, she had to be fierce. He seemed to like strong characters. Could I ever be that strong?

With the shake of his head, Dalton walked away, his head down like he was deliberately not looking in my direction.

"What was that about, Jenna?" Brendon asked, his eyes on Dalton's back. "Giving you something and completely ignoring Cora?"

Jenna tucked the paper into her back pocket. "Just some notes from a class we have. You know Dalton. Not really the talkative type." She cleared her throat and stared at the gray linoleum floor.

"What class do you have together?" I didn't know they had a class together. But then again, I'd never asked.

"Huh?" Jenna ran her hand behind her ear, tucking away hair that wasn't there. She had it pinned up, as usual. "Oh, uh, history."

"I have history with him," I said, confusion in my tone.

She shifted back and forth, tapping her fingers along her leg. "Did I say history? I meant science."

What was going on with her? I'd never seen Jenna look nervous. Maybe the test answers had been on the paper. She said they had science together . . . if she was even telling the truth about that. The thought of them working together made my insides coil into a tight ball. Jenna was supposedly my friend. I didn't want to believe she was capable of something like that.

"Are you Cora?" a soft voice said.

I turned to see a girl, probably a sophomore, staring at me with hopeful eyes. I slowly nodded, wondering what she wanted.

She grinned, revealing slightly crooked teeth. Her eyes skittered to Jenna and Brendon before they came back to me. She went up on her tiptoes. "Do you have any more of those cell phone holders for sale?"

I couldn't stop the matching smile that burst across my face. Taking hold of my backpack, I swung it in front of me and opened the zipper. I pulled out a few cell phone bands I'd made during the night. I hadn't been able to fall asleep after Brendon had dropped me off outside my window. The breaking and entering, almost getting caught, and *kissing* him had left my mind whirling. I couldn't shut it off.

The girl pointed to the bright fuchsia one with zebra stripes. "Can I buy that one?"

"Sure." I handed it to her and set the others back in my bag.

She handed me a ten-dollar bill. Her glossy eyes danced. "Thanks so much!" She practically skipped toward her friends near their lockers. They formed a circle around her, their excited hands fighting over who got to touch it, and they all squealed in excitement.

"You're getting quite popular," Jenna said as she nudged

me with her elbow. "Just remember, I was your friend first."
Was she my friend? She pulled her phone out of the band on
her arm. "Speaking of which, let's hang this weekend. I'm
really needing a girl's night." Her fingers flew across her
phone. "Heather is in." Her fingers kept on moving. "So is
Jillian." She glanced up at me. "You're in, right?"

I bit the side of my lip. She wouldn't like my answer.
"I can't."

Jenna sighed. "Let me guess. Busy." She put her phone
back in the holder. "Are you ever *not* busy?"

"Not really."

Jenna pointed her thumb at Brendon. The neon green on
her thumbnail was done so well it looked professional. "If
you'll just admit you have plans with your boyfriend, then I'll
understand. I'll encourage you. One of us needs to be getting
some action."

My lips warmed, thinking about my kiss with Brendon. If
I told Jenna I'd kissed him, she'd die. After she finished
squealing and hugging me to death. I didn't want to be
responsible for a murder-suicide.

I was about to deny our involvement once again when
Brendon draped his arm over my shoulder. "If you must
know," Brendon said, "I asked Cora to be my girlfriend, and
she said yes."

The squealing commenced. So did the hugging. I feared
that Jenna would squeeze the life out of me and at least the
murder part would come true. The burns on my back
screamed in protest, and I had to bite back a yell.

"Alright," Brendon said, pulling me and Jenna apart.
"We're all excited that Cora landed an awesome guy like me."

Jenna snorted. "Please. You're the lucky one. Cora is
amazing." She clapped her hands in excitement, her nails
clicking together. "Oh! Did you guys hear about the break-in
last night?"

Brendon and I exchanged a look before he spoke. "What break-in?"

Jenna glanced around to make sure no one was listening. "While I was working in the front office, I heard some teachers talking about a window being broken in the back of the school."

"Was anything missing?" Brendon asked. He looked so relaxed and calm. The complete opposite of me. I was trying my best to act casual, but I wasn't doing a very good job. Luckily, Jenna was too excited about her news that she didn't seem to notice.

"Not that they could find," Jenna said. "The cops think it was just a prank."

My eyes went wide. "Cops?" They'd called cops?

"Well, yeah," Jenna said. "The school had to file a report."

I swallowed, my mouth completely dry. "Are they going to do an investigation or something?"

Jenna waved her hand. "I highly doubt a prank is high up on the cops' list of things to do. But I'm dying to know who did it and why."

Brendon squeezed my arm. "As exciting as this all is, we need to get going." He winked at me. "We have some studying to do."

Jenna squealed again and put her hand on my arm. "I want all the details tomorrow! Promise!"

Promise. I had once only used that word with Daddy. Now the list was expanding. "Promise."

Brendon steered me away from a still giddy Jenna and led me to the doors leading outside.

"Sorry about that," Brendon said, dropping his arm. "If she thinks we're together, you can use that as an excuse to get out of things. Just let me know when we're *hanging out*." He used air quotes. "So we can get our stories straight." He turned my shoulders so I was facing the exit. "Now, hurry and place the bag by the flagpole and get to your dad. You're already late."

Daddy would be suspicious. I'd have to make up an excuse as to why it took me so long to come out after school had ended. It was starting to happen way too often, and I didn't like it.

I didn't get to thank Brendon. He'd gone out of the school without looking at me, like we hadn't been talking just seconds before.

As I walked to the flagpole, all I could think about were Jenna and Dalton. They had seemed highly suspicious with the note exchange. They skyrocketed to the top of the list, pushing Brendon and the others lower.

I hated that I couldn't trust anyone. I needed to go home and talk with Noah. Or better yet, get in trouble so Daddy would put me in timeout and I could speak with Sally. She'd know what to do.

CHAPTER 22

*W*hen I arrived at Daddy's van, it was empty. I scanned the area, searching for any sight of him, but he was nowhere to be seen. Where was he?

My stomach lurched. Had he seen me with Brendon? Or Jenna? He couldn't know they were my friends. If anything happened to them because of me, I'd never forgive myself – even if Jenna was the person who stole my journal. She didn't deserve to fall into Daddy's hands.

"Where were you?" Daddy's deep voice rumbled behind me.

I spun around, slamming my back into the side of the van, flinching slightly from the pain. "Ttt . . . talking to a teacher."

Daddy stepped up close. "Why are you so nervous, angel?" His hand wrapped around my arm and squeezed tight. "Were you doing something you weren't supposed to?"

"No," I whispered.

He twisted his hand, gripping where my bruises were from before. "Were you with someone you shouldn't be around?" His hand kept rubbing back and forth.

Tears pricked at the corners of my eyes from the pain. "No, Daddy."

What was happening with him? He'd never lost that much control out in public. He was usually careful about how people perceived us.

His eyes searched mine. "Promise?"

I hated lying to Daddy. But I didn't want Jenna or Brendon to get hurt. "Yes, Daddy. I was just talking to a teacher about a project. I'm sorry I was late, but I felt it important to discuss things with her."

His grip slowly loosened from my arm. "Don't let it happen again. You can talk to your teachers during break or lunch."

"Yes, Daddy," I whispered.

He walked around to his side of the van and got in, not opening the door for me like he normally did. I desperately wanted to rub my arm where he'd hurt me, but I resisted and slid into the passenger seat, shutting the door firmly.

"What project?" he asked as he drove.

After years of living with Daddy, sticking with truthful things worked the best. So I picked a science project I was working on. I just hadn't talked to my teacher about it. But it seemed to satisfy Daddy.

His mood flipped again the second we pulled into the driveway. He hurried to open the passenger door for me. "I have a surprise for you."

Had he changed his mind about the piano? "What is it?"

He waggled his finger at me. "It's a *surprise*." He unlocked the front door, took my backpack from me, and swept his arm out for me to go in first.

A quick look around the front room told me it wasn't a piano. The tiny spark of hope that had been in my heart fluttered away.

He wrapped his arms around me and covered my eyes with his cold hands. "Walk forward."

A little bit of panic set in. Where was he taking me? But I did as directed, following his every command until we'd stepped out into the backyard. The early summer warmth wrapped around me.

"You ready?" he asked.

I nodded in response.

He lowered his hands. "Surprise!"

He'd finished the swing set he'd been working on – the one I begged for when I was little. Though, I hadn't asked for it in the longest time because I didn't want it anymore. But so much excitement danced in Daddy's stormy eyes. I hadn't seen him that happy in the longest time. His sudden mood swings unsettled me. Why did he randomly feel the need to finally give me my swing set at the age of fifteen? Especially when he had been so mad at me.

He made it with a dark wood, the stain rich and warm. Two wooden seats hung from thick ropes, giving me two swings. The thought of the second swing broke my heart. I'd never have a friend to sit there. No one to swing with me aside from Daddy.

"Thanks, Daddy!" I clasped my hands together in pretend excitement. "It's all mine?"

He cradled my cheek. "Come on. Let me push my little girl on her swing."

His little girl. He wanted the young version of me back. The girl who didn't go to public school or have friends. The girl who hadn't reached puberty or caused problems.

Forcing a smile, I sat on the swing and let Daddy push me. I swung my legs with the movement and tried to focus on the breeze against my cheeks.

"See how nice this is?"

"Yes," I said.

He made sure to avoid pushing my back and used the ropes instead. "Just me and my angel girl. Why would I need anything else?"

So much had changed in a matter of a few weeks. Before, I would have agreed with him. Just me and Daddy. No one to interfere with our lives. But I never knew having a friend could be so nice. I had no idea what I was missing out on.

"Just me and you," I whispered. Always.

Dread settled inside.

But it kept my friends safe. It wasn't about me – it never had been. If anyone were to find out mine and Daddy's secret, I would be taken away from my friends anyway. I'd never see Daddy again. I'd be all alone in the world with no one to protect me.

"Angel," he said, giving me a push. "How's everything at school?"

I kept my eyes on my spotless white tennis shoes as they swung in the air. "Great. I'm learning a lot."

"That's good." He paused. Every second that ticked by let the storm grow. I didn't have to see his eyes to know the clouds were rolling in. "I talked with your school the other day."

Fear squeezed me tight. Had Mr. Mendoza called?

"What for?" I asked.

"You're so ahead of the other kids. You don't belong in tenth grade. So I've been debating what to do."

I didn't belong in any of the grades. I never would. "What are you thinking?"

He let go of the ropes and sat on the swing next to me. "We could move you ahead. By your grades and knowledge, your counselor thinks we could start you in twelfth grade next year." So Mr. Mendoza had called.

My wide eyes went to him. "Do you think that's a good idea? People would notice me. Pay attention."

He nodded. "Exactly." He started to swing. "I don't think you need to be in public school anymore. I had thought you could learn more there, but you're so smart you can teach yourself. If I get all the right books, you could do it alone and be done with high school next year." His smirk left a sour taste in my mouth. "Then we can focus on our future."

Our future. It made me sick to my stomach. What did that entail? Would he ever let me have a job, drive a car, or go to college? Or would I be stuck at home, locked in my room, until the day he died? Then what would happen to me?

"Are you pulling me out of school?" My voice was so quiet.

He put his feet down to stop swinging and wrapped his hand around my swing rope. "At the end of this school year. It will be less noticeable that way."

"But I like school," I said, daring to look in his eyes. The storms were hovering in the distance, waiting to move in. If I didn't play it smart, the forecast could be deadly.

"I know, angel." The normal dark, gravelly tone had been replaced by something sweeter. Almost like honey. Goosebumps broke out on my arms despite the nice day. I almost preferred his rough voice – it was less creepy.

"But this will be better," he said. "It's less risky. Plus, this way you won't be exposed to all the bad stuff high school has to offer. You'll be safe at home."

I couldn't fight with him or demand to stay in school. So I put on my sweet smile. I'd have to figure a way out on my own. "Okay, Daddy."

He returned my smile, used my swing rope to pull me close to him, and kissed me on the forehead. "I'm worried that I've been losing my little girl. I think being out in the world has taught you some bad habits. But I can fix them and make you perfect once again." He sighed. "I couldn't live without you, Cora. You're my world."

I leaned my head against the swing rope, trying to appear innocent and happy.

"I'm going to make dinner tonight. Why don't you enjoy some time out here and come in the house in a bit?"

"Thanks, Daddy." I swallowed down the thick lump in my throat. "For the swing and always looking out for me."

"I love you, Cora. I'll always protect you and do what's best for you." The next words were muttered under his breath, so quiet I almost didn't hear them. "Unlike *him.*" With a cold smile, he left me alone in the backyard, something he'd never done before.

I wanted to ask him what had changed. Why his mood kept swinging all over the place.

If he took me out of school, I'd never see Jenna or Brendon again. No more guitar lessons from Dalton. But if any of them had taken my journal, they weren't the friends I thought they were.

There would also be no more blackmailer trying to ruin my life.

Maybe it would be for the best, but I had no way to know.

CHAPTER 23

*A*fter dinner, Daddy headed down to the basement to finish repairing the pipe. The hallway was still bare, so I'd kept my shoes on so my feet wouldn't get dirty. I took them off the second I got into my room. Daddy only wanted socked feet on the carpet.

"How was your day, Cora Nora?" Noah asked from the bed.

Something inside of me ignited, and I rounded on him. "Why did you call me that?"

"I always rhyme your name with things. It's what I do."

A disturbing feeling settled inside me, but I wasn't sure why. "Well, don't do it anymore."

"Fine." He cleared his throat. "How was your day, *Cora.*"

I sat cross-legged on the floor, keeping him in my vision. "Not good." Reaching over, I wrapped my hand around the top handle of my backpack and dragged it to me. Normally I'd pick it up, but lifting anything heavy caused my back to flare in pain.

"Why not?"

Leaning forward, I peered out the open door, checking to

make sure Daddy wasn't nearby. I didn't need him eaves-
dropping on my private conversation. But if I closed the
door, he'd be suspicious.

"Oh, more secrets." Noah chuckled. "You know how I love
a juicy secret."

I rolled my eyes as I settled back into place. "Everything
with you is a secret. You can't repeat anything you hear."

"Ouch. Right to the heart."

"Do you want to know or not?" I asked, shooting him
a glare.

He sighed. "Alright, tell me."

"I'm thinking Jenna might be involved with the whole . . .
situation."

"That's the girl that was in your room, right?" he asked.
"With the weird metal stuff on her teeth?"

I nodded at the elephant on my bed. "Yes. And they're
called braces."

Noah growled. "I knew there was something bad about
her. You should tell your father what happened."

"No!" My gaze snapped to the door. I remained quiet until
I was sure Daddy hadn't heard me. I kept my voice low. "He
can't know what happened."

"Don't worry. My lips are sealed."

"Ha. Ha." I opened my math book. "I just don't want to
believe it's her. She's been the closest thing to a friend I've
ever had."

"Wow. You're really going for the heart tonight."

"I mean a *human* friend," I said, narrowing my eyes at him.

"And now you just drove a stake through it. Not sure
what I did to deserve that."

Nothing. But no matter what I said, he'd still be hurt.
Every word out of my mouth was burying me deeper and
deeper, and I couldn't afford to lose him as a friend.

The phone in the kitchen rang, breaking the uncomfortable silence. On the second ring, I stood and went to the top of the basement stairs, leaning my hand against the door frame. "Daddy! The phone's ringing!"

"Go ahead and answer it," he shouted up.

"Are you sure?" I asked. He rarely let me answer the phone. Especially without being able to check the caller ID.

"Of course."

I hurried to the kitchen and checked to see who was calling, but it only read *Unknown Caller.* My insides tightened. Were they calling again?

"Hello?" I kept my voice as steady as I could.

"I got the test answers," the rumbly voice said through the receiver.

"Good," I said, keeping my voice low. "Don't call here again." I moved to hang up the phone, but they spoke loudly, catching my attention.

"Because Daddy wouldn't like it?"

My heart hammered through my chest at the usage of Daddy, but then I remembered they had used it before. It kept throwing me off. "No, he wouldn't. Stop calling."

"That's not how this relationship works, Cora," the raspy voice said.

I peered down the hall to make sure Daddy hadn't come up the stairs. "This isn't a relationship at all. You're just a felon who gets off on torturing people." Once it came out of my mouth, I cringed. I'd heard someone use the phrase *gets off* at school, and by the recipient's reaction, it had been a mean thing to say. But I had no idea what it meant. Gets off on what? Or where?

"I was just calling to thank you," the voice said, anger dripping from every word, "but now I think I'll add another demand."

"No," I said through clenched teeth. "Stop doing this to me. I'm not your slave."

"You don't have to do anything I ask. I'll just tell precious Daddy everything."

My hand gripped the phone tight. "Go ahead. It'll be your funeral."

"You really want to take that risk?"

I took a few breaths to calm my nerves, pinching the bridge of my nose. "What do you want?"

"Money," they rasped.

There were so many things they could ask for, but I hadn't thought about money. I had none. They had to know that about me. Where would I get money?

"That's not possible." I leaned against the counter and pulled at the collar of my shirt, wishing I could undo the top button and fan myself. "Think of something else."

They breathed deeply into the phone. "Anything is possible if you try. Five hundred dollars. In an envelope. Tape it to the inside of your locker door. You have one week."

They hung up before I could protest. How could I possibly get that much money in a week? How would I get that much money at all?

I replaced the receiver, grabbed a glass from the cupboard, and filled it with apple juice from the fridge.

"Who was on the phone?" Daddy ambled into the kitchen and washed his hands.

I took a long drink of juice. "Wrong number." I'd have to sell a lot of cell phone bands. But I didn't have enough material to make fifty of them. Or time.

"Really?" he asked.

I placed my empty glass in the sink. Maybe I could steal it.

"Then why did the call last three minutes?" Daddy asked, looking at the phone.

I froze, unsure of what to say or do. I'd just thrown myself into a pit I couldn't escape. My pulse throbbed in my ears as I worked moisture back into my mouth. "What?"

He placed his hand under my chin and yanked my face toward his. "The call lasted three minutes, Cora."

Panic rippled through me. I wanted to back away, but his grip was too strong. "I must have forgot to hang it up all the way." I clutched the side of the counter as paid radiated in my jaw.

His fingernails dug into my chin, breaking the skin. Blood trickled out. "And they did the same?"

"Daddy." I couldn't think of what to say. Anything out of my mouth would be a lie. My chest heaved in and out. Trying to breathe was like trying to wrap my hand around something just out of reach.

"Who was it, Cora?" he yelled, the words slamming into me. If he hadn't been holding on so firmly, I probably would have stumbled back. When I didn't respond, he seized my arm and dragged me down the hall. "Why do you lie to me? After everything I do for you."

"Daddy, please!" I pushed my feet into the now bare floor, hoping to slow our progress, but without the carpet, I had nothing to really dig my toes into. My legs burned in protest.

He pushed me onto the stairs, and his hand tightened around the door. I shoved forward, trying to stop the door, and Daddy, from shutting me out.

"Don't make this worse," he growled.

I threw my body against the door so he couldn't close it. "Please don't lock me down here! I'm sorry!"

A hurricane landed in his eyes, the blue and gray splashing all around, so fierce and uncontrollable. I'd never seen that kind of rage on him. Seconds after he flipped on the light, his coarse hands found my arms and hauled me with him. He was able to run down the stairs, but my body bounced along the banister and steps as he forced me to the bottom.

When we arrived on the cold, concrete floor, he threw me down, my palms slamming down and burning my wrists.

"If you want to be raised how I was, then so be it!" His strong hand fisted the collar of my shirt, and he yanked, the buttons flying off along with the rest of my shirt.

I looked down in horror as I stood there in my bra. Coldness and embarrassment engulfed me. He'd never taken off my clothing – boys and men weren't supposed to see me like this.

Taking me by the braid, he wrenched me toward the wall and threw me against the mattress leaning on it, my arm smashed awkwardly between me and the mattress. Urine and sweat attacked my senses. The water had enhanced all the horrible smells. Before I could move my arm, he'd removed his belt and slashed it against my already bandaged back.

My wail echoed throughout the basement. Strike after strike came, peeling back the bandages and ripping open my flesh, causing more pain than I had ever felt in my life. Warm blood slithered down my back as I tried to grip onto the sides of the mattress, but he was going too fast for me to grab hold. When my knees gave out and I fell to the ground, Daddy started taking things from the shelves and throwing them all around.

Screwdrivers, hammers, scraps of metal, used car parts, all the different, random items Daddy had collected over the years collided with the walls and floor. I threw my arms over my head for protection.

"You're the worst mistake of my life!" His eyes bulged as he chucked a picture frame above me. It slammed into the mattress before it bounced off and shattered to the ground. He reached his arms in a shelf and swept them to the side, all the boxes falling one by one to the floor.

When he finally stopped, his hurricane eyes whipped about as his chest heaved in and out. His perfectly gelled hair was disheveled, loose locks falling against his sweaty forehead.

He pointed a shaking finger at me. "No more lying, or I'll . . ." His eyes closed tight as he drew deep breaths. Moments later, he snatched my ruined shirt from the ground, pounded up the stairs, and turned off the light as I sat shaking on the floor. He would what? I probably didn't want to know.

With a mighty shove, he slammed the door, cloaking me in darkness. The lock clicked into place. I thought about trudging up the stairs to turn on the light, but I liked the thought of basking in the blackness. Maybe by staying in the darkness, I wouldn't have to see the reality of what Daddy was.

CHAPTER 24

$\mathcal{I}$'d never been so humiliated in my life. Why had he taken off my shirt and then left me without any cover? It took at least a half hour before my heart had steadied and the overwhelming fear that clawed at me had faded to a dull throb. The sting in my back had dwindled to a bearable state. I would need to re-bandage it when Daddy let me out.

If he left me out.

Daddy had mentioned his father in the past, but I had no idea he'd been this violent. No wonder Daddy hated to talk about him. It made me wonder where his father was now.

I needed to focus on something else before I completely broke down and lost it. Talking to Sally would help.

I forced myself up the stairs, gritting through the pain, and flipped on the light before I descended, gripping the handrail tight and trying to force my wobbly legs to calm.

Because of the water leak and Daddy's meltdown, everything in the basement had been moved around. I wondered if I'd even find Sally among all the debris. She could have been broken apart, or worse, thrown away. If I still had all her pieces, I could put her back together.

Before I searched for her, I needed something to cover myself with. Even though no one could see me in the basement, I didn't like being half naked. I went to a tote I knew held some old clothes – I'd created Sally's dress from a shirt inside – and found an old, stained T-shirt of Daddy's and slipped it on, sucking in a sharp breath when the cloth pushed against the cuts on my back.

Once the sting subsided, I searched the room, climbing over the mess and moving things around, trying to find any signs of Sally.

"Sally, where are you?"

No response.

"I need your advice." I searched inside a crate on one of the metal shelves in the corner of the basement. When it proved empty, I went to another shelf, checking every single box. I moved things around with a little too much force, including a creepy looking nutcracker with red eyes, but I didn't care. I needed to work out some of my frustration and fears.

I dragged out a tote from the bottom of a shelf. "Sally, I need you. Daddy has completely lost it." And possibly my one human friend had betrayed me. I didn't want to believe it, but her interaction with Dalton left me wary.

Jenna and I weren't incredibly close. We couldn't be. Since I couldn't hang out with her outside of school, and since she had other friends she usually hung out with at lunch, our time together was limited.

But still. To take my journal, ask me to steal test answers, and now demand money? It didn't make sense. But she'd lied to me about what Dalton had given her. Why did she have to cover it up? What was it? Dalton was already high on my suspect list. He knew things about me that no one could have known unless they read the journal.

Dalton did need money. That was why he agreed to give me guitar lessons. It would make sense that he'd demand money from me.

Out of the corner of my eye, I saw a wrench sticking out from under the metal shelving unit. I replaced the lid of the tote, shoved it back under the shelf, and went to where the wrench sat. Bending down, I picked it up and brushed off the dirt.

"Sally," I said. Half her wired hair was gone. Her dress was stiff from water damage. But she was still with me – I hadn't been completely abandoned.

"Do I still look pretty?" Sally asked.

I smiled as I curled one of her wires with my finger. "You'll always be pretty, Sally, no matter what."

"But my hair and dress." She sighed. "I look horrible, don't I? You're just being nice."

I sat down on the cement floor, the chill biting into my legs, and leaned gently against the shelf. "You don't need hair or a dress to be pretty. There's beauty in everyone if you look in the right places."

"Enough about me. Why are you down here?"

"I lied to him," I whispered. But what could I have told him? That it was a blackmailer on the phone? Demanding money that I'd probably have to steal?

"Will you ever learn, Cora?"

I shook my head. "Apparently not."

I updated Sally on the journal and blackmailer situation. She remained quiet the whole time, even the times I had to pause to collect myself. Anger and hurt were two emotions that had overtaken me thanks to everything that was going on.

"You can't steal," she said. "It's a bad habit of yours."

"It started out as something so simple."

"It always does."

All I'd wanted was to have something that was mine. Journals that held my life and thoughts. It made me feel like I was still in control of some part of my life. But it didn't mean I liked stealing. I knew it was wrong and that I could be arrested for it. Yet, I couldn't stop.

"How else can I get that money?" I banged the back of my head against the shelf a couple times. Frustration took over my body, heat erupting in my veins.

"Make more cell phone holders," Sally said. "Ask Brendon for help."

Brendon did have a lot of plastic bottles for me. With all the fabric from Jenna's mom, I probably had enough to make fifty holders. I still had plenty of paint. If I could get them assembled, I'd just have to find a way to sell all of them. That would be even more difficult than the assembly.

The broken picture frame on the floor caught my eye. I crawled over to it and carefully removed the photo from the broken glass. The picture had been torn straight down the middle so only half remained. A little boy with sad, blue/gray eyes stared at me. The chubby man next to him towered above him, his hand gripping the boy's shoulder tight. The man's face had been ripped off as well.

The lock unlatched, and the basement door flung open. I stuffed Sally behind the mattress since it was the closest thing to me, and scrambled to my feet.

Daddy tromped down the stairs holding my backpack. "The school called. They're worried that you're missing too much school." His jaw clenched tight, and he shook my backpack at me. "I can't have them getting suspicious. You'll be going to school tomorrow. But I'll lock you back up in the basement when you get home." He tossed the bag at me.

I caught it and held it tight against my chest. At least that meant I had Husky as well.

His glaring eyes took in the T-shirt I was wearing before he saw the picture gripped in my hand. He blew out a long breath. "That's me as a boy. I was better than you've even been, and my father treated me so much worse. You're lucky, Cora. Remember that." He motioned to my bag. "There are bandages and cream in there – something I never got."

I wasn't sure how he expected me to apply them myself, but I didn't want to start another storm, so I kept my mouth shut.

He stood tall with his chin tilted up. "Do your homework. Make your teachers happy." He started up the stairs.

I swallowed, a thick lump moving against my throat. "My mattress is ruined. Can I have something else to sleep on?"

His hand wrapped tightly around the handrail. "Why would you think you deserve that?" He stormed up the stairs and slammed the door.

I shivered as the lock clicked into place, my hand wrapping tightly around Husky.

CHAPTER 25

*I*t had taken a while, and a lot of weird angles, but
I'd managed to get some cream and bandages on
my back. The next morning, Daddy fixed them all up for me.
He had calmed, but he didn't say one word to me all through
breakfast and the drive to school.

During break, I found Brendon in the hallway talking
with Jake and some of their other friends. I hated going over
there with so many people watching, but it couldn't wait.

Jake grinned when I approached. "Hey, Cora. Nice to see
you again."

I forced a return smile, even though I was eager to talk
with Brendon. "Hi, Jake."

Jake leaned against the locker they were near and folded
his arms. "When are we going to hang out?"

"Soon." I hated lying to him, especially since he seemed so
nice, but I couldn't really tell him my daddy wouldn't allow
it. I tugged on the sleeve of Brendon's shirt. "Can we talk?"

Brendon's eyebrows pinched together in worry, but he
nodded. "Yeah, sure."

Before he could say anything else, I motioned for him to

follow me down a short hallway near the bathroom. There wasn't much traffic, so there was a smaller chance of being seen.

His shirt had a big, green, angry looking guy on it. "Oh, hey, look," he said, pointing to it. "It's your dad. On a regular day, he's a nice, small guy. But then . . ." He threw up his hands and made a sound like an explosion. When I frowned in confusion, he grinned. "I was kidding."

"I need your help," I said, wanting to change the subject. He'd described Daddy perfectly.

Brendon rubbed the back of his neck. "That seems to be your favorite thing to say to me."

A blush crawled up my neck to my cheeks. I wasn't used to asking for help. But with hardly getting any sleep on the cement floor, I was running on fumes."I don't have anyone else I can trust."

"Don't get me wrong. I'm glad you come to me." He tapped my arm. "I just like to see you blush."

The blush deepened, and I stared at the black flecks on the linoleum tile.

He gently touched my chin. "What happened?"

"What?" I ran my finger along the nicks from Daddy's fingernails. "Oh, I scratched myself."

He narrowed his eyes like he wanted to say something, but stopped himself. He picked at a fraying Band-Aid on his finger. "What can I do to help?"

"They called me again," I whispered, keeping my eyes unfocused on a fleck on the ground.

"Who? The person who has your journal?"

I nodded. "They have another demand."

He swore under his breath. "What is it now?"

"Money." Taking hold of Husky, I rubbed him with my thumb. A part of me wished I had snuck Sally out of the basement so I could've had her with me. But the other part wanted her with me when I was locked down in the cold basement. She helped me through it. Kept me from exploding in frustration and loneliness.

Brendon took my free hand and warmth ignited in me. My hand fit so perfectly in his. "I hate this. They're demanding impossible things."

I finally looked him in the eye. "It's better than them revealing all my secrets to the world."

He stepped in close, our body inches from each other. "Would that be such a bad thing? I don't like the way your father treats you."

Letting go of his hand, I pushed him away. "Yes, it would be a bad thing. I love Daddy. I don't want to be taken from him." I had no idea why I was defending him, but I couldn't stop myself. I still cared for him – he had done a lot for me. Suddenly, I found it hard to breathe. I wanted to run home and lock myself in the basement, curl up on the floor with Sally and forget everything. Not deal with school, blackmailers, and storms I couldn't control.

Although, it wouldn't fix anything. If I locked myself away, the person would reveal the truth. I'd be taken from my home, Daddy would be thrown into prison, and I'd be alone. I didn't want that.

Brendon took a tentative step toward me. "I'm sorry, Cora." His jaw clenched like he wanted to yell or something, but he just briefly closed his eyes and took a deep breath. "How much money do they want?"

"Five hundred." I leaned against the wall. "I was thinking I could make a bunch of cell phone bands and sell them."

"That's a good idea." He ran his hand over the top of his hair. "How long do you have?"

"A week."

He pulled out his phone and moved his fingers across the screen. I'd never had a cell phone, so I had no idea what he, or anyone else, were doing when they looked at their phone. It seemed to hold a lot of information for them.

"There's a big basketball game next Tuesday night." His thumb continued to move along the screen. "How about I come over this weekend and help you make them?"

"Dad would never allow you to come over."

He stuffed his phone into his band he always wore on his arm. "I know. That's why we won't tell him. I'll come over at night when he thinks you've gone to bed."

I folded my arms close against my chest. "I don't know exactly when it will be every night. He doesn't have a regular schedule." I always thought he'd kept things random on purpose. That way I'd be off guard at all times.

Smiling, Brendon pulled a phone from his backpack and held it out to me. "That's why I got you this."

I stared at the cell phone in his hand. It was small and simple and looked way different than the ones he and Jenna had. "You got me a phone?"

"It's just a burner."

I looked up at him, my eyebrows scrunched together. "A burner?"

A tiny smile pulled at his lips. "It just means it's not registered under anyone's name. It's not traceable. You use it for a little while and then throw it away. It doesn't have a lot of minutes on it."

I took it from his hand, our fingers grazing each other. The warmth lingered, and I wished it would never leave. "Minutes?" I turned it over, trying to understand how it all worked.

Brendon took a deep breath and then explained it to me, showing me what all the buttons did and how I could call him. He'd stored his number in the phone for me.

"Use it to let me know when I can come over this weekend," he said. "Otherwise, just use it in case of an emergency. I'll come right over."

A weird sensation took over my heart. It felt warm, and my heartbeat was unsteady, beating wildly. My skin tingled all over, but all in a good way. I'd never had someone do something like that for me. Bought me something so valuable or cared about what happened to me.

I gently put the phone in the bottom of my backpack and then threw my arms around him. "Thank you."

Brendon held me close, holding strong and sure. "You're welcome."

My back stung from the beating I'd received from Daddy, but I didn't care. All I wanted was to be in Brendon's arms and feel his warmth around me. He looked after me and didn't ask for anything in return – he didn't demand anything from me.

"Why?" I whispered in his ear. "Why do you keep helping me?"

He pulled back enough so he could look at me. "Because you don't deserve anything that's happening to you. You're smart, sweet, and beautiful." He yanked on my braid. "Because I like you. You're stronger than you think you are." He placed his warm hand on my cheek. "Don't ever forget that. You deserve to be happy."

That overwhelming sensation to kiss him came rushing back, paralyzing me. I finally understood what Daddy always said about hormones. How they'd overtake your body and leave you confused. He told me I could never trust my hormones since they were uncontrollable and unreliable.

For the moment, I didn't want them to be controlled. I wanted to remember the feeling forever.

Brendon leaned in close, and when I didn't pull away, he pressed his lips to mine. He moved softly, not forcing any of it like I'd worried a kiss could be from a guy. My hand found the way to the back of his neck and rested there, feeling the heat of his skin under my fingertips. Way too soon, he pulled away.

"I'll get the fabric from Jenna, and we can start making the bands tonight," he said, still holding me close. "Will that be okay?"

I nodded, unable to find any words. My heart hadn't calmed. My blood burned, my lips pulsing with the pressure of his lips.

"Everything will be okay, Cora. I promise. We'll figure this out together." He clasped his hands behind me, between my shirt and my backpack. It stung ever so slightly, but I didn't say anything. Being in his arms felt safe, like nothing – and no one – could harm me.

A thought occurred to me. "We can't make them in my room."

"Your dad won't catch me, I promise."

"It's not that. The bars." I glanced down, embarrassed. "No offense, but I don't think you could fit through them."

He frowned. "Ouch."

My cheeks flared. I opened my mouth to apologize, but Brendon let out a small laugh.

"It's okay. There's hardly any room. I'm amazed you fit through there." His fingers tapped against my back. "How about I come get you, and then we can go back to my place and make them?"

I'd never been in a boy's room. It would be in the middle of the night. The thought scared me. "Okay." I hated what the blackmailer was making me do. Too many uncomfortable things and situations.

"Where's the drop off for the money?"

"In my locker in the locker room."

"Maybe I could hide out," he said. "I'll wait around to see who comes and gets it. I tried to watch the flagpole at the last drop off, but there were way too many students around for me to get a good look. Any one of them could have grabbed the bag as they walked by."

A smirk appeared on my lips. "You just want to hang out in the girl's locker room."

Brendon shrugged like he didn't care, but laughter danced in his eyes. "Minor benefit."

"I think they'd notice a guy hiding out in the locker room. Whoever's doing this to me is clever."

"We could ask Jenna to do it. She'd have more of a reason to be in the girl's locker room than me."

I sighed. "I'm starting to suspect Jenna."

"Really? Why?"

I told him all my suspicions about the exchange between her and Dalton.

Brendon rubbed his eyelid. "Yeah, that was a little weird, but I just don't think Jenna's capable of something like this. She's your friend. My money's still on Dalton. I don't trust him."

"I can stand watch. I'll stay in the locker room to see who comes and gets the money."

"You can't be late. Your dad wouldn't like that. It has to be someone who can stay after school." He smiled brightly, his blue eyes lighting up. "Just let me do it. I promise I won't spy on any girls in there. I'll only watch your locker."

His smile was contagious. A big one landed on my lips. "Okay. But it's not my fault if you get caught by a teacher."

"I won't get caught," he said, rubbing my arms.

The bell rang, breaking us apart. I had no idea how I'd gotten so lucky with meeting Brendon, but he was starting to be the best thing that ever happened to me.

CHAPTER 26

*W*e were sitting at the dinner table, almost done with our meal. Daddy had started speaking to me again, his current mood calm as an ocean breeze. He hadn't brought up what happened in the basement, and I certainly didn't want to bring it up and give him a reason to do it again.

"Is everything okay, angel?" Daddy asked.

I'd barely spoken. My mind was buzzing with theories and worry. I had five hundred dollars to somehow obtain in only a few days.

The thing that worried me most, though, was sneaking out of my bedroom again. If Daddy found out, I'd be in serious trouble.

But I couldn't come up with the money myself. I didn't have all the supplies to make the cell phone bands. I wasn't involved with the school to know there was an important basketball game where I could sell them.

I twirled the spaghetti around my fork. It was a meal we both loved. "Just thinking about school."

"Are you having problems?" He took a bite of his spaghetti, his eyes on me the entire time. He had that way of reading into your soul and knowing things about myself that *I* didn't even know.

I hated lying to Daddy, but I had no other choice. If I didn't lie, didn't take care of the blackmailer, we'd be exposed, and he'd be thrown in jail. I wasn't quite sure if he deserved that harsh of a punishment. Although, after what had happened the night before, maybe he did.

But then I'd be left all alone, tossed back into the system and placed with some random family probably far away from where I currently lived. They would never love me like Daddy did. No one could.

"I'm not doing so well in P.E." There was truth behind that. My physical abilities were terrible.

He patted my hand. "It's okay, angel. It's one class. And not even an important one at that."

My hand tensed under his. If he was relaxed about it, he wouldn't buy into my lie. "It's worse than you think. I could fail."

His hand tightened around mine as a small flame of anger lit behind his eyes. "Are you trying, angel?"

My bones ached, begging for relief. "Yes, Daddy. But there's an opportunity to earn some extra credit."

His rough grip loosened ever so slightly. "How?"

I wished the storms in his eyes would calm, but they brewed, ready to shower down. If he didn't agree to it, there was no other chance to get to the game. I put on the sincerest smile I could muster. "Go to a sports game at the school."

His hand squeezed mine hard, and the storms flew in. "What game?"

I forced my smile to stay where it was, even though I wanted to cry from the pain in my hand. "A basketball game on Tuesday night."

"It's at the school?"

I nodded.

"What time?"

I wanted to lick my lips to wet them, try and work moisture in my mouth, but I couldn't show signs of anxiety. "Seven."

He stared at his plate of half-eaten spaghetti. His hand stayed tightly wrapped around mine. His fingers on his other hand drummed along the table. "I have an appointment Tuesday night. I can't go with you."

It hadn't crossed my mind that he would try to go with me. That would have ruined everything.

"I could ask Jenna to go with me."

His eyes shot toward mine, and the storm thundered.

"She's the one you met at the store," I hurried on. "She's very nice. I'd be safe with her. We'd go straight to the game and then straight home."

The silence stretched on. I'd blown it. He would never agree to let me go to a basketball game with Jenna. I wasn't allowed friends, to have fun, or be out in the world without Daddy. *He* was supposed to be my world.

He *was* my world. All I had. I hated that the blackmailer was making me break my trust with him. Making me lie to him and deceive him. They were turning me into someone I wasn't and someone I never wanted to be.

"Straight there and straight home," he finally said.

I was so lost in thought, it took me a moment to process what he said. I nodded. "Yes. Of course, Daddy."

"And this will help your grade?" The thunder-storm bounced around in his dark gray eyes, and I worried it would never die down.

"Yes."

"This will help get you off your teacher's radar? I don't

like them paying too much attention to you." The clouds in his eyes broke apart, and the storm calmed.

I couldn't believe what was happening. Was he going to let me go to a school function? Without him and with a friend? I forced myself to nod. "Yes."

He took a bite of his food, chewing slowly and staring at his plate. Each second that ticked by was agonizing. If he didn't agree, I'd have to find another way to sell all the cell phone bands. I needed that money, and I didn't have much time.

"Only Jenna would go with you?"

"Yes, Daddy."

"Not that boy from the pizza place?" he asked, his hand holding his fork frozen above his plate.

Brendon. I thought back to our hug and how his arms burned against my back. I'd barely been able to conceal the pain. He was getting too close to the truth. I didn't want him wrapped up in all my problems. "Who?"

Something flashed in his eyes, but it was so quick that I couldn't pin it down. "The one in your class. In your French group."

"Oh, him?" I scrunched my eyebrows. "Why would he go?"

He stared at me. I worried he could see right through me and know that I'd been hanging out with Brendon. Know that I liked him. That I'd kissed him. That I'd be sneaking into his bedroom later that night.

"Just making sure," Daddy said. "You can't trust teenage boys. They only have one thing on their mind." He finally lowered his hand.

"What?" I asked, twirling the same piece of spaghetti around my fork.

His jaw tightened. "Doesn't matter. Just stay away from them."

"Okay, Daddy." I smiled at him before I forced myself to eat. My appetite had completely gone, but I'd somehow convinced him to let me go to the game. He didn't know it, but it was helping save our family. In the end, it would be worth it.

CHAPTER 27

*D*addy stayed up late. For hours, he clomped up and down the basement stairs, mumbling to himself the whole time. He'd pass by my room, toss something heavy in the entry, then make his way back down the hall and into the basement. Maybe he was cleaning it out. He didn't like clutter, and he'd made a mess down there.

I almost fell asleep a few times, but luckily Noah kept me awake. He wouldn't stop talking. I bet Jenna would be the same way if we'd ever had a sleepover.

Suddenly, something slammed into my bedroom door, rattling it. I pushed back against my headboard and clutched Noah in my arms.

"We wouldn't be in this mess if it weren't for you!" Daddy bellowed. He threw another heavy object at my door. "Be a good little girl, that's all I ask." What sounded like his fist punched the door before he went back to cleaning.

I stayed safe on my bed, surrounded by my canopy, working hard to control my breathing. My body tensed every time his footsteps came close to my door.

It was almost midnight when the hallway light turned off.

I picked up the phone Brendon had given me and turned it over in my hand. Was it too late to text him? I had no idea when he went to bed.

My thumb hovered over the buttons. The thought of Brendon coming to break me out of my room in the middle of the night sent my stomach whirling. What if Daddy caught him? What if he was secretly outside my door, waiting for me to step out of line?

My heart pounded, my blood rushing through my body like it couldn't get to its destination fast enough. It suddenly felt hot in the room.

"Are you sweating?" Noah asked.

I wiped my forehead, the moisture absorbing into my hand. "It's hot."

"No, it's not."

"Hush." I glared at him. I wasn't in the mood for his attitude.

I tiptoed over to the door and pressed my ear against it. After a few minutes, Daddy's snores echoed down the hall, releasing some of the tension in me.

Before I could talk myself out of it, I texted Brendon. *It's safe.*

I didn't know what else to say or how much I could send in a text. I didn't even know if I'd done it right. Did it get to Brendon? Or someone else? My shaking hand dropped the phone when it buzzed.

See you soon, Brendon wrote.

My hands shot up to my hair. Did I look okay? Scrambling off the bed, I rushed to the mirror. My pale skin was unusually red. Heat erupted all over my body. Sweat glistened on my forehead, and I did my best to wipe it off. I didn't own makeup or anything to do my hair. Just a brush . . . that was in the bathroom.

But I was locked in my room. I undid my braid and did a

fishtail braid instead. It was the only thing I could think of. I could change it back when I got home.

My window rattled, causing me to jump. I hadn't expected Brendon to come so fast. Smoothing out my hair and clothes, I took a few deep breaths before I went to the window and pulled back the curtain. I'd already taken out the loose bar so I could escape.

A smile spread on my face when I saw Brendon standing there, grinning at me. But then my smile slipped off, falling to the ground with an obvious thud. Jenna stood next to him. She was dressed in black, completely clashing with her personality. She'd even put on black eye shadow. Her hair hung loosely around her shoulders.

I creased my forehead, confused. Brendon shrugged, his happy smile switching to an apologetic one. I opened the window.

"Like my look?" Jenna somehow whisper shouted. "I was going for a criminal feel." Her gaze settled on the bars on my window. "What's with the prison style window?"

"It was here when we bought the place." The words tumbled out of my mouth. I took a breath to calm myself. "Daddy never got around to removing them."

Brendon held out his hand to me. "Let's get this party started."

I handed Jenna my backpack and then let Brendon help me through the window.

"Isn't that a fire hazard or something?" Jenna asked, pointing at the bars.

"That's why I removed one," I said. "So I could escape."

Brendon leaned in close, whispering in my ear. "Sorry. When I went to get the fabric, she insisted on coming along."

"It's okay," I whispered. Only, it wasn't. It was one more person I had to worry about getting hurt.

Brendon took my hand, and the three of us walked over to his house. A few houses had their porch lights on, but the others were dark and uninviting, making me want to hurry on by.

When we arrived, I was surprised how close he lived to me. Only a couple blocks away. His house looked like all the others in the quaint neighborhood. Daddy had driven by Brendon's house every day on the way to school, and I'd never known. It was one of the houses I imagined knowing the people who lived inside, and now I truly did.

Brendon opened the front door and walked in, pulling me in with him. The TV in the front room was on. A guy who looked a couple years older and had the same red hair as Brendon sat on the couch in a T-shirt and boxers. Nothing else. Was that normal? Why didn't he have on pants? I blushed, doing my best not to look. The thought of Brendon in the same thing lit a fire inside and my blood practically boiled. Stupid hormones.

The guy looked up, smiling wide at me and Jenna. "Two girls?" He looked at the clock. "After midnight. I'm proud of you, bro."

Brendon rolled his eyes. "Shut up, Dylan."

Jenna tucked her hair behind her ear and smiled shyly, making sure her braces didn't show. "Hi." Her eyes were on Dylan.

Dylan had his eyes on the TV, though. "Hey."

"You don't need to know my brother," Brendon said. He squeezed my hand and then took us toward the stairs.

I stopped and stared at a picture on the wall. Brendon, Dylan, and their mom and dad smiled back at me. They all wore green. It was the first time I'd seen Brendon in a button-down shirt – and I liked it.

They looked like the happy family I'd always imagined. Was it real? Or forced? The pictures next to it were the four of them goofing around, all laughing and making funny faces for the camera. Definitely real.

Their mom had red hair and freckles, just like Brendon's. She looked so friendly and kind. When my focus landed on his dad, all I could see was Daddy. I shivered and looked away.

"Mom makes us do these pictures every year," Brendon said. "And we happily oblige since she's the best cook in the world."

He tugged on my arm and guided us upstairs. I'd expected to sneak up there, walk quietly and carefully, but Brendon just went up like it was no big deal to be bringing two girls into his room in the middle of the night. A light came from a room down the hall, and I could hear the faint sound of a TV.

"Here we are." Brendon let go of my hand and plopped down on his bed, landing on the side of his arm. The bed was much bigger than my own. He wasn't a big guy, so I wasn't sure why he needed so much room while he slept.

Brendon's bedroom walls were covered in posters, filled with people I didn't know. I moved in close to one and noticed the spider logo he once wore on a shirt. The guy was completely covered in a red and blue costume, hanging upside down from a building. It said Spiderman on the bottom.

"Nice room," Jenna said, sitting down on the carpeted floor. She placed some Velcro and her bag of fabric next to her and began pulling it out, arranging them by colors.

I sat down next to Jenna and took the paint out of my backpack. Brendon turned on the radio and then grabbed a soda from a mini fridge next to his bed.

"You ladies want a drink?"

We both shook our heads no, so Brendon sat down close to me, popped open the can of Dr Pepper, and gave me a small smile. He already had the plastic bottles ready on the floor.

"This is kinda cool," Jenna said. "It feels so mysterious, like we're in some sort of secret club." She held up a piece of pink argyle fabric. "I love this one. You have to use it."

I took it from her and set it in front of me. I'd started to sweat from being in a guy's room, so I undid my top button and rolled up my sleeves, making sure to stop at the elbows. Anything above that would expose my bruises.

Jenna whistled. "Look at you, showing some skin." She leaned toward me. "You should seriously do it more often. I've never wanted to say anything because you have your look set in stone, but a little variety wouldn't hurt. I could let you borrow some of my shirts if you want."

We had a lot to do in a very limited window of time, so I just smiled politely at her and went to work. Jenna kept up the conversation, pretty much talking the whole time. Brendon and I stayed quiet, me intently working, Brendon keeping his focus mostly on me.

The heat in my cheeks wouldn't go away. Any time I glanced at him, he smiled in a way that melted me.

But boys were bad – Daddy said so all the time.

So why didn't Brendon seem bad?

"How many times have you been in here, Cora?" Jenna's gaze passed back and forth between me and Brendon.

The heat flared all over my face and neck. I wanted to undo another button. When I stole a glance at Brendon, even he had the smallest blush on his face. That never happened to him.

"I've lost count," Brendon said, replacing his blush with a smirk.

"Five times," I said, gluing down a piece of fabric against the plastic. Making the bands became easier with each one. Only silence answered me, so I looked up to find both

195

Brendon and Jenna staring at me. I'd said something wrong again.

"You've seriously counted?" Jenna finally asked.

I raised my eyebrows at her. "Wouldn't you?"

A small laugh escaped her mouth, and she didn't bother hiding her braces. "You know I would."

Just like that, Brendon covered up his mouth to hold back a laugh, and the tension in the room disappeared.

"You going to the game Tuesday night?" Jenna asked. Her eyes told me she was waiting for me to say no.

"I was hoping we could go together."

Jenna's jaw dropped in surprise, and then a smile burst across her face.

Brendon pulled back in surprise. "You're going?"

I nodded. "Yes. Daddy . . . Dad said I could. If I went with Jenna."

Jenna clapped her hands. "Yay! I finally get you out of the house." She glanced around Brendon's room. "And not in your boyfriend's room."

My cheeks warmed. Boyfriend. Such a strange word to me. One I thought would never be used regarding me. He wasn't my boyfriend, but Jenna thought he was.

"You're so cooped up at home," Jenna said. "You take homebody to a whole new level." She pulled out her phone, and her fingers went to work. "This will be so much fun. I'll invite some of my friends. We can grab a bite to eat afterword."

"I can only go to the game," I said.

Jenna stopped typing long enough to gape at me. "Why?"

"School night," I said, forcing a smile.

Rolling her eyes, Jenna went back to her phone. "Your dad is like a freaking Nazi, I swear. He won't let you do anything. You should seriously call child protective services because it's so wrong."

I froze, holding tight onto the cell phone band I was currently working on. Fear worked its way through my bones, latching on. Jenna knew more about me than I thought.

Brendon placed his hand on my knee, making me look at him. He gave my knee a little squeeze and smiled at Jenna. "Very funny, Jenna."

Jenna waved her hand. "I can be funny, you know. It happens."

She had been joking. A joke that rang so true.

Brendon didn't move his hand, and I didn't stop him. It calmed me, having him there. He helped me be normal. Guided me through things I didn't quite understand. Having friends was foreign territory I never thought I'd roam.

It was a little after two in the morning when I completed number twenty.

"I'm so done," Jenna said, standing up. "I'm freaking tired and want my bed."

Brendon stood. "We should get you home, too, Cora."

They helped me gather everything together. Brendon put all the completed bands in a bag. As Jenna went out the door, Brendon pointed at the bag on the floor. "I'll keep these here and bring them Tuesday night."

I threw my arms around his neck. "Thank you. You've helped me more than I deserve." Lowering my arms, I kissed him on the cheek.

Brendon smiled at me. "It's worth it just for that." He took my hand. "Let's get you home."

Darkness surrounded my home when we reached my window, which I hoped was a good sign. Sweat slid down the small of my back. I wasn't sure what I'd do if Daddy was in my room. I wouldn't put it past him to sit in the dark and wait. I almost told Brendon to leave, but he reached out and rolled down one of my sleeves. My breath caught in my throat. Once he buttoned the cuff, he lifted my other arm and softly kissed the inside of my forearm before he pulled down the sleeve. My stomach fluttered in the most perfect way.

Going onto my tiptoes, I pressed my lips to his. It was starting to feel natural, expressing my feelings like that. And if Daddy were waiting for me in the room, it might've been the last time I ever got to kiss Brendon.

Brendon put his warm hands around my waist and helped me back into my room.

"See you tomorrow," he said.

I smiled. "Thanks for your help. Goodnight."

I waited until he was out of sight before I put the bar back in place and closed the window. One scan of my room showed no signs of Daddy. Everything remained still in its place, neat as always. The night had been a success. We'd gotten a lot done, which gave me some relief. I changed my braid back to the normal three-strand way and rested it over my right shoulder.

Sitting down on the bed, I took Noah into my arms. "Maybe having friends won't be so bad after all."

"I'm not so sure about that," Noah said.

The lock on my door clicked, and the door swung open. Daddy turned on the light in my room. "Who are you talking to?"

Storms flashed in his eyes. He stepped into the room, his eyes darting everywhere, his hands in fists.

"Myself," I said, holding onto Noah. I made sure he covered the area below my neck so Daddy wouldn't see that the top button of my shirt was undone.

His eyes shot toward me. "Why are you still dressed? Why aren't you sleeping?"

"I wasn't tired." I rubbed Noah's fur, willing myself to stay calm. He'd only know I'd done something wrong if I let him know.

He moved toward my bed, bending down to look under it. I took the moment to fasten my top button. He stood and walked to the other side. In my pocket, my phone vibrated. I didn't know how to turn it off, and I hoped he wouldn't hear.

He stared at the floor on the other side of my bed for a moment before he went over to the closet. "You aren't lying to me, are you, angel?"

"No, Daddy," I said. "I couldn't sleep, so I was talking to Noah, and . . ."

He whipped around, the storms in his eyes exploding. "Noah?" He rushed to my side, taking me by the arm. Noah fell from my arms, landing softly on his head.

I pointed at the stuffed elephant on my bed. "Noah. Remember? You gave him to me?"

He slowly loosened his grip. He stared at the elephant. "Yes. I remember." He let go of me, and my anxiety fluttered away. "Get in your pajamas and go to bed, now. No more talking with Noah."

"Yes, Daddy."

He glanced around the room once more and stormed out, slamming the door closed and locking it from the outside.

Letting out a long sigh of relief, I sat down on my bed and pulled the phone out of my pocket.

I had fun tonight, Brendon wrote.

Me, too.

Sleep well.

I was about to put the phone in my backpack when the screen lit up again.

P.S. I love when you blush.

For the first time, I didn't blush. Instead, I fell onto my bed with the biggest smile on my face.

CHAPTER 28

Tuesday night Daddy dropped me off at the school in front of the gym. I shut the passenger door and waved goodbye, thinking he would drive way, but he waited, his unsure eyes staring at me. With a forced smile, I turned toward the gym and calmly walked inside, knowing he watched me the whole way.

The second I walked in the door, I forgot about Daddy. The place was packed. It was a sea of black and gold shirts and uniforms, the colors of our school. A few maroon shirts weaved in between the crowd. I assumed it was the color of the other team. I pulled a little on the bottom of my light blue shirt. I wasn't aware I was supposed to wear school colors.

A lady bumped into me, sending me forward. The next thing I knew, I was standing in front of a table.

"Ten dollars," a guy said. He looked maybe a year older than me. He had black and gold paint on his face that looked rather silly. I couldn't peel my eyes off it. His eyes widened in annoyance, and he held out his hand. "I said that will be ten dollars."

I licked my lips. "What?" I didn't realize I had to pay to get in. No one had mentioned that to me.

The guy let out a deep breath. "If you want to watch the game, you gotta pay. Otherwise, get out of the line. You're holding it up."

I had no money to give him.

"Excuse me." Brendon's friendly voice came from my right. He pushed himself between an elderly couple, offering an apology as he did. He held out a five-dollar bill to the guy at the table. "She's a student, so it's five." He was wearing his black shirt with the bat on it.

The guy stamped my hand with a basketball in black ink.

Taking my hand, Brendon tugged me out of the line and away from the crowd. I had a second to peer inside the gym. Brendon wasn't kidding about it being an important game. I'd never seen so many people crammed in there, even during an assembly. The players were warming up on the court while the cheerleaders waved their pom-poms and chanted at the crowd in the stands. I stared at their shiny, smooth legs and all of a sudden, the hair on mine weighed me down. Maybe I could sneak one of Daddy's razors. But he'd be so mad if he ever caught me shaving my legs.

Someone waved from the crowd, and I looked over to see Jake sitting with all his friends, his smiling eyes on me. I waved back before I turned to Brendon.

He wrapped his arms around me, but quickly released me. "Sorry. Is it okay if I hug you?"

We'd done more than that. It was all happening so fast, but I felt so comfortable with him. I smiled. "Of course."

"Thank goodness." He pulled me close.

I sank into him, letting the warmth embrace me. I didn't want to let go. He felt safer than Daddy, which took me by surprise. It was a blanket of security, like nothing could ever hurt me again. It was overwhelming. Pushing him away, I dropped my arms and looked around. "Where's Jenna?"

He pointed his thumb behind him. "We have a table set up over here. Hope you don't mind, but we already opened shop." He had a fresh Band-Aid covering his thumb. I wondered if he'd ever stop cutting his fingers while he folded pizza boxes at work.

"Really?" I couldn't see the table from where I stood. There was a long line blocking it from view.

"We were going to wait, but someone asked about it, and the next thing we knew, people were wanting to buy them." He shrugged. "Didn't want to turn customers away." He took my hand into his and guided me to the table. He raised my arm in the air. "The designer is here!"

A small applause broke out, more polite than anything.

"Cora, these are selling like crazy," Jenna said. She'd chosen gold as her color, which was much better than the black. Her gold, glitter eye shadow glimmered in the light. "We only have twenty left."

"What?" A guy in the line stood on his tiptoes to see us. "You only have twenty left?"

Brendon smiled at the guy. "For now. We'll be making more and selling them at other events."

I squeezed his hand to get his attention, but he just squeezed it back, smiling the whole time. I wanted to tell him that it wouldn't be likely I'd be attending another school event. I was lucky Daddy let me attend the basketball game.

The people shoved forward, crowding around the table. Customers were pushing their money toward me, reaching for a band at the same time.

The first person handed me a twenty-dollar bill. I reached for a ten in the cash box, but Brendon put his hand over mine to stop me. He leaned in, whispering in my ear. "We're selling them for twenty."

"Why?" I asked. It seemed like a lot. Why would they want to pay that much for my bands?

"Supply and demand," Brendon said. "Besides, we can't let the blackmailer get all your money. You deserve to walk away with some cash as well. Plus, I had to buy some supplies, so this will help cover that."

I didn't understand why people would pay it, but I wasn't about to argue. It would be nice to get some money out of the situation.

"I find it interesting you've never mentioned this hobby of yours." Mr. Mendoza approached the table, his hands in his jeans' pockets, eyeing the cell phone bands.

"Did you call my dad?" I asked.

He looked surprised by my question. "He called the school. I thought you would've known."

"He mentioned talking to the school, but not who made the call."

He eyed the line of customers. "He wanted to know if public school was giving you all you need."

"And you said no?" I stared up at him, trying to read his face.

Mr. Mendoza was stoic. Not the type of person I could gauge what he was thinking or feeling. He took his hand out of his pocket and rubbed his goatee. "I said you were too advanced for the tenth grade. Suggested we move you up next year."

I didn't want to tell him that Daddy had decided to remove me from public school, so I took a cell phone band from the table and handed it to him. "It can be yours for twenty dollars."

He studied the band. "Twenty bucks? What do you do with all that money?"

"Supplies. Also, investing in my future. That's what you wanted, right?"

"Saving up for college?" He rifled through his leather wallet and handed me a twenty. "I can support that. And buy my niece a birthday present in the process."

"You have a niece?"

He folded his wallet and placed it and the band in his pocket. "Does that surprise you?"

"Yes," I said with a nod. "Not sure why, though."

"Siblings," Mr. Mendoza said. "They'll give you nieces and nephews."

I rubbed my arm. "I'm an only child."

He folded his arms. "Well, if one day you get married, your spouse might have siblings, which could get you nieces and nephews." He cracked a small smile. "Easier than having your own children, if you ask me."

"I don't want kids." The words flew from my mouth.

The smile on his face fell. "Didn't even hesitate on that one. There a reason why?"

I glanced at the line. "This really isn't the time, Mr. Mendoza. Besides, not everyone has to have children."

"Or need a reason to *not* have them." Jenna leaned on the table next to us. "Kids gross me out." She rested her chin on her fist. "I want to travel the world. Taste different countries. Take lovers."

Mr. Mendoza took a step back. "And that's my cue to leave. You ladies enjoy your night." He left without looking back.

Jenna winked at me. "Always scares the adults off when you use the word *lover*."

"I'll have to try that sometime," I said with a smile. The likelihood of that happening was slim to none.

"Do you have any left in blue?" A man asked.

I playfully shoved Jenna away and turned my attention to the man before me. He had soft blue eyes, and his mouth turned up into a fraction of a smile. Something about him seemed so familiar like I knew him from somewhere, but I couldn't pinpoint it.

"Blue is my favorite color," the man said. He stuffed his hands into his trouser pockets like he didn't know what to do with them.

"Mine, too," I said. On the table, there were only a few bands left, none of them blue. "Looks like we're out of blue."

The man pulled his phone out of his pocket. "Do you mind if I take a picture of one to show my daughter?"

"Of course." I picked one up and held it out to him.

"Do you mind modeling it? So my daughter can see how it's used?"

I tugged the band over my arm, twisting it so he could get a good angle.

The man lifted his phone and snapped a picture. "Thanks. My daughter will be excited." He tucked his phone in his pocket. "When do you think you'll have more blue ones available?"

Brendon wrapped his arm around my shoulder and gently squeezed. "Our talented artist will be making more soon. Come to the next game, and we'll have lots of blue bands to choose from."

"I'd like that." The man cleared his throat. "I mean, I'd like a band. A blue one." He smiled at me. "You're very talented. Does it run in the family?"

"I don't know," I said.

The man furrowed his eyebrows. "You don't know?"

Brendon scooted closer to me, his stance turning stiff. "You have a son on the basketball team or something?"

The man tore his gaze from mine and blinked at Brendon. "Uh, a nephew."

"Who's your nephew?" Brendon asked. "I know all the guys on the team."

The man shifted where he stood, stealing a glance inside

the gym. He took a few steps away from the table. "Number twelve. I better get back inside." He hurried through the doors and out of sight.

"That was creepy," Brendon said. He didn't lower his arm around me.

"What was?" I asked, pulling on my braid.

"Do you know who number twelve is?"

Of course I didn't. I didn't know anyone on the basketball team, let alone any sport teams at our school.

"It's Jamaal Howard," Brendon said. "Our star player. And most definitely African-American and that creep was definitely white."

"So," I said with a shrug. "Maybe he married into the family."

Jenna sat down on the now empty table. All the bands had been sold. Aside from the one on me. Jenna slipped it off my arm. "That man was a total perv."

"Why?" I asked.

Jenna twirled the band around her hand. "He took a picture of you."

I pointed at the band. "He took a picture of that."

"That was just an excuse," Brendon said. "So he could snap a pic of you."

My eyes darted to the gym, expecting to see the man, but he was nowhere in sight. "Why would he want a picture of me?"

"Because he's a creep," Jenna said. "Probably some sick pedophile. I'll bet you a blue cell phone band he doesn't even have a daughter."

"What's a pedophile?" I asked.

Jenna dropped the band. "Are you serious?"

Brendon gave my shoulder a little squeeze and then lowered his arm. "How about we go enjoy the rest of the game?" He crammed the cash box in his backpack and slung it over his shoulder. Slipping his hand in mine, he smiled like everything was going to be okay. "Ready?"

"Sure," I said. I let Brendon guide me into the gym. We squeezed into a tight spot near the top of the stands.

Brendon put his arm around my back and held me close, not that there was much of an option. Everyone was packed in the gym – Jenna was practically sitting on top of me.

The excitement of being so close to Brendon vanished when my hair pricked. I had an overwhelming sensation that I was being watched. I scanned the gym, trying to find the source. On the other side, near the bottom, I spotted the man. He had his phone up but lowered it when I looked at him. He shifted his gaze to the game and clapped, pretending like he was paying attention, but I knew he hadn't been. He'd probably taken another picture of me.

Was he the blackmailer? I'd never seen him before and knew nothing about him, so why would he want to know so much about me? Unless he really was a creep like Brendon and Jenna had said.

"You okay?" Brendon asked.

I turned to him, our faces close. "That guy was staring at me. I think he took another picture." I pointed him out for Brendon.

"I'm not leaving your side until your dad gets here," Brendon said. "I don't like how interested that man is in you. Something's not right about him."

I rested my head on Brendon's shoulder, willing myself to stay calm. My life had become way too complicated, and I didn't like it one bit.

Brendon rubbed my back a little too roughly over one of my recent cuts from Daddy. My back stiffened and I winced from the pain.

"You okay?" Brendon asked. His new favorite question.

My back felt like it was on fire. I needed some space. We

were shoved in too tight. Everything closed in on me, and it suddenly was hard to breathe. I'd never been surrounded by so many people. I felt claustrophobic, and I wanted out.

"I have to use the restroom," I said, standing. I pushed down the stands, muttering apologies I didn't mean. When I cleared the last person, I took off out of the gym, bypassing the bathroom, and headed straight for the front office.

I didn't belong there, stuffed in that gym, surrounded by people whose world was nothing like mine. I'd never had to experience creepy men or uncontrollable feelings before I started public school. But if I didn't belong there, and I didn't belong with Daddy, where *did* I belong?

My hand wrapped around the handle and tried to yank open the door. It was locked. I needed to call Daddy. I needed to go home, lock myself in my room, and hold Noah.

"Cora!" Jenna ran up to me and put her hand on my arm. "What's wrong?"

"I need your phone." I glanced behind her, expecting Brendon to show up, but he was nowhere in sight.

"He stayed in the gym," Jenna said, handing me her phone. "He wanted to keep his eyes on perv man."

I stared at the screen, a pair of puppy eyes staring back at me. How did you call someone on it? Where were the numbers? It was nothing like the phone Brendon had given me.

"That's Louie," she said. "My newest pup. You should come over and meet him! He's the most lovable thing ever."

I didn't care about a dog. I wanted to go home. "I need to call my dad."

When I continued to just stare at the screen, Jenna pressed a button on the bottom, and a screen of numbers popped up.

My fingers fumbled over the phone. I wasn't used to

using a cell phone with a touch screen. Once our home phone was entered, I glanced up at Jenna. "Now what?"

Her jaw dropped. "You've seriously never used a cell phone before? What year are you living in?" She pressed a button.

I stared at the screen, waiting for something to happen.

"You need to hold the phone to your ear if you want to hear your dad," she said, her eyebrows furrowed.

"Right. I knew that." I put the phone to my ear.

"Uh huh." She folded her arms and stared at me like I was crazy. Maybe I was.

Daddy's voice rang out from the phone. "Hello?"

"Daddy?" I licked my lips. "It's Cora. Can you come get me?"

"Is the game already over?"

"No," I said. "But I've seen enough. I just want to go home."

He sighed. "I knew it was a bad idea to let you go. Too overwhelming." He paused. "Whose phone are you calling from?"

"Jenna's." I put my hand on my forehead. "Can you come now?"

"Of course, angel. I just finished with my appointment. I'll pick you up outside of the gym where I dropped you off."

"Just hurry." I didn't know how to end the call, so I handed the phone back to Jenna.

She pressed a button on the phone and tucked it in the band on her arm. "He won't hurt you."

Sweat formed at my temples. I craved air, even though we were outside, the temperature perfect. "Why would my dad hurt me?" Did she know? Had she seen the scars? Maybe Brendon had mentioned something to her.

Jenna frowned. "The perv. Why would you think I'm talking about your dad?"

I forced a laugh, the sound unnatural. "No reason. I

should probably go wait out in front of the gym." I took off at a fast pace.

Jenna ran to catch up with me. "Are you nervous or something?"

"Nervous?" My legs somehow carried me forward. The rest of me felt like collapsing. "Why would I be nervous?" With a strange man taking pictures of me and constantly lying to Daddy about what I was doing, I was a pile of nerves, about to crumble to the ground.

"About kissing Brendon," Jenna said. Her short legs worked hard enough to keep up with me that she almost stumbled when I stopped walking.

I just stared at her. Did she know about our kiss? I couldn't imagine Brendon telling her. I'd thought about talking to her about my crush, but I was too embarrassed to bring it up.

"Now that you're officially together, this means you'll have to kiss at some point." She rubbed my arm. "Don't stress about it. I'm sure it'll be amazing." She squeezed my arm. "I'm so jealous! I've been dying to get my first kiss but haven't had any options." She pointed at her braces. "These aren't helping, either."

The smallest sigh escaped my lips. She didn't know.

"I really need to be less picky," she said. "The guys at our school gross me out. They're so immature." Her eyes widened. "Not Brendon, though. He's wonderful." She sucked in her breath. "Not that *I* want to be with him. I meant for you."

A laugh bubbled up and burst out.

She slapped my arm. "Don't laugh!" She glared at me for only a moment before she busted out laughing as well.

"You'll find someone."

Jenna smiled, her eyes sparkling. "I hope so. It better be romantic."

A honk broke up our fun.

I gave her a quick hug. "I'll see you tomorrow." I took off, running straight for Daddy's van.

He had the passenger door open. He was leaning toward me, watching me run.

I hopped into the van and shut the door. "Hi, Daddy."

"You okay?" he asked, giving my leg a little squeeze.

I nodded. "Better now that you're here. My teacher better be happy I went. Basketball is so not my sport."

I stared out the window as he drove away from the gym. The creepy man stood under a tree, watching us leave. He snapped another picture before we were out of sight.

CHAPTER 29

*R*ubbing my eyes, I held back a yawn. Every few nights I had been sneaking out and burning a few of my journals. It cut into my sleep. But they needed to be destroyed.

My hands shook as I taped the envelope of money to the inside of my locker. A part of me wanted to be there when the person picked it up. The other part didn't want to know the truth. I just wanted it to end. Go back to my normal routine and not have to worry about any of it.

I wasn't sure if I wanted Brendon to tell me who it was. But I had to know so I could stop them from blackmailing me further.

"Snow!" My P.E. teacher's booming voice broke me from my trance. "You going to join us today? Or do you have another excuse?"

Shaking my head, I shut my locker door and ran past my teacher and her snarl. She hated me. I didn't blame her. I was a terrible athlete and came up with excuse after excuse as to why I couldn't participate in P.E.

We were playing volleyball on the asphalt courts outside.

It was a nice day, the sun shining, but not too hot. I looked up at the blue sky and soaked in the warmth. Daddy had bought me a cotton, long sleeve shirt to wear underneath my gym clothes so my arms would be covered . . . along with my bruises. I always changed in the bathroom stall where no one could see me.

"You better help today," Dalton said. He stood next to me, hugging his arms close to his chest. "Last time, Easton practically had me burned at the stake for not picking up your slack."

I frowned at him. "It's not your job or anyone else's to handle my position."

He grunted. "Well, you certainly can't do it."

I punched him in the arm like I'd seen guys do with their friends. "It's just P.E. Why do you guys take it so seriously?"

He rubbed his arm where I hit him. "It's our grade. We actually want to pass P.E."

I rolled my eyes. "Why does it matter if I'm athletic or not? It's not like I'm going to be playing professional volleyball after high school." Or ever.

"Ain't that the truth," Easton said, walking up to us. "It's not about being athletic. It's about staying in shape." He ran his fingers through the top of his brown hair. He had the sides completely shaved, which was the style for some strange reason. I didn't get it. Then again, I didn't get a lot of the trends.

Easton gathered our team. "I'll start as server. We can rotate." He looked at me, opened his mouth, and then snapped it shut. He probably realized no matter what he said, I wouldn't be a good player.

I stood next to Easton so I'd be the last server in the rotation. Easton's plan was to get us as far ahead in points as we could before I had to serve. I wanted to let him know that it wouldn't help, but I decided to keep my mouth shut as well.

No point in arguing about something neither of us could change.

For the first few serves, I stood in the back, keeping out of the way. Our teacher gave me some disapproving shakes of the head. She thought being a terrible participant was better than not participating at all.

When I circled to the front, my invisibility decreased. I became a target for the other team. Before the other team served, Dalton put his hand on my shoulder. "You over think it. Just hit the ball when it comes at you." He demonstrated a few different techniques, showing me how to use my hands. "The ball won't kill you, I promise."

I'd been watching the other players, trying to learn how to play. The reason I wasn't any good was because I had no experience. Before I'd gone to public school, I'd had no chances to play sports. Daddy didn't play any with me and he didn't watch them – starting P.E. had been a big eye opener.

"Cora, hit it!" Dalton said.

I glanced up to see the ball sailing toward me. I'd seen the tall girl on the other side of the net stick her fingers straight up and hit the ball that way. They'd called it a set.

Taking a deep breath, I raised my arms, stiffened my fingers, and connected with the ball. It soared back up, and Dalton hit it hard, forcing it over the net and whacking into the asphalt.

Dalton held his fist out to me. "Nice job!"

A fist bump. Knuckles. Or something like that. That was what he wanted. So I fisted my hand and hit his. Not too hard, though, like when I'd high fived Julien.

"Where have you been hiding that?" Easton asked.

I shrugged as I stepped back. My foot connected with a crack in the asphalt and I stumbled to my spot.

Easton smiled at my clumsiness. "Just do the same thing again."

Each time the ball came at me, I set it so Dalton could spike it. It was something simple I could do. The P.E. teacher actually smiled at me. Smiled. *At me.* So rare.

When it came my time to serve, both Dalton and Easton crowded close.

"Okay, Cora," Easton said. "Just swing your arm back and then forward, using your fist to hit the ball."

I furrowed my eyebrows. "You throw it up and then hit it with your palm."

Easton snorted. "Let's start the easy way. Just because you've done a few decent sets doesn't mean you're a professional now." He slapped my shoulder.

Dalton gave me another fist bump.

I hated that something insignificant got me so nervous. It was high school P.E. volleyball. Yet my palms were sweating so bad I had to wipe them on my pants a few times.

My fist shook as I held the ball out, ready to strike. It was just a serve. Just a ball in my hand. For some reason, though, I felt like the moment meant so much. It was approval from my peers. Approval from my teacher who loved nothing more than to shake her head at me and mumble things under her breath.

You can do it, Cora. Sally's voice came into my head. *I'm with you in spirit. I always will be.*

A smile found its way to my lips. I wasn't alone. It was just a ball, and I could hit it hard enough to go over the net.

Swinging my arm back, I pictured myself doing it, and then let my arm fly forward, my fist connecting with the ball. It soared up into the air and over the net.

Everyone was so surprised, even the other team, that they let the ball fall to the ground. Easton, Dalton, and the rest of my team cheered. Out of the corner of my eye, I saw my teacher do a little fist pump.

I couldn't wait to get home and tell Noah. "I did it!"

Easton pointed his finger at me. "You did. But don't let it go to your head. The game isn't over yet."

My next few serves were a little shaky, but they went over the net. So, I wasn't completely hopeless. I'd still never become a professional athlete, but I had a chance at passing high school P.E.

We'd just rotated spots when my skin pricked. The smile on my face fell and shattered on the asphalt. I scanned the field, searching for something – someone. I could feel them.

Behind an ash tree, I spotted him. The man from the basketball game. He barely peered out, but I remembered his calm and self-assured stature. His frame. I'd tried to memorize everything about him so I'd never forget.

My hand wrapped around my braid. The man wore a hat and shades, but it was him. Staring at me. At my school, watching me play volleyball. Watching *me.* What did he want? He couldn't do anything on the school property. Not with that many witnesses. But him standing there, one hand in his pocket, the other holding his cell up, and his gaze on me was enough to terrify me.

Pain radiated through the side of my head and I stumbled back.

"Cora!" Dalton ran over to me and took hold of my arm to keep me from falling.

"What were you looking at?" Easton asked.

The side of my face stung. I pressed my hand to my cheek. The volleyball had smacked right into me.

"Dalton, take her to the nurse," the teacher said. She patted my shoulder. "It's going to be okay, Cora. Just put some ice on it." She squeezed my shoulder. "And pay attention. No day dreaming."

As Dalton escorted me off the court, I looked over my shoulder at the tree, but the man was gone.

CHAPTER 30

The right side of my face had swollen. The nurse had given me an ice pack and some ibuprofen. She was nice enough to let me stay in the office until school ended. For some reason, I wasn't ready to face the truth behind the blackmailer. I'd find out from Brendon later.

"What happened to you?" Daddy asked.

I sat down in the passenger seat of his van and shut the door. "Volleyball." The immediate smell of sweat and grease overwhelmed me.

His nostrils flared, and his knuckles around the steering wheel turned white. "Why didn't they call me?"

I gently pressed my fingers against my swollen skin. The ibuprofen seemed to be helping. I wished Daddy let me use it. "Getting hit in the face with a volleyball doesn't qualify for alerting the parents. This kind of stuff happens all the time."

The day before, Dalton had taken a volleyball to the groin. He'd fallen down, curled up, and grimaced in pain. For some odd reason, I'd found it funny.

"You're probably going to get a black eye," he said.

A car behind us honked.

Daddy reached his hand out the window and flipped them off, which was completely out of character. He pounded his palm against the side of the van. "They should have called me."

"Daddy, it's okay," I said, still touching the swollen skin. "I've been hurt worse. This is nothing."

I sucked in a sharp breath. Why had I said that? It would only make him angrier, which was never good for me.

He peeled out of the parking lot and rushed home. He rarely drove fast. He always insisted on obeying the law and driving safe. But he flew through stop signs and took sharp turns.

The second he turned off the ignition, he turned to me. "Inside. Now."

My hand fumbled on the door handle. A part of me wanted to run and never look back – scream and shout for help – but fear sealed my lips. My whole mouth went dry. Would he beat me again? I fisted the front of my shirt, worried he'd ruin this one as well.

If I did run, where would I go? Now I knew where Brendon lived, but going there would be admitting something was wrong at home. I wasn't sure if I was ready for that, either.

Grabbing my backpack, I hurried into the house and hung it up on the hook next to the door.

Daddy slammed the front door closed, took me by the arm, and dragged me down the hall. I expected him to throw me downstairs, but he tossed me to the floor in the middle of the hallway.

"We're going to finish installing the wood flooring, and then you can spend a few nights in the basement." He bent down and lifted my chin, squeezing tight. "Cora, you call me when you get hurt. You tell me right away."

"Yes, Daddy," I managed to get out through the aching pain from the wounds in my back and his hold on my chin.

His cloudy eyes stared into mine, somehow stripping me of my innocence. "Change into work clothes and then we'll get started."

I desperately wished my door locked from the inside and not the outside. I wanted to lock myself away from Daddy – away from the world. I wanted to be alone, safe and warm on my bed, with no one to stop me.

Instead, I changed and met Daddy in the hallway, and we went to work.

What was going on with him? Something bothered him deeply, and I wished I knew what it was. Did he know the truth? That I kept a journal and it had been stolen? It didn't seem likely. He would have said something by now. It had to be something else, which somehow worried me more.

Daddy sent me to the basement at one in the morning. My whole body ached. Installing wood flooring was harder than I expected. It required certain muscles I didn't have.

The one light bulb flickered above me. He had locked the basement door and closed me off. It wasn't the kind of alone I wanted. It hadn't been *my* choice – it was Daddy's. It was always Daddy's choice.

My stomach rumbled – a mix of worry and hunger. He'd never fed me dinner. I still didn't have a mattress. The old one was so ruined, we'd thrown it out. All I had in the base ment was hard concrete floor – no blanket or warmth. How my life was destined to be forever. I'd never be safe. I'd never be able to make my own choices, have friends, be a teenager, or be a real person.

Until Daddy died.

I had a feeling he never would. He'd make sure I went with him when he did. He wouldn't want to leave me alone in the world.

My feelings feuded with each other. There was still the part that wanted to be under Daddy's control. It took some stress out of planning a future, worrying about what college to go to and what to major in. I could count on my life staying the same. Always provided for and looked after. Fed – usually. A roof over my head.

All I had to do was be better. Be careful. Get rid of Brendon and Jenna in my life – Dalton as well. We'd grown closer from the guitar lessons. Not totally close, but enough to consider him sort of a friend. He was nicer to me and didn't tease me. He treated me like a person.

Me being out there in the world put them in danger. It put *me* in danger. So many bad things could happen. So many people could take advantage of me, like that man who was following me. Whatever he wanted couldn't be good.

The good thing was he couldn't find me in the basement. He couldn't snap pictures of me or stare at me. The cold, concrete walls provided a barrier.

I went to the wall and pressed my palm against it. At least I had a permanent home. I wasn't tossed from place to place like I was worthless. Daddy loved me. I knew he did. He got angry with me, but it was because he loved me so much. Some people didn't know how to control their emotions. It overtook their body.

That was Daddy. That was why he never married. He said a romantic relationship was more overwhelming than a family one. The emotions were too hard to control. The mind and heart would make you do irrational things.

With the way Daddy treated me, I never wanted to see how he'd treat a wife.

My phone buzzed. I'd forgotten I'd hid it in my bra. Jenna said it was a good hiding spot because no one would ever check there.

Removing my hand from the wall, I wiggled the phone out from the side of my bra and read the text.

It was from Brendon.

I came over tonight, but the lights were still on, he wrote.

We were installing the hardwood floor.

That late?

~~*Daddy,*~~ I erased it. *Dad wanted to get it done.*

We still have lots of cell phone bands to make. There's another big game on Friday night.

Even if we'd made the bands, I couldn't go to the game. I was locked in the basement until Saturday at the earliest. Daddy would probably let me out on Sunday so I could make him dinner.

I can't. It'll have to wait until next week.

Why? Did something happen?

I got hit in the face with a volleyball. After I'd done pretty well. I wasn't as bad an athlete as I thought. I had just needed experience and practice.

Did you see who took the money from the locker? I couldn't believe I hadn't asked that first thing. With everything that happened after P.E., I'd completely forgotten.

No, Brendon wrote. *I was waiting, hiding behind a locker when everything went black.*

They knocked you unconscious?

Yes.

Are you okay?

Just mad, Brendon wrote. *I should've known they'd be looking for a spy. They aren't stupid.*

No, they weren't. At least I'd met their demands. I honestly didn't think I'd be able to do it. Five hundred dollars was a lot. But I did it and had a couple hundred dollars left for me at the end. I shared some of it with Brendon and Jenna for their help.

The phone buzzed, but not from a text. Someone was calling me. It didn't match Brendon's number. Had he given the number to someone else? Like Jenna? Or had the blackmailer found it?

I decided to answer. "Hello?"

"Thanks for the money," a deep voice said.

"Please leave me alone. I did what you wanted, so leave me alone." My finger hovered over the hang-up button, about to press, when they spoke louder.

"One last thing and then we'll be done. *Promise*."

Why should I believe them? They were deceitful.

"What?" I should've hung up, but they would've kept calling back. I could destroy the phone. Would they call the house? Would Daddy answer? He'd be so mad.

"Next Friday is my birthday," the voice said. "I want to celebrate. With you."

My whole body shivered. "What do you mean?" I didn't want to know. I didn't want to go anywhere near them.

"Meet me behind the school. Ten o'clock. Come alone."

"No," I said, my hand trembling. "I'm not going anywhere with you."

"Then I release your journal. Everyone will know the truth."

That couldn't happen. I didn't want Daddy to go to jail. I didn't want to go back to the foster system.

Maybe hanging out with them wouldn't be that bad.

I grabbed hold of my braid. "I can't stay out long."

The voice laughed. "Don't worry about that." They paused. "If it'll make you feel better, bring Noah and Sally with you. I've been *dying* to meet them."

My eyes sought out Sally. She was in the basement somewhere. I'd hidden her behind a storage tote. I worried Daddy might have taken it out the other night during his clean-up, but I spotted the tote in the corner.

I stumbled toward it and reached my arm around, grabbing Sally. With her and Noah with me, I wouldn't be alone. I'd have my two closest friends.

"What are we going to do?" I asked.

They laughed again. "We're going to celebrate my birthday. You'll have fun. Promise."

I just wanted the whole thing over with. After next Friday, I'd be in the clear. I could go back to my life and drop out of school. Cut off ties with Jenna, Brendon, and Dalton. They'd be safe. I'd be safe. Somewhat.

"If I do this," I said, "it'll all be over? You'll give me back my journal?"

"Of course," the voice said. "But if you tell a soul that we're going to meet up, the journal will be released. If you don't show up or are a minute late, the journal will be released."

"I understand." Who would I even tell? Brendon and Jenna wouldn't understand. They'd try to stop me and ruin everything.

"Good. See you next Friday, Cora."

The line went dead.

I had a ton of text messages from Brendon, but I didn't care. I didn't want to read them. Anger boiled up inside to the point it almost overflowed. Why was all of this happening to me? It was unfair and wrong. I didn't deserve any of it.

I'd done everything that had been asked of me. I'd broken every rule I'd created to keep me and Daddy safe. My fist tightened around the phone. I'd been a good girl. Good girls were rewarded, not punished. Yet, the stupid blackmailer was acting like none of that mattered.

My breathing sped up, making it difficult to control. My body shook in rage. I stared at my hands. Was this how Daddy always felt when I'd done something wrong?

An uncontrollable urge pushed its way to the surface and

broke free. Holding in a roar, I threw the phone against the wall, shattering it, cutting off my only link to the outside world.

CHAPTER 31

*S*ometime, late into the night, sleep tugged at my exhausted body. I had nowhere comfortable to lie, nothing to keep me warm, so my body fought the exhaustion, refusing to give in. I picked up every single broken piece from the phone and scattered the remnants throughout the remaining boxes in the basement so Daddy wouldn't see.

The right side of my face ached from the volleyball hit – the ibuprofen had worn off. I was grateful there wasn't a mirror. With how tender my skin felt under my touch, I knew there had to a be a large bruise, in addition to the swelling. It wouldn't be pretty.

I must have dozed off at some point because when I opened my eyes, sun shined through the tiny window. Daddy had placed a bowl of oatmeal on the top of the steps. He hadn't even checked on me or spoken to me.

"What did you expect?" Sally asked. "A warm morning greeting? A kiss on the check?"

"Hi would have sufficed."

Sally was leaning against a metal shelf near me. I had

slowly crept up the stairs, my muscles fighting the entire time, to retrieve the bowl of oatmeal and brought it back down. No spoon, of course. Just my hands.

"Is he worth it?" she asked.

I licked some oatmeal off my fingers. "Who?"

"Your father. Is he worth living like this?"

I stared at her. My living arrangement wasn't all that bad. I had a home, my own room, a bed, shower, clothes, and food.

But no freedom.

"You're not in your room," she said. "You're in a cold basement using your hands to eat."

Sally wasn't the one who was supposed to make me feel bad. Noah did that. She was supposed to be my friend. An ally.

"No shower, no toilet," she said. "No change of clothes. No sink."

"But a nosey friend," I mumbled, stirring the cold oatmeal with my finger.

"Is that so bad? To have someone that cares about your wellbeing? Jenna and Brendon would be horrified to find you down here."

"I was bad. I keep lying and putting our family at risk."

"You're putting your father at risk. You're not bad."

"I am." I set the half-eaten bowl of oatmeal on the floor. I couldn't eat any more. "This whole mess is my fault. If I'd never had a journal, this never would have happened. No one would know who I am. I wouldn't be locked in the basement."

"You still would've been hit in the face in P.E.," Sally said. "You'd still be here."

"Not true," I said, glaring at her. "I was distracted because a creepy man was watching me. A man who's probably my blackmailer." I had no idea why I was arguing with her. Deep inside, I knew she was right. But it was hard to admit out loud.

"Stop making excuses. No matter what, your father would have found a reason to be mad at you. Before all this journal mess, it was over stupid things like a scratch on a spoon or dropping the trash on the floor. The reasons have just changed. If anything, they're more legit and make more sense."

I picked her up, ready to throw her across the room. All she was doing was confusing me.

"Now you're going to get rid of me?" Sally asked. "Just like the phone?"

My fist squeezed tight around her. I wanted so badly to ruin her – destroy her. She made me think bad things, and I couldn't control the anger taking over me.

"Or true things," she sang.

"Daddy loves me!" I yelled. Was I turning into him with this uncontrollable anger?

"Interesting. I never said he didn't, but you went there. Why?"

"This isn't a shrink session." Putting my thumb and fore-finger in the hole on the bottom of the wrench, I swung her back and forth, hoping to annoy her like she was doing to me. "You can't get into my head and try to figure me out. Solve all my problems."

"Why not? We can start with your problem of not using full sentences."

I stopped swinging her. "Now you're bringing grammar into this?"

"Fine, let's skip to the major problem. You can't meet up with your blackmailer."

"Why not?" I wanted it over. Ended. It was the only way

to do it. I would meet up with the person, celebrate with them, get my journal back, drop out of school, and go back to my normal life.

"This isn't normal, Cora. You're locked in a basement, starved and dirty."

"I don't want to be thrown into the system!" I screamed, my fist clutching her tight. I yanked one of the wires off her head.

"You'd rather meet your blackmailer in the middle of the night, by yourself, let them torture you, rape you, do whatever they want, and then if they keep you alive, you'll go back to this lifestyle."

I tore off another wire. I hated her for being right.

"This is your solution? Destroying me? Are you feeling better?"

I stood, took a deep breath, and threw her at the wall with every bit of strength I had left in me. The wrench stayed fully intact. With a fierce battle cry inside, I stormed over, picked her up, tore off her clothes, the rest of her hair, and buried the wrench deep down inside a water-stained cardboard box in the corner of the basement.

Fuming, I went to the middle of the room and paced, yanking at my braid. How had I gotten here?

"You really thought that would work?" Sally asked.

I whipped around, staring in the direction of the box she was buried in. "Shut. Up. You're dead."

"I can never die, Cora. I'm not a wrench. I'm in your head."

"No. You're my creation and used to be my friend. I could only talk to you down here, so you're not in my head."

She chuckled. "Is that what you truly think? You could have talked to me at any time. You heard me earlier today during P.E. You could talk to Noah right now if you wanted."

"That's not true," I growled. I couldn't speak to him

whenever I wanted. He had to be present, just like she did. "Wait. How do you know about Noah?" I'd never talked to them about each other. I liked to keep them separate.

"Leave me out of this," Noah whined. "I don't want to get involved in your little girl quarrel."

"Noah?" No. I shook my head. He wasn't here. Sally was gone. She couldn't torment me.

"I'm not tormenting you," Sally said. "I'm trying to show you that you could have a chance at a normal life. One where you aren't beaten and abused or locked in basements in horrible living environments."

"It's much nicer up here," Noah said. "But I must admit, I like having the bed all to myself."

Sally snorted. "You would."

"Can't a guy enjoy his space?" Noah let out a sound like he was stretching. "Just the men upstairs, ruling the lair."

"You're an elephant, Noah," Sally said with a flat tone. "You don't live in lairs."

I slapped the sides of my head, wanting to turn them off so I could think.

"We should," Noah said. "I view Cora's bedroom as my lair. The walls could use some fresh paint, though. There's *way* too much pink in here."

"What do you have against pink?" Sally asked, her tone incredulous.

"Nothing," Noah said. "It's just not my favorite color."

Sally scoffed. "Anything else?"

"The bars on the window need to go." Noah clucked his tongue. "Although, if it keeps out that guy and girl Cora has made friends with, keeping them might not be a bad thing. He tried to come in last night, but the bars stopped him."

"Shut up!" I pulled at my braid. "Both of you. I want to be alone." I fell to the floor, tucked my legs in close, and rocked.

Sally hummed, but I blocked her out.

They couldn't control me. Daddy couldn't control me. I was in charge of myself and my own decisions.

Wasn't I?

CHAPTER 32

*L*oud thumps from above pulled me from my restless sleep. Upstairs, someone was moving around, dragging something. Feet pounded across the ground. What was Daddy doing? He was never that loud. From all the noise, I would have thought more than one person was up there, but that was impossible. He never had people over.

The basement door clicked unlocked. I was too stiff, too cold, to move from my position on the cement floor. Every bone and muscle ached. I tried to turn onto my back, but it stung. So I stayed on my side, holding back tears that wouldn't come because my body was too dry. I'd hardly had anything to eat or drink for a couple days.

"Get up." Daddy had come down the stairs and was standing right behind me.

I didn't want to get up. There was nothing good for me upstairs. Nothing to care about.

"I said, get up." He reached down, grabbed me by the arm, and yanked me up.

I cried out in pain.

"We need to get you upstairs and cleaned," he said, dragging me to the stairs.

"Why?" I managed to squeak out.

He tightened his grip around my arm and tugged me up the stairs like a doll. I didn't help, but I didn't exactly fight him. I just let him drag me over the stairs, down the hall, and into the bathroom.

He tossed me on the floor. "Take a shower and get dressed."

Hanging on the towel rack was a brand new full-length dress. It was baby blue with a white floral design. My fingers trailed along it. I could tell it was expensive by the material and style. Light blue flats were under the dress.

I slowly pulled myself up, using the counter for help. It took way more effort and energy than it should have. I was so weak.

"Don't take too long." He pointed to the counter. "I hope you have everything you need."

Mascara, eye shadow, blush, and a lip gloss were next to the sink. He never let me wear makeup.

I turned to him. "What's the occasion?"

"Your birthday." No smile. He normally went all out for my birthday – made my favorite dinner, baked me a cake, and bought me a present. He'd dress up in a fancy suit. He was always happy and laughing, showering me with love.

None of that was in his eyes. All that sat behind them was anger.

With everything that had been going on, I'd completely forgotten about my birthday. Honestly, I couldn't remember the current date.

"Is today my birthday?"

He nodded. "Yes. Now, shower and get ready." He took a deep breath. "I just want you to think about one thing today: *I* am the one in control."

He shut the bathroom door, leaving me alone. He'd always ingrained that in me, so why did he feel the need to remind me?

The hot water rained down on me. I didn't want the shower to end, but Daddy had said I had to be quick. Lifting my head, I let the water spray onto my face. I wished it could wash everything away. My worry, my lies, my pain.

But it couldn't. Nothing could.

It took me a while to put on the makeup. I'd never worn any. I'd seen some girls at school applying it on, so I did my best to mimic what they had done. The bruise covered my high cheek bone, circling under my eye. It was visible under the makeup, but I'd minimized it and the scratches on my chin. A lot.

I went to put my hair in a braid, but I stopped myself. It was my birthday. I had no idea what the future held, so I was going to do what I wanted. My hair had a slight curl to it. After brushing it and then running my fingers through it to fluff it a little, I put in some mousse. I'd stolen it from the store a while back and stashed it under the sink, hoping that one day I would use it.

It took me a while to work myself into the dress. The pain in my back made it hard. But it fit like a glove.

I stared in the mirror and didn't recognize myself. The girl that stared back at me was pretty. She had kind, bright eyes, and shiny lips. She wasn't real.

Closing my eyes, I took long, deep breaths to calm my heart. Daddy may have been spoiling me with the new clothes and makeup, but he wasn't happy about it, which left me unsettled.

I opened the door, turned off the light, and walked down the hall.

A lovely melody played from a piano. Had Daddy turned on some music? He normally liked to dance on my birthdays.

All the smells hit me at once. Cookies, garlic, pasta, chicken, oregano, cake. Those were the ones I could pin down. He had made me dinner.

But why was he so upset by it? Was he really still mad at me? Usually his anger would fade, especially after a few days. I hadn't complained once when I was locked in the basement. Never put up a fight or tried to argue. I'd been as pleasant as I could.

Something was off about him. Different. I wished I knew what had changed.

The music cut off, followed by soft clapping.

"Play another song."

Jenna? I shook my head. I must have heard wrong. There was no way Jenna . . .

I rounded the corner and stopped so abruptly, I almost fell forward.

"Surprise!" Julien blew into a party horn. He wore a glittery birthday hat way too small for his head.

"What?" Jenna's wide eyes landed on me. Her blouse, skirt, makeup, and jewelry were a rainbow of bright colors. "Cora! I didn't know you were here." She ran to me and gave me a tight hug. "Totally ruined that for you. Sorry." She let me go. "I got lost in Dalton playing the piano. He's so talented!"

Dalton blushed and stood from the piano bench. "I'm better at the guitar." He gave me an awkward hug. "Happy Birthday, Cora." His usually shaggy hair had been gelled back. It made his green eyes stand out.

Julien hugged me next. "Happy Birthday!"

I was in too much shock to respond to anyone. Why were they in my house? And where had the piano come from?

"Yeah, Happy Birthday, or whatever." Sydney stared at her phone, her fingers moving rapidly over the screen. She held it up for a second, probably snapping a picture of me. Why was she here? She wasn't even a friend. Actually, neither was Julien.

Brendon was the last one. He wore the button down green shirt I'd seen in the picture. He looked so handsome in it. He stood the farthest away, his jaw dropped, staring at me.

I'd done my makeup wrong. I probably looked like an idiot. A clown.

"Who did your hair and makeup?" Jenna asked, beaming. "You look so beautiful! We finally get to see you without a braid. You should do your hair like that more often. And your dress!" She squealed. "It's so nice!" She gave Daddy a thumbs-up. "Way to go, Dad."

Daddy's hands were clasped behind his back. He stood in the kitchen, watching over everyone and their greetings to me. He was probably trying to get a feel for how close I was to everyone. Which was why I was happy Brendon stood so far away.

But Brendon hadn't taken his eyes off me, which Daddy certainly noticed.

"Happy Birthday, Cora," Brendon said. He smiled, but it looked strained. He was probably as worried as I was.

Daddy had invited all of them over.

And something terrible was about to happen.

CHAPTER 33

"That's it?" Jenna asked, narrowing her eyes at Brendon. "No hug or kiss or anything? She's your girlfriend!"

All the air inside of me rushed out. I teetered where I stood. It didn't help that I was completely famished. Julien, who stood closest to me, put his arm around my waist.

"Are you okay?" he asked.

Daddy's glare shot between Brendon, who also looked like he might pass out, and Julien, who had his arm around me.

I pushed away from Julien. "I'm fine." I forced myself to look at Daddy. "We have a piano."

"It's my birthday present to you." The words, so calm and natural, wouldn't faze my friends. But the storms brewed behind his eyes, fierce and nasty. When the tornado landed, I worried there would be nothing salvageable. "I know you've wanted to learn how to play."

He'd bought me something expensive, but he was mad at me. He'd denied me a piano before. Why was he giving one to me? What had changed?

Dalton smiled. "That's awesome! If she's as good as she is with the guitar, she'll be a natural at the piano."

If I thought the air had rushed out before, now it had been completely sucked from every crevice of my body. Everything I wanted to remain hidden, close to my heart and kept all to my own, was now exposed. Falling free at every turn. Exposing me. I wanted to grab Noah, rush into the basement, lock the door, crawl into a corner, and wait out the storm.

Daddy's hand tightened around a kitchen knife. He clenched his jaw and then forced a smile onto his face. "Cora, why don't you and your guests sit down? Dinner's almost ready."

"It smells so good, Mr. Snow," Jenna said. "Like, amazing."

She sat down at the table next to Dalton and winked at me. Sydney plopped down next to Jenna, still on her phone. Julien took the spot next to Sydney and threw his napkin at her face.

"Are you ever not using your phone?" Julien asked.

Sydney glared at him, throwing the napkin back. "No."

"Can't you put it down for today?" Dalton asked, looking over at her. "It's Cora's birthday. We're about to eat."

"Like I care," Sydney said.

Why had she come? She'd put herself in danger for no reason. She didn't like me and didn't want to be at my party. So, why?

"Do you need any help, Mr. Snow?" Brendon asked.

Daddy still held the knife. "No."

"Sit down, Cora," Jenna said, motioning to the table. She sat tall in her seat. "You, too, Brendon."

With a deep breath, Brendon held out the chair next to Julien for me. "Cora?"

Jenna's smile widened. For once, she didn't seem to care

her braces were showing. "Such a gentleman. You should be happy, Mr. Snow. Cora got herself one of the good ones."

I sat down, not looking at Daddy or Brendon. Jenna didn't realize she'd probably just gotten Brendon killed.

Brendon sat down next to me and squeezed my hand. I finally looked at him, and he gave me the smallest smile. Sweat lined his palms. He was scared. Nervous. Yet, he'd still put himself between me and Daddy at the table.

Daddy.

When I looked up at him, he took the knife and drove it into the cutting board.

"Seriously, Cora," Jenna said, leaning forward with a sparkle in her eye, "you look gorgeous. Love that color on you."

"Thanks," I whispered. I had no idea if I'd be able to eat. Nausea had taken over my body.

Daddy brought the food to the table, set it down, and then took the last seat between Dalton and Brendon. Sydney surprised me by tucking her phone into the cell phone band on her arm and turning her attention to Daddy.

"I didn't know we were supposed to dress nice," Sydney said. She wore jeans and a shirt, just like Dalton. Julien wore jeans as well, but he had his typical dress shirt buttoned to the top.

Daddy had put on a shirt and a tie that matched the color of my dress. He smiled at Sydney, one that sent shivers down my spine. "If I wanted you to dress up, I would have told you. Just the birthday girl needed to."

"And yourself," Jenna said. "You look handsome, Mr. Snow." She licked her lips, staring down at her food. "This looks and smells so good!" She also wore her cell phone band. In fact, they all were wearing their bands. I was flattered. But then it was replaced by worry. What if Daddy asked about them? He didn't know I made them. Another secret to unfold.

It took a lot of effort for me to force down the food. I worried it would come back up. Daddy was up to something.

"So, Mr. Snow." Sydney poked at her artichokes with her fork. "May I call you by your first name?"

"No," Daddy said.

Sydney raised her eyebrows but didn't comment. Instead, she continued. "What do you do for a living?

Her interest in Daddy took everyone by surprise. Sydney wasn't one to pay attention to the world around her. Maybe that was what happened when she didn't have a cell phone to occupy her time.

"I'm a repairman." He took a bite of his pasta, his cloudy eyes on me the entire time.

I swallowed, forcing down the food in my mouth.

"What do you repair?" Julien asked. Out of everyone at the table, he was the happiest. He smiled without a care in the world. Like he didn't find it odd to be having dinner at my house even though we weren't friends. Like everything was perfectly normal.

"Whatever people need." His dark gray eyes snapped to mine. "I like to fix broken things."

Brendon's hand tightened around his fork to the point his knuckles turned white.

"Where's Cora's mom?" Sydney asked.

"Syd!" Jenna turned her wide-eyes to her. "You can't just ask questions like that."

Sydney set down her fork. She'd barely touched her food. "Why not?"

"Because it's rude," Dalton said through clenched teeth. "And none of your business."

Daddy wiped his mouth with a napkin. "It's okay. Cora's

mom died during child birth." The usual certainty in his eyes faltered for a second.

I looked at him, surprised. He'd told me my birth mom had abandoned me. Was he lying when he told me, or lying to Sydney to spare my feelings?

"I didn't know that," Jenna said, frowning at me. "I'm so sorry, Cora."

I pushed my food around the plate. "It's okay. I never knew her." Which was true. But if she really had died while giving birth to me, that changed things. I always thought she'd left me – abandoned her daughter – which made me angry. Made me hate her. But if she died, there was still a chance she had wanted me. A chance she would have raised me and loved me.

"So, it's just the two of you then?" Sydney asked.

Brendon, Dalton, and Jenna all turned to her. They were just as shocked as I was. Why all the questions?

"Yes," Daddy said. "I'm a lucky man."

"Why didn't you remarry?" Sydney folded her arms, clearly not knowing what to do with her hands.

"Holy rude, Syd," Jenna said. She smiled sheepishly at Daddy. "So sorry, Mr. Snow. When I invited her, I didn't know she'd act like this."

Jenna had invited Sydney? Why? She knew I didn't like Sydney. Had she invited Julien as well?

Daddy finished off his plate of food, silence in the air. When he'd taken his last bite, he wiped his mouth with his napkin and set it on his plate. "I wanted to focus on raising my daughter. She's the only girl I need in my life."

"That's so sweet," Jenna said with a grin.

"Thanks for cooking dinner, Mr. Snow," Julien said. "It was delicious." He'd cleaned his entire plate before everyone else had. He'd eyed the kitchen like he wanted to go check if there was more, but he'd remained in his seat.

"You're welcome," Daddy said. He stood, so I did the same. I moved to pick up his plate, but he shook his head at me. "The birthday girl doesn't clean up." He stared down at Brendon. "Why don't you help me clear the table?"

Brendon quickly stood, picking up his plate and mine. Julien got up as well, grabbing his and Sydney's plate. Sydney had hardly eaten a thing. Julien stuffed some of it in his mouth before taking the plates to the kitchen.

Jenna sauntered over to me and pulled me toward the piano. "I hope you don't mind I invited everyone. I've been working on this party for a while. I thought it would be a good opportunity to invite all the suspects." She eyed Sydney who'd gone back to her phone. "She seemed awfully interested in your dad, don't you think?"

I nodded. "I've never heard her talk that much."

Dalton joined us, his hands stuffed in pockets. He checked over his shoulder before he spoke. "That was weird, right? Sydney asking all those questions."

Jenna stared at him, her eyes glowing. She had a crush on him. Jenna giggled and placed her hand on his arm. "We were just saying that!"

Dalton got this goofy grin when Jenna touched him. He quickly cleared his throat and covered it up. "Knowing her," he said, his annoyed gaze flitting over to Sydney, "it probably has something to do with her social media followers. It always does."

I wished I could be as calm and happy as Jenna, but she had no idea she'd been invited into the eye of a storm. I glanced around the room, taking them in. Brendon moved cautiously in the kitchen, his tension painfully obvious. His shoulders were stiff, his hands working carefully on each dish he dried and handed over to Daddy. Daddy's scrutinizing gaze kept flitting over to Brendon like he could pick apart his motives for me.

Sydney was leaning against the counter, showing Julien something on her phone as he washed the dishes. For once, she was smiling, happy that Julien was interested in whatever they were looking at. Dalton and Jenna shared an embarrassed glance. Jenna swayed side to side as she bit her lip. Would any of them come out unscathed?

"Dalton," Daddy called from the kitchen. He finished drying off a knife with a towel and shoved it back in the knife block. "Did you bring your guitar?"

"Yes." Dalton shoved his hands in his pockets. His cheeks had the smallest taint of pink. "It's out in the car."

Daddy tightened his jaw. "Why don't you go get it? I'd love to hear my angel play a song." His voice had strained when he said "angel."

Dalton flashed a grin at Jenna before he walked away, a lightness in his step.

"Do you think he likes me?" Jenna asked, staring after Dalton as he closed the door behind him, her eyes filled with hope.

"How does my dad know about me playing guitar?"

Jenna's smile faltered. "When he called me, he asked who I was inviting to your party. I mentioned Dalton and how you two spent lunch together playing the guitar."

"When did he call you?"

She pulled out her phone and scrolled through it. "Uh, two days ago?" She tucked her phone away. "I've been planning this for a while. Remember when Dalton brought me that note at school?"

"Yes," I managed to get out. I still found it difficult to breathe. I could feel Daddy's eyes pinned on me.

"It was plans for the party," Jenna said with a sly smile.

So it had nothing to do with the journal or test answers. I leaned against the piano to keep myself from falling over. "How did you get my dad on board?"

She waved her hand. "Worked my charm. He seemed hesitant at first, but then I told him how you deserved a party with all that's going on."

I placed my palm against my chest like it could calm my wildly beating heart. "All that's going on?"

"Yeah." She leaned against the piano next to me. "All your awesome grades, guitar skills, cell band making artistry, all while balancing a boyfriend, a guidance counselor breathing down your neck, and a perv stalking man?" She patted my arm. "You're my hero. You look stunning and graceful through it all."

I plopped down on the piano bench. "You told my dad *all* of that?"

"Well, yeah," Jenna said with a slight frown. "Considering how close you two are, I knew he'd already know and want to help me celebrate your awesomeness."

No wonder Daddy had snapped.

"Did you tell him about the journal?" I whispered.

She put one hand on her hip, the other on her chest. "Do you think I'm an idiot? Of course I didn't! Fathers shouldn't know about their daughter's journals. It's like their one private outlet."

Dalton strolled back into the house with the guitar. He set his case on the coffee table and opened it up, a small smile spreading across his lips. A comfort washed over him as he held his guitar in his hands.

"Is there anything stuck in my braces?" Jenna asked, lifting her lips so I could see her teeth.

"No," I said. She wiggled her eyebrows at me and practically skipped into the other room, fawning over Dalton.

Julien chatted away as he, Daddy, and Brendon joined Dalton and Jenna in the family room. Sydney had gone back to her seat at the table, and I was still frozen on the piano bench.

Aside from the journal, Daddy knew everything.

With his angry mood swings, ripping off my doll's head, shattering my snow globe, tearing off my shirt, I was coming to the conclusion that maybe Daddy was capable of darker things than I'd originally thought. Had Daddy brought everyone to the house to torture them? Torture me? I wanted to believe that maybe he'd turned a corner and wanted to let me get out more. Have friends and be a regular teenager. But by the scary gleam in his eyes, as he sized up everyone in the room, that couldn't be further from the truth. I'd never have a normal life with him as my father.

"Syd, you going to join us?" Jenna asked, a slight impatience in her tone.

With a reluctant glance at me, Sydney went into the family room and flopped down on the couch. She took off her shoes and rested her feet on the coffee table.

I sat there, staring at Daddy with my closest things to friends. He watched them all, smiling and laughing, and clapping Brendon on the shoulder. Brendon flinched under Daddy's touch.

Only I could tell the smile and laugh were forced. Unnatural. What did Daddy plan to do? Lock us all in the basement? Pull off his belt and lash me? Or just lash them and make me watch? That would be worse than getting lashed myself.

"Cora," Daddy said, "come play your father a song."

I forced my feet to move, away from the piano, passed the kitchen table, and toward the couch. My feet were heavy, like iron weighing me down. By the time I reached the family room, I was out of breath.

Dalton handed me the guitar and patted the spot next to him on the loveseat. I didn't want to sit near him. Daddy would hate it. But I didn't have a choice. I had to pretend like all was normal. Like having my friends over, laughing and playing the guitar was a commonplace occurrence in our home.

With shaking hands, I strummed the latest song Dalton had taught me. A song that Daddy loved. One he used to sing to me every night before tucking me into bed.

Sydney stayed glued to her phone, fully engrossed like there was no one else in the room with her. Any time I messed up a note, Dalton would encourage me and place his hands on mine to show me the correct way to do it. Julien seemed to be one of the few actually paying attention and enjoying the music. He clapped along the entire time, mouthing the words with a smile. Jenna was too busy staring at everyone as she tried to uncover the blackmailer. Worry sat in Brendon's eyes, his focus drifting between me and Daddy.

The storm in Daddy's eyes calmed. He hated me having friends, learning things without him, lying to him, but I'd learned his favorite song, and he couldn't overlook that. I'd done something horrible, but I'd done it for him.

Halfway during the song, I started singing. I'd never sung in public. I had no idea if I was good or not. But Jenna stopped investigating to look at me in awe. Brendon's worried eyes changed to wonder. Sydney looked up from her phone.

And a smile. A real, genuine smile landed on Daddy's lips.

When I finished, everyone clapped, including Daddy.

"That was amazing!" Jenna squealed. "You have to teach me to play, Dalton." She gazed longingly at him, and if I wasn't sick to my stomach, I would have smiled and been happy for her.

But my eyes were on Daddy and his sudden change.

The calm before the storm.

CHAPTER 34

With shaking hands, I gave Dalton back his guitar. What was Daddy going to do? My dinner churned in my stomach, and I hoped it would stay down.

"Mr. Snow," Jenna said. "Since you've already given Cora your present, can she open ours?"

Daddy smiled, so natural and normal. "That's an excellent idea."

Jenna clapped her hands. "Mine first!" She placed a large, pink bag in my lap, bright fuchsia tissue paper spilling out.

"It looks like it threw up," Sydney said, glancing up from her phone.

Jenna glared at her. "Just like your face."

Taking the tissue paper, I tossed it at Dalton. It piled on top of him. No matter what was inside, I had to pretend to be happy. Jenna was overly excited, and I didn't want to let her down. Daddy would be upset regardless, so my focus was on Jenna.

I pulled everything out. Glitter pens. A pink journal with a *C* on it. Lip gloss. Breath mints. Spearmint gum.

"You can thank me later for the gloss, Brendon," Jenna said. "It tastes like strawberries!"

"I'm allergic," Brendon said, his eyebrows furrowed together. To everyone else, he probably looked upset, but to me, I could see the sarcasm behind his eyes.

Jenna frowned. "To artificial flavoring?" She threw up her hands. "I can get another flavor."

Brendon smiled. "I was kidding, Jenna."

She let out a long breath. "Whew! Good. It tastes so good, trust me." Her gaze landed on Dalton. He used some of the tissue paper to cover his bright red face.

I picked up the journal and flipped through the pink pages. Something lay between two pages near the middle.

Jenna knelt next to me and whispered. "Get that later." Her eyes were urgent. Warning me of something, but I had no idea what.

Dalton moved the tissue paper and looked over my shoulder, opening the journal. "What is . . ." His face burned bright. "Oh." He glanced at Brendon and then sat back against the couch, creating a distance between me and him.

"Well, now you have us all curious," Julien said. "What's in there?"

"Later, Cora," Jenna said through clenched teeth. "When there's a smaller audience."

Daddy stepped closer to us. "Are you hiding something in there?"

"Just a girl thing," Jenna said, her laugh strained. "Who else got Cora a present?" She glanced around at everyone, her eyes begging for someone to take the focus off the journal.

Julien reached over and snatched it from my hands before I could react.

"No!" Jenna said, falling forward, scrambling to get to Julien.

Julien held up a piece of thin, red material. "Oh, this just got good."

"What is that?" I asked.

Brendon's face flared, matching Dalton's. Sydney glanced up from her phone for a second, but then snapped her head up when she saw what Julien was holding. She took a picture with her phone.

Daddy yanked it from Julien's grasp and took it into the kitchen, throwing it away in the garbage.

Jenna frowned. "That was expensive. I was trying to hide it so you'd find it later." She patted my leg. "Sorry. I didn't mean to get you in trouble."

"What was it?" I still had no idea, but everyone else in the room seemed to know.

Jenna leaned in close to me. "A thong."

"A what?" I asked.

Dalton stood and moved far away from us.

Jenna tilted her head to the side. "Are you being serious right now?"

Everyone in the room, well aside from Julien and Sydney, were completely embarrassed, but I had no idea why.

I shook my head in confusion.

Jenna darted a glance at Daddy, who fumed in the kitchen, and then turned back to me. "It's underwear."

"That was underwear?" There had hardly been any material. Not enough to cover me or to make it useful.

Julien leaned toward us. "You've never worn a thong before?"

Sydney held up her phone. "This is so great. Everyone keep on talking."

"Are you recording this?" Brendon asked.

When Sydney shushed him, he grabbed her phone and pressed a button.

"Hey!" Sydney reached for her phone, but Brendon held it

away from her, scrolling through it. I assumed he was trying to delete it. She huffed. "I was live streaming. Can't erase what the world has already seen." Her eyes lit up. "I'm going to get so many new followers."

Live stream? What did that mean?

"Seriously, where are you from?" Jenna asked. "A convent? It's sexy underwear. For your man."

"Brendon's supposed to wear it?" I whispered, the heat finally flooding my cheeks.

Jenna's eyes went wide. "No! You are! For him." She shushed Julien, who had busted up laughing and clapping his hands. Tears trickled out of his eyes.

"What did she say?" Sydney asked. She was still trying to wrangle her phone from Brendon. "My followers are missing all the good stuff!"

I helped Jenna onto the couch next to me and whispered, trying to keep everyone else out of the conversation. "What's going on?"

Jenna patted my hand. "You wear it when you're alone together. Just you and him. When you're ready for that phase of your relationship."

That phase? I'd never reach a *phase* of a relationship where I'd want to wear only a tiny strip of material on my body. My cheeks and neck burned, putting Dalton and Brendon's embarrassment to shame.

"I said when you're ready," Jenna said. "It doesn't have to be tonight. I wasn't sure where you two were at in your relationship, but now you'll be ready when the time comes. I almost got the matching bra, but I couldn't stuff it in the journal. Plus, it was too expensive."

"Did anyone else get Cora a present?" Daddy stood near the coffee table, his arms folded and back straight. His chin was tilted up.

All the laughter in the room cut off.

"I did," Dalton said, his body tense. "But I'm afraid to give it to her now."

Sydney finally yanked her phone away from Brendon and sat down. "Did you get her lingerie too?"

Dalton shook his head a little too vigorously. "Nope." He handed me a small, wrapped box. "Nothing awkward, I promise."

With shaking hands, I tore back the wrapping paper and opened the box. Guitar picks with the initials C.S. for Cora Snow.

"Thanks, Dalton," I said.

He flushed. "No problem."

Julien smiled sheepishly from the couch next to me. "Sorry, Cora. I didn't get you anything."

"Neither did I," Sydney said with bored eyes. Or maybe they were annoyed. Or both. "But I'm not sorry about that."

I smiled at them. "That's okay. You didn't have to."

Brendon handed me a small box. He glanced at Daddy. "Totally appropriate."

"I'm really sorry," Jenna said. "It was just a joke." She waved her hand in a casual manner, trying to downplay the situation.

Sydney chuckled. "Way too late to lie about it."

I took the box from Brendon, my fingers brushing against his. My cheeks flared, and Brendon snatched his hand away and hid it behind his back.

"Wow," Jenna whispered. "I really ruined things."

I gave her a soft smile and opened the box. Inside was a gold chain. A flower pendant hung from it, an emerald in the center. "My birthstone."

Jenna gasped. "It looks so expensive!" She whispered in my ear. "You've so reached the level. Dig that thong out of the trash and wear it for him."

I pushed her away, making her laugh. I pulled it out of the

box and held it up. Jenna clasped it around my neck, the chain cold against my burning skin. My fingers brushed along the flower laying against my chest. A real present that was all mine. "Thank you, Brendon."

He wet his lips. "You're welcome."

Clouds blew through Daddy's eyes, quick and fleeting, like the time we met Brendon at the pizza parlor for the first time and Brendon knew my name. Daddy was upset but trying to hide it.

Jenna put her arms around me, squeezing tight. "You're so lucky."

Sydney suddenly stood, snapped a picture of me and Jenna, and tucked her phone into her band. "My mom's here. Happy Birthday, Cora. Thanks for dinner, Mr. Snow." She trudged out of the house, knocking into the coffee table as she passed it, not noticing what she did. It had shifted on the floor, and Daddy hurried to put it back in its proper place. Something inside me snapped. I needed answers, and I couldn't believe she'd come to my house just for the party. With all her questions at dinner, she had to be the blackmailer.

I pushed out of Jenna's embrace and ran after Sydney, careful not to bump anything on the way out. I stopped her outside her family's minivan.

"Did you take it?" I asked, setting my hand on her arm to get her attention.

Sydney swung around and put her hand on her hip. "Yes, I did."

I hadn't expected her to admit it so easily. "Why?"

Brendon and Dalton jogged out of the house. Brendon went close to Sydney, looking down on her. "Why did you take it?" Anger stirred in his eyes. Different from Daddy's, but anger nonetheless.

Sydney backed away from him with an annoyed huff. "What's the big deal?"

"The big deal?" Brendon clenched his fists. "How could you put her through that? Threaten her?"

The passenger side window on the minivan rolled down. "Syd, dear, let's go." Her mom tapped her fingers along the steering wheel, eager to leave.

Sydney sulked to the van and put her hand on the handle. "It's a picture. Get over it."

"How . . ." Brendon pulled back in confusion. "What? What picture?"

"The one I took of Jenna and Cora hugging," Sydney said. She pulled her phone out of the band and showed me and Brendon the picture. "I didn't know you'd freak out about it so much. I won't make a meme, okay?"

"A what?" I asked.

Sydney scoffed. "You're seriously so weird."

"Why did you come?" I asked. "You obviously hate me."

"I don't *hate* you." Sydney pointed at her band. "You're pretty talented and can be funny at times. You're just weird. I almost said no when Jenna invited me, but I couldn't pass up the opportunity to see your home life. I wish I could have live streamed the whole thing, but my fans will just have to deal with my play by play tonight." She looked past me at Daddy, who'd come outside with everyone else. "Your dad kind of creeps me out."

"What about the journal?" I asked through clenched teeth. The more she spoke, the angrier I became. I was a joke to her.

Sydney furrowed her eyebrows. "What journal?"

"*My* journal," I said, stepping up to her. "That you *stole*."

Sydney backed into the van. "You keep a diary?" She laughed. "I shouldn't be surprised."

Brendon leaned forward. "So, you didn't take it?"

"Why would I?" Sydney asked. "Like I'd want to read about her boring, weird life." She opened the van door, got in, and snapped at her mom to drive.

Dalton lingered at my side, his eyebrows furrowed. "Your journal was stolen?"

If it wasn't Sydney, Dalton was next on my list. I wanted to find out the truth.

"Was it you?" I asked him.

Surprise passed over Dalton's eyes. Then hurt. "You think I'd do that to you?"

"You knew I wanted to learn to play the guitar." I stood tall. "I never told anyone that. It was in my journal."

Out of habit, Dalton lifted his hand to brush hair out of his eyes, but then remembered it was gelled. "Like I've said, I can't remember who told me. I just overheard it somewhere." He put his hand on my shoulder. "I'm telling you the truth." He lowered his hand and his lips curved into a smile. "I'm not really into reading girls' journals. It's not my thing."

Should I believe him? Every emotion on his face, in his eyes, told me he was being genuine and truthful. "So, who did?"

Daddy clapped his hands together, jolting me. I whipped around to see him standing just a few feet away. I'd dropped my guard. Dropped everything. He knew the truth. Knew I kept a journal and it had been stolen from me.

But he only knew of the one. I somehow had to burn the others before he found out there were more. Although, none of that mattered if I didn't get the journal back from my blackmailer.

"Time for cake!" Daddy said. The lightning behind his eyes flashed.

CHAPTER 35

Once we were all back inside the house, Daddy held out his hand and motioned for me to join him. The focus and determination that settled in his eyes told me he'd finally decided what he wanted to do. I wondered if the whole party had been some sort of test and I'd failed miserably. I smiled at him and went to Daddy's side. He took my hand in his and whispered in my ear. "You have a journal?"

"I did," I said. "Someone took it."

"This is all your fault. Remember that." He cleared his throat, speaking loud for everyone to hear. "Thank you all for coming to celebrate Cora's birthday. It's nice to see she has so many friends." His tone twinged on the last word, but I was probably the only one who noticed.

Daddy dished out the cake and ice cream, plastering on a fake smile the entire time. The only one who seemed wary aside from me was Brendon. As they were eating at the table, Daddy pulled me off to the side.

"I'm going to leave it up to you," he whispered.

"Leave what up to me?"

He nodded his head at the table. "What we're going to do

with your friends. They know too much now. We obviously can't stay here. Do we let them go, or get rid of them? Carbon monoxide poisoning would be a clean, simple route."

My eyes widened, surprised he'd suggest such a thing. I didn't want to believe him capable of murder. "Don't hurt them, Daddy. They don't know anything. They aren't the ones who look my journal." At least I hoped that was true. Sadness gripped me tight to the point I had to force the words out. "We'll just leave and never look back."

He put his arm around my shoulder. "You really believe that? None of them took it?"

I watched my friends, Julien, Dalton, Jenna, and Brendon, eating their cake and ice cream, all smiling and laughing. Even Brendon has loosened for the moment. He laughed at something Julien said, and I smiled, though it hurt.

"They're innocent," I said. "If they disappeared, the cops would come after us. We'll leave." We could go back to how things were at the beginning when it was just me and Daddy. They'd stay here, go on with their lives, and forget about me.

Sorrow tugged at my heart. I never thought I'd miss anyone, but I would miss Jenna and Brendon. They really had become my friends. But they deserved to live and have a free life to be whoever they wanted.

Daddy stayed tensed next to me, probably mulling over my decision. Killing all of them would cast a bigger spotlight on us. If we just disappeared, after some time, no one would remember us. No one would remember me.

Like I never existed.

"Just know," he whispered, "I'll never forget that you did this to our family." He cleared his throat and took my hand, his cold skin rough against mine. "Cora and I are moving."

Stunned silence filled the room. I wished I could tell them it would be good for everyone. I'd be out of their lives, and they'd be free from danger.

The only one who'd suffer was me.

If it meant saving them, then it would be worth it.

Jenna completely deflated like a popped balloon. "What?" She frowned as her shoulders drooped. "You can't move! Why are you moving?"

"Where are you moving?" Dalton asked. Surprisingly, he looked sad as well.

"I got a job opportunity out of state." Daddy waved his hand out in a nonchalant manner. "We leave next weekend."

Brendon's eyes were unfocused on his plate. His whole body went rigid for a few seconds before he started shaking. He rushed to his feet, the chair sliding out behind him, and he bolted outside, slamming the door behind him.

I wanted to follow him, but Daddy's hand held mine tightly to the point my blood circulation cut off.

"Did you know this?" Jenna asked me. Tears welled in her eyes.

The only thing I could do was shake my head, letting her know I hadn't.

"Worst birthday ever," Jenna mumbled. She pushed her unfinished piece of cake away from her. "I mean, I'm happy for you, Mr. Snow. But I don't want to lose Cora."

Julien waved his phone with hope in his eyes. "Technology. We can stay in touch."

Jenna clasped her hands together in a plea. "This means you'll get her a cell phone now, right Mr. Snow?"

Daddy squeezed my hand, which I didn't think was possible with how tight he was already holding it. "Unfortunately, we're moving to a place with limited coverage. You'll have to say your goodbyes tonight."

Tears trickled down Jenna's cheeks. "This is the worst news ever!" She stood and ran at me, throwing her arms around me.

It hurt. So bad. Everywhere. My body ached from the

lashings and sleeping on the cold, cement basement floor. Jenna squeezed way too tight. I wanted to scream out in pain, but instead I wrapped my arms around her and took it. Pain I could manage. Losing the only friend I'd ever had would be much more difficult.

Dalton walked by, patting me on the shoulder. "I'm going to talk to Brendon." He sulked out the front door, closing it quietly behind him.

Julien gave me a hug like we'd been friends forever. "Good luck, Cora!" He waved at Daddy. "Thanks so much for dinner. I wish you both the best."

Daddy's eyes lingered on the stripes shaved into the side of Julien's head, but he gave him a friendly wave in reply.

Outside, I found Brendon and Dalton huddled near the old crabapple tree on the park strip. Brendon had his hands on his head like he was trying to hold himself together. Dalton looked up when I cautiously approached, my hands gripping the sides of my dress.

Dalton squeezed Brendon's shoulder. "I'll let you two talk." He wrapped an arm around me and I gently side-hugged him back. "Don't stop practicing the guitar now that you have a piano."

"I won't," I said with a forced smile. I wouldn't be using any instrument ever again.

I turned to Brendon. Brendon. My heart hurt at the pain in his eyes. It wasn't only about my leaving. I could see the worry there, too, for my safety.

Brendon's heartbreaking gaze landed on me as he swept me into his arms and I melted into him. "Please, let me say something." He held me close, his arms so strong and steady. "Let me go to the police."

"No." I pulled back enough so I could look him in the eyes. "I'm going to be fine. This is good for everyone." Even though I wanted Brendon to remain in my life, if staying with Daddy protected him and my friends, then I'd do it. Once we moved, I could figure another way out and maybe back into Brendon's life.

His eyes snapped behind me, probably to where Daddy stood. I didn't want to turn around to see Daddy's expression. It would ruin my last moments with Brendon.

"Is it? Will it be okay for you, Cora? You think about everyone but yourself."

"Is that a bad thing?"

His body tensed. "In this case, yes."

I lowered my arms and took a step back. "I'll be alright. Daddy found a new job and we'll relocate and . . ."

He pointed a shaking finger behind me. "You really think he got a new job? He's just trying to get you out of here. He doesn't want you to be happy."

It was like Brendon could see right through our facade.

"Yes, he does." I folded my arms. Really, everything Daddy had done for me was for my happiness. He'd taken me out of the foster care system and given me a home. A stable home. He'd loved me, protected me, and provided for me. It hadn't always been easy, but before I'd lost my journal, things were fine. We just needed to get back to that. "I had a rough childhood. He's just looking out for me."

Brendon furrowed his eyebrows. "What are you talking about? What happened to you as a child?"

"I think it's time for you to leave," Daddy said, suddenly right behind me. I was surprised I didn't feel him.

Everyone else had gone. Brendon gave Daddy a weird look and then turned to me, his voice low so only I could hear. "Remember that you're stronger than him. You're brave, Cora." Brendon wrapped me in his arms and whispered. "I'll come by tonight." He slipped something into my pocket. "Here's another phone just in case. The other one stopped working."

Because I had smashed it into a million pieces. "Don't come." I wouldn't be in my room. The basement was where I'd be until we moved. I pushed out of Brendon's arms. "Thanks for coming to my party." I swallowed down the tremble in my throat and blinked away the tears. "Hope you have a nice life." I stepped far away from him, creating a large distance like the first night we met.

Pain and worry rushed to Brendon's eyes again. He shot Daddy a glare before he stormed off down the street, his fists clenched at his sides.

~

*D*addy placed the last dish in the cupboard and closed it. He'd made me sit at the table the entire time he cleaned.

I did as told, waiting for him to finish. The whole time I had to sit and think about all the things he would do to me – how he'd torture me. Were we really going to move to another state? Or was my new home going to be six feet under? I'd never thought him capable of killing me, but after his reference to using carbon monoxide poisoning on my friends, now I knew there was a possibility he could snap in the heat of the moment.

I'd ruined everything. All because of a journal. All because I couldn't keep my feelings to myself. I'd let everyone down, especially Daddy. I'd hurt him after everything he'd done for me.

But I didn't want him to punish me. I didn't deserve it. Was Brendon right? Did I need to think about myself for once?

"Stand." He stared down at me, the storms in his eyes wild and tumultuous.

I wanted to argue but did as told. He clutched my arm

and yanked me down the hall. The basement. Just like I thought. I'd spend the week there until Daddy released me to move. Would he pack my things? Were we taking anything with us? Or would everything be left behind? Or just *my* stuff left behind.

It might not be needed in the future.

I needed to stand up to him. Stand up for myself. Did I have the strength to overpower him?

Daddy threw me onto the floor of my bedroom.

My fingers gripped the carpet. "Not the basement?"

He clenched his fists. "After the scene you caused?" He scoffed. "I don't think so. Too many people have been sniffing around and asking questions. You'll stay in here until we move. You'll eat, stay clean, and be a good little girl. I'll deal with your punishment when we're free of this place."

"What people?"

"I've had men calling me, Cora. A counselor from your school. Another man who won't identify himself. All asking about *you*."

Another man? The perv man, as Jenna had labeled him. Why was he calling? I had hoped Mr. Mendoza wouldn't talk to Daddy again, but I wasn't surprised he did.

"Why wait?" I eyed Noah on the bed, wanting his comfort.

He stepped farther into the room, towering over me. "It'll be too suspicious if we up and leave overnight. Because of you, we must pretend like we're happy and everything is fine. Pretend like you didn't put our family in jeopardy."

"I'm sorry, Daddy." I got on my knees, grabbed Noah from the bed, and wrapped him in my arms.

"Sorry?" He put his hand on his belt, wanting to rip it off, but he stopped himself. "All I wanted to do was make you happy. I provided for you, gave you a life you never had, and you betrayed me."

I clung to Noah. "No, Daddy, I . . ."

"Enough." He put his hands on his head, his stiff hair crinkling under his fingers. "Enough lies, Cora. You kept a journal? And someone stole it?" He stared at me, waiting for an answer.

I slowly nodded.

"What did you write in there?" The storms raged, whipping and fierce. Uncontrollable.

"Just normal teenage girl stuff." My stomach clenched and I held in the bile that wanted to escape. I had been way too careless. "About school and Jenna."

Daddy ripped Noah from my grasp. "I said don't lie to me. You wouldn't be so worried about it being stolen if it was little girl stuff."

"I needed an outlet!" The words flew from my mouth, smacking into Daddy.

He stumbled back like he had been hit. "An outlet? For what? All the happiness and comfort I've provided you?"

"I . . ." What could I say? He'd never believe my lies. The truth would hurt him.

"Who took it, Cora?" Daddy asked, clutching Noah in his hands.

"How did I get dragged into this?" Noah asked through clenched teeth. He was in pain, and I couldn't stop it.

"I'm so sorry," I whispered to Noah.

Daddy cackled, the sound sending prickles through my skin. "You're sorry? Who took the journal, Cora?"

I licked my lips. "I don't know. I've been trying to figure it out, but there aren't many options. I don't have a lot of people in my life."

Daddy pointed Noah at the door. "Then who were all those *friends* of yours at your party?"

"They're just students at my school."

"Oh, really? Then why do they know more about you than I do? Why were they crying about you moving?"

"Only Jenna cried." I threw up my hands. "She'd cry at anything."

He shook Noah at me. "And Brendon? Your *boyfriend*."

I stood, my fists clenched at my sides. "He's not my boyfriend. We only told Jenna that so she'd stop asking to hang out with me."

The gray clouds in his eyes somehow darkened. "Why would he agree to that, Cora? What does he know?"

My jaw tensed. "Nothing, Daddy. I told him I didn't want to hang out with Jenna, so he agreed to say he was my boyfriend to keep her away." The lies were intertwining, creating too large of a web. Everything was getting crossed and confusing.

"No teenage boy would agree to that without wanting something in return."

"He didn't. He's nice, Daddy. He was just being kind. He wanted nothing in return."

He laughed, staring up at the ceiling and shaking his head. "You're so naive, Cora. Of course he wants something. I've seen the way he looks at you!" He tossed Noah on the ground and seized me by the arms. "What have you done with him?"

Heat flared in my cheeks and neck. "Done with him? Daddy! Nothing!"

He shook me. "I said no lies. I saw what Jenna bought you and the necklace Brendon gave you. I saw the way you hugged. Did you kiss as well? Did he touch you anywhere he's not supposed to?"

"No!" I screamed. If Daddy hadn't been gripping me, I would have crossed my arms over my chest. "That hug you saw was the first one. He was just wishing me a Happy Birthday." If Daddy found out about the kisses, oh, I didn't even want to think about what would happen.

"He looked at you with . . ." He growled, a war raging in

his eyes. "He's infatuated with you." He shook me again. "Did you have sex?"

The heat erupted. My skin was on fire. "Daddy! How could you ask such a thing? You told me to not let boys touch me like that."

He raised his fist as if to strike me. I stared straight into his eyes and waited for the pain. For his hard fist to connect with my bony face. If he wanted to hurt me, he'd have to see me watching. I wouldn't cower away this time.

With a shaky breath, he lowered his hand. He let go of me, picked Noah up off the floor, and went to the door. "Well. We'll have to go to a doctor to make sure you're still a virgin. I know a guy who won't ask questions." He rested his hand on the door knob. "We'll go next week. For now, you're staying in this room until we move. You only come out when I say you can."

He slammed the door and locked it.

He still had Noah with him.

Leaving me all alone in my room.

CHAPTER 36

*A*fter crying for a few hours, I finally forced myself from my bed and over to the closet. Using my backpack, I stuffed a couple dozen journals inside, which didn't leave too many left. After tonight, I'd just need to make one more trip, and then all the journals would be destroyed. Except for the one the blackmailer had.

I'd created a larger hole in the closet and hoped Daddy wouldn't notice. But it would be better for him to find the empty hole than a stranger to find all my journals. If Daddy was caught, he'd find a way to torture me, even from prison. He'd find a way to hurt my friends. I needed to protect them.

I'd just zipped the backpack closed when a knock sounded on my window. I quickly put my hair in a braid and rested it over my right shoulder.

Brendon stood on the other side of the window. He had changed into his Wonder Woman shirt.

I slid open the window. "I told you not to come."

"I had to see you again." His tone was gentle. Kind. "To make sure you were okay. Your father looked really upset when I left."

264

I started to close the window.

"Please, Cora. Don't shut me out."

His eyes were so different than Daddy's. There were no storms. No anger or hatred. They held something else – something I'd never seen before. I had no idea what it was. Daddy had said love, but that was impossible. Daddy loved me, and I'd never seen that look in his eyes before.

I wanted to shut the window, but for some stupid reason, I found myself removing the bar and helping him into my room. It took a while for him to squeeze between the bars. One of the other bars came loose in the process. Since we were moving, I didn't care.

Brendon stared down at my full backpack on the floor. "Are you going somewhere?"

"I have to destroy the rest of my journals."

"I can do it for you so you don't have to leave. I'll bring your backpack back when I'm done."

"No!" I slapped my hand over my mouth. I waited as the seconds ticked by, hoping Daddy hadn't heard me. When I was certain he hadn't, I lowered my hand. "I'm sorry, Brendon, but I have to do it myself. I won't be satisfied until I see them burn." Plus, I wasn't sure if I could fully trust him. I wanted to so badly, but people were deceiving.

He furrowed his brow. "I understand. But I'm going with you."

I rocked on my heels. He'd already risked too much. "I have to do this alone." My hand wrapped around the pendant on the necklace he'd given me.

"No." He stepped toward me. "There's still a creepy guy out there who's following you. Plus, you have a black-mailer. There's no way I'm letting you go alone." He took another step, closing the distance between us. He placed his hand on my cheek. It was so soft and warm, and I found myself leaning into it. "Please let me come with you. I know you can take care of yourself, but I make the best sidekick."

I had no idea what he was talking about, but those eyes of his were going to be the death of me. How could one person have so much emotion behind their eyes?

Daddy did – but it was so different. His were storms. Unending and unwavering.

Brendon's held concern and loyalty. Compassion.

Or was I wrong? He was my first encounter with a boy. Maybe I was just being stupid and irrational. Letting hormones take over my life.

"Please, Cora," he whispered.

I moved the pendant back and forth on the chain. My eyes went to his lips as my heart pounded. Heat rushed everywhere, consuming me. Hormones. That was all it was. It meant nothing. Brendon meant nothing to me.

He couldn't.

I couldn't.

Nothing made sense any more.

I pushed away from him and sat down on my bed, putting my hands over my face. Everything was out of control, and I had no idea what to do.

I could run. Away from it all. From everyone and every-thing. But I had nothing. I couldn't take care of myself. And Daddy would hurt my friends if I did.

Daddy would take care of me. I'd made him mad, but I had years to make it up to him. We could move somewhere secluded like he wanted and I could go back to being the best daughter. I could cook for him and take care of him. He'd protect me and provide for me.

I wouldn't be able to go out into the world again, but was that such a bad thing? People were bad. I couldn't trust them. They'd take advantage of me. Use me.

Not like Daddy.

Lowering my hands, I glanced over at Brendon, who had sat down next to me. He put his arm around my waist and pulled me close. Letting out a deep breath, I rested my head on his shoulder.

Brendon had never taken advantage of me. He'd been kind and caring. He'd done what I wanted to do, even though he wanted to go to the police. Brendon didn't even know the whole truth. If he did, he'd turn Daddy in, and that would be the end of my life.

"It's going to be okay," he whispered. "We'll get rid of all your journals so you can breathe easy and not have anyone blackmailing you."

"But we're moving."

He rubbed my arm. "I know. That part really sucks."

"I'll never be able to talk to you again." I sniffed. "I'm actually sad about that."

Brendon chuckled, moving his body up and down. "It's nice to know you care."

I looked up at him. "I do care. You've been so nice to me."

He placed his hand on my cheek. "I care about you." He swallowed. "I like you. A lot." He leaned his forehead against mine. "I'm going to miss you."

"I'll miss you, too. You've been a good friend."

He stiffened. "Friend, huh? That's it?" He lowered his hand, and I instantly wanted it back.

"I don't know anything about having relationships," I whispered. "But I do know I've enjoyed being around you." Heat rushed to my cheeks. "And the kisses were nice."

He smirked. "Yes, they were." Softly placing his finger under my chin, he lifted it so our eyes were level. "I'll always remember you, Cora Snow. If you ever need something, someone, you can call me."

My eyes went back to his lips and the freckle in the

corner. Was it just hormones? Or something more? We were so young, and I was so inexperienced.

Brendon leaned in and paused, waiting to see my reaction. When I didn't back away, he pressed his lips to mine. At first it was soft, just like our other kisses. But then he pulled me against his body and opened his mouth. His lips moved all over mine, his tongue sneaking into my mouth.

His hands moved up and down my back, faster and harder. It hurt against my wounds that were still healing. Wounds he didn't know about.

I arched my back to relieve some pressure, but that somehow heated him. He lifted me into his lap, kissing my neck and cheeks. His hands wandered over my back and sides, exploring my body.

Was this what Daddy had talked about? What a boy would want and do to me? Was Brendon just using me? Did he expect something more from me?

A small moan escaped his mouth, and I pushed away from him, stumbling back until I was on the floor.

"Cora." He reached down for me, but I scrambled away.

"Don't touch me," I said between pants of breath.

He creased his eyebrows. "I'm sorry. I didn't mean to upset you."

"Is this what you had planned all along?" Tears pricked at the corner of my eyes. "Were you just using me?" My hands tightened into fists.

"What? No. I like you, Cora. I thought you liked me too." He took a step toward me, so I scooted away from him. With a deep breath, he stepped back. "I'm not going to hurt you."

"What were you going to do to me?" The tears fell down my cheeks as my body shook.

"Do to you?" Brendon ran his fingers through his hair. "Nothing. I mean, yeah, I enjoyed kissing you, but I wouldn't have pushed for more if you hadn't indicated you wanted more."

My cheeks flared. "I never said I wanted more."

He pulled his shirt down. I hadn't noticed it had ridden up through the whole ordeal.

"You arched your body into mine. That's kind of a girl's way of saying she wants more."

I hurried to my feet and glared at him. "You were hurting my back."

"What?" Worry flooded into his eyes, and he looked like he wanted to move toward me, but he stayed in place. "Did he hurt you again?"

I pointed my finger at him. "Leave Daddy out of this."

He threw up his hands. "Daddy? Cora, you're not five. Look at what he's done to you. You're scared of me." He motioned to himself. "*Me*. I would never hurt you or take advantage of you."

"Oh, really?" I huffed. "So you didn't want to have sex with me?"

He pulled back in confusion. "Sex? It was a kiss, Cora. It's not like clothes were coming off."

"But your hands." I pressed my arms close to my chest.

"Only went to your back and sides," he said, holding up his hands. "They never went to the no zones."

I furrowed my eyebrows. "The no zones?"

His eyes went to my chest, and then he quickly looked away. "I would never force you to have sex. Ever. I'm not even ready for that."

"You aren't?"

All teenage boys were. That was what Daddy had said.

Brendon sat down on my bed. "I'm not going to lie. A lot of boys want that. We think about it a lot." He sighed. "But I'm not a rapist. Even if *you* had said you'd wanted to have sex tonight, I would have said no. You're not ready. I don't think you'll be ready for a long time. You have some issues with men to work out."

"I do not have issues." My hands clenched into fists.

He tilted his head toward me and swept his hand out. "You still call your father 'Daddy.' You pushed me away from only a kiss. It took you forever to even let me touch you. You sometimes look afraid of me, Dalton, and your dad. Basically, any guy." He slowly stood. "I'm sorry if I upset you. I just came here to make sure he didn't hurt you." He stuffed his hands in his pockets. "Which, obviously he did."

"He didn't touch me tonight. Daddy didn't hurt me." He'd wanted to but stopped himself. Although, he'd make up for it when we moved.

He licked his bottom lip and let out a loud breath. "Physical abuse is not the only abuse. There's also verbal and emotional."

"Daddy loves me."

"Love sometimes makes people do crazy things." He took his hands out of his pockets. "Let me see your back."

I backed away from him. "No."

"Why not?"

"I said I didn't want to have sex."

He rolled his eyes. "This isn't about that. I want to see why your back hurts."

I stood tall. "I pulled something. It's fine. Nothing for *you* to worry about."

Brendon backed toward the window. "I've kept my mouth shut for way too long. I've been stupid and careless." He reached down and picked up my backpack. "I've let you control me with those beautiful eyes of yours. I'm not making the same mistake I did with my friend." He threw the backpack out the window.

"What are you doing?" I asked, panic rising. It wove through me, clutching tight.

"What I should have done a long time ago." He wiped a tear off his cheek. "I really didn't want it to end this way." He pushed the loose bar free and hurried out the window before I could stop him.

He grabbed my backpack from the grass and took off running.

What had I done?

CHAPTER 37

My fists pounded on the door. "Daddy!" I screamed as loud as I could. I yelled and thrashed against the door, hoping Daddy would hear me and come.

"Daddy!" Pain erupted in my toes as I kicked against the door. I didn't care. I needed Daddy. We had to stop Brendon before he went to the police.

The door clicked unlocked and then swung open. Daddy stood on the other side. "What's wrong, angel?" His eyes swept past me to the open window.

"Brendon was here," I gasped.

Anger fumed in his eyes. "What?" He scanned my body. "Did he hurt you?"

I didn't know why, but my head moved up and down in a nod. "He kissed me like you said he would." I wrapped my arms tight around me. "He stole more of my journals."

"More?" He clenched his jaw. "You had more?"

I pointed to the closet. "There's still a few more. But, Daddy, he has about twenty of them." That was two years of my life he had. I had no idea which years they covered, but that really didn't make a difference – they were all damaging.

He took me into his arms and stroked my hair. "How far did he go with you?"

"Not far. I stopped it before it could."

"That's my good girl." He kissed me on the forehead and hurried to the closet. "Where are the journals?"

I pointed to the hole in the wall. He tensed next to me.

"How many more are there?"

"About a dozen," I whispered. "I think."

He reached inside as if to start grabbing the journals, but I stopped him.

"Daddy, that's not important right now. I think Brendon is going to the police."

All the color drained from his face. He ran his hand over his head. "Okay, here's what we're going to do. You're going to get all your journals out from the wall. Tear the thing down if you need to."

"Okay," I said, heart pounding. Why had I been so stupid? I'd put me and Daddy in grave danger.

"I'm going to get Brendon before he makes it to the police station."

"Do you really think you can get there before he can?"

"Yes. He's on foot." He put his hands on my arms. "You did good, Cora, by getting me. Just get the journals out and then grab the emergency bags from the hall closet. It has everything we'll need."

"Need for what?"

He ran his hand down the side of my head. "To get away and never look back."

I wrapped my arms around him and tried to push down all my feelings inside. My lips still burned from Brendon's kiss. Jenna's laugh flashed through my mind, and I had to shove it away with everything else. They couldn't be in my life. "I'm so sorry, Daddy."

He held me tight. "I know, angel. It's going to be okay. Daddy is going to fix everything. You'll be safe. I promise."

He gave me another kiss on the forehead before he left and a calm washed over me. Daddy and I could survive this together. We always did.

As Daddy peeled out of the driveway, I went to work. If I paused for even a second, I'd think about all the things he'd do to Brendon, and I couldn't afford to do that. It would weaken me.

I found an ax in the garage and ripped open the wall. It hurt my back, but I pushed through the pain. There was no time to waste. I had to retrieve all the journals before Daddy got back.

Drywall dust scattered in the air. I coughed and waved it away. After I tore off the last piece, I saw at least twenty journals jammed inside. All of them were filled with words. *My* words. Sorrow, happiness, pity, joy, regret, love. Every emotion possible weaved through those pages, telling my story. My journey. But it was about to end. No one could know. Every single page had to be burned to ash.

I ran into the kitchen, grabbed a trash bag, and threw the journals inside. I dragged the bag out into the hall and into the entryway – it hurt too much to lift it.

Before I went back to my bedroom, I checked the driveway to make sure he hadn't come back. In my room, I retrieved all the hidden bags with my treasures I'd collected, like the invitation to Jenna's party. There was a bag taped under the dollhouse, one under the night stand, and one under the bed. To anyone that found them, they'd just been random, meaningless items. But to me, they were everything.

I added the presents I received for my birthday to the bags. With a sigh, I ran the pendant back and forth on the chain before I decided to take off the necklace Brendon had given me and put it in a bag. I didn't want to give Daddy the opportunity to rip it from my neck.

Before I left my room, I remembered the cash I'd earned from my cell phone bands. I'd put it in a plastic storage bag, cut a slit in my pillow, and stuffed it inside. There was no way I was leaving that behind. Maybe it would help with an escape in the future.

After I got it, I retrieved the emergency bags from the closet, took them to the entryway, and stuffed my treasures into the bottom of the emergency bag that had my name on it. It was packed with new clothes, bathroom supplies, and books.

I was about to close it when I remembered Noah. I couldn't leave without him. He was my only friend left.

"Noah!" I ran toward Daddy's bedroom. "Where are you?"

I searched all the dresser drawers, under the bed, and then went to the closet. Daddy wouldn't be coming back in, so I threw everything out the door and scrambled through his stuff. In the bottom right corner, I found Noah buried under some old clothes.

Noah coughed. "So happy you found me. It's quite dark and boring in here."

With a kiss on the trunk, I ran down the hallway and gently placed him in my bag. I'd barely zipped the bag closed when the door burst open, and Daddy rushed in

"Did you find him?" I asked.

He nodded, his frantic eyes scanning the entryway. He wasn't his usual, composed self. "Let's grab all these bags, put them in the van, and get out of here." He lightly squeezed my arm. "You did good, angel."

With a tense smile, I grabbed the first bag and heaved it over my shoulder. Wincing through the pain, I carried it outside and threw it in the back of the van.

My breath hitched, and I pressed my palms against the floor of the van for support when I saw Brendon laying up front near the bucket seats, not moving.

Daddy threw another bag in the back.

I pointed at Brendon. "Is he?" I couldn't stand the thought of him being dead, no matter what he'd tried to do.

"Just unconscious." He rubbed his jaw. "The boy put up quite the fight."

Relief ran through me. "You aren't going to kill him, are you Daddy?"

He sighed, fixing my braid so it rested perfectly along my right shoulder. "You didn't really leave me a choice, angel, now did you?"

I stared at the concrete beneath my feet. "He's nice, Daddy. He doesn't deserve to die."

He kissed my forehead, the cold causing me to cringe. "Oh, my Cora. Always looking for the good in people, even if there isn't any to be found. This boy tried to take advantage of you. He tried to expose our family and get me thrown into jail. He tried to tear us apart. Is that what you want?"

"Of course not, Daddy. That's why I yelled for you." But that didn't mean Brendon deserved whatever was coming for him.

"That's why you're my good girl," he said, looking me in the eyes. "Now, let's hurry and get the rest of the things. I'm sure it won't be long until the boy's parents notice he's missing."

Together, Daddy and I filled the back of the van with the rest of the bags. He switched out the license plates. Why did he have those? Was it part of his emergency supplies? Did he know that one day I'd screw up and we'd have to run?

He helped me into the passenger seat and went back into the house to do a run through. He didn't want to leave anything behind that marked who we were. He'd probably see the mess I made in his room, but hopefully he'd be too anxious to care.

I stared at Brendon, unconscious on the floor of the van. Did he deserve to die? He had seemed so nice. I always felt safe in his arms. He treated me so kindly and knew how to make me laugh. He was gentle and warm.

But he'd deceived me, just like Daddy said he would. He used me and took my journals. He'd probably stolen the first one and used it as an excuse to get close to me. Each blackmail had required his involvement. He'd shown up the night I needed to break into the school and offered to go with me. He'd tricked me into kissing him that night. He'd held me close under the counter, long after the janitor had left.

Then he demanded money. Made it so we had to spend night after night in his room, making the cell phone bands. He probably hadn't planned for Jenna to get involved, but it would have been suspicious to say no to her.

He'd been the one who wanted to watch the blackmailer get the envelope. But it was him. He'd never been knocked out. I never saw a bump or bruise on his head. He'd given me an expensive necklace for my birthday. He probably used the five hundred dollars to buy it. No way he could afford it otherwise.

He probably knew the man who'd approached me. Probably paid him to pretend to watch me. I'd never met his father. When I'd looked at their family pictures, all I could see was Daddy. I strained to remember, but Daddy's face showed up in every family picture. Could the man be his father? Helping his son trick a girl into liking him? His eyes had looked familiar – they were the exact same shade of blue as Brendon's. That man had to be his father. Brendon had been so protective of me. He and his dad were sick.

I'd been so stupid. It had been right in front of me. All of a sudden the day my journal was stolen, Brendon had inserted himself into my life. Paid attention to me when before that day, he hadn't said a word to me. Not even looked in my direction.

He'd put his hands on me. Kissed me. Took away my innocence. I'd bought into all his lies and let him trick me.

I slapped my palm against my forehead. How could I have been so stupid? So foolish? All for a boy? A deceitful, sick, twisted, boy.

The van door slammed shut.

"It's all set," Daddy said, starting the van.

Tears ran down my cheeks. I tried to wipe at them, but they kept on coming. I needed to be strong for our family.

Daddy reached across and put his hand on my cheek. Just like Brendon had. I yanked away from him, my eyes darting down to Brendon.

He sighed. "He can't hurt you anymore, angel. You're safe. Daddy will take care of you."

Orange flames licked the side of the house. The front window and door were ablaze with light, our home burning before my eyes. The fire expanded to the garage. Smoke rose into the night sky, telling the world of my betrayal. Of my sins.

"Did you set the house on fire?" I asked, staring out the window in horror. Sally was in there. Daddy had the key to the basement, so I couldn't have gotten her. But I figured the next family would find her and love her. Except, all they'd find was a wrench since I'd torn her to pieces. How could I do that to my best friend?

"I didn't have time to rid the house of our fingerprints." He pulled out of the driveway and stopped in front of the house so we could watch the flames rise. "I poured gasoline everywhere and lit a few matches."

"Why didn't we leave the journals in there to burn?" I held in the sobs that rattled my chest.

"We can't take the risk of firefighters putting out the fire before every page has had a chance to burn." Daddy glanced at Brendon. "He has your other journal. We need to get the truth out of him, and then we can burn them all."

"Oh, Daddy." I pressed my hand to my cheek, the heat burning my skin. "I've let you down. I did this to our family."

He patted my leg. "We all make mistakes. It's how we handle them that proves the type of people we are." He pointed at Brendon. "Angel, you could have let him run. Could have let him do more than kiss you. But you were strong. You got me and let me handle the situation. You fixed your mistake."

I knew he was right, but I couldn't shake the guilt that had set fire to my body. I was like the house, slowly disintegrating into nothing. "It's not fixed yet." I wasn't sure if it could ever be truly fixed.

He put the van into drive. "Then let's go fix it."

He sped away from the burning house.

CHAPTER 38

*D*addy drove us to an abandoned field in the middle of nowhere. We took the bag of journals – plus the ones in my backpack – and threw them in a pile. We poured gasoline all over and lit a match.

"You do the honor," Daddy said.

I held the burning match in my hand. The second it landed on the pile, I'd be gone. No more Cora Snow. The flame burned dangerously close to my fingers. I was being wiped from the face of the earth.

With a forced smile, I threw the match on top of the pile, and the flames erupted, lighting up the night. It hurt to see my entire life being erased. There was nothing left to prove my existence in the world. I watched for a moment before I went back to the van.

Brendon grunted as I was closing the back doors.

A part of me wanted to rush to him and make sure he was okay and see if we could figure a way out. But Daddy would be furious if he caught me near Brendon, and I knew from experience that Daddy could overpower me. Best to go along with it for the moment.

"Daddy!" I yelled. "He's awake!"

Daddy opened the side door of the van and grabbed Brendon by the ankles. I thought he'd pick him up, but instead he yanked him out of the van and dragged him toward the fire. I couldn't do anything but watch. Daddy came to a stop near the blaze and let go of Brendon's legs.

"What are you going to do to him?" I asked, staring down at Brendon's bloody body. I hadn't noticed before that Daddy had beaten him badly. It had been so dark in the van.

"Add him to the fire," Daddy said like he was just another journal.

My eyes widened as I clutched the collar of my shirt. "Don't burn him!"

Daddy's eyes snapped to mine. "Why not?"

I stared down at Brendon. He was sweet and kind. Loyal and compassionate. He had an impure mind at times, but didn't all guys?

Dying by fire. That seemed so cruel and heartless. I wasn't heartless. Neither was Daddy. I folded my arms close to me and rubbed my arms. "Does he have to die, Daddy? We can just leave. You burned down the house. We burned the journals. No one will ever find us."

"What about the stolen journal?"

"Oh." I bit my lip. That was still out there. "I was supposed to get it back from the person next Friday."

"We can't wait that long." He stepped back from the flames that had grown larger. "We need it now."

I welcomed the heat from the fire. It matched my insides. "We can search his room. Before we leave. I bet it's there."

Daddy looked at me. "And if it isn't?"

I glanced at Brendon. "It has to be. Where else would he hide it?"

Brendon moaned, turning his head in the dirt. His eyes

fluttered open. His lips were dry, and blood caked the side of his head.

Daddy had tied up his hands and feet so he couldn't escape. He knelt in the dirt in front of Brendon and slapped his face. "Where's the journal?"

Brendon turned onto his side, spitting blood out of his mouth.

"Where's Cora's journal?" Daddy yelled.

Brendon squinted at Daddy. "What?" His voice was raspy and dry.

"The journal!" Daddy slapped Brendon hard across the cheek. My hands flew to my mouth in shock. He really was capable of hurting someone else. My stomach flipped at the sight.

"I." Brendon licked his lips. "I don't have it."

"Liar!" Daddy punched him in the stomach. I winced and wrapped my arms around me.

Brendon grunted in pain, curling into a ball.

"Daddy." I didn't like watching Brendon get beaten. He'd made a mistake, but there was still good in him. I'd seen it.

Daddy's eyes snapped up to me. "We have to find that journal, Cora. We won't be free until we have it." Daddy squeezed Brendon's knee like he did mine when he wanted the truth. "Where's the journal?"

Brendon screamed out in pain. I yanked on my braid as the nausea rose inside. *I am strong. I am brave.*

"Where is it?" Daddy asked.

"I don't have it." Brendon's eyes found mine and my heart melted. "Cora. Please. Don't let him do this to me. I didn't steal your journal."

"Don't lie to my daughter." Daddy punched him in the stomach again, and I couldn't take it anymore. If Daddy hurt me, oh well. It was worth it to end Brendon's suffering.

I dropped down next to Brendon. I remembered the day

we first spoke at the pizza place. He looked at me like I was any other normal girl at the school. His smile held so much sincerity and life. "Why did you steal it, Brendon? Just to get close to me?"

Brendon squinted up at me. His eyes were swollen, masking the soft, calming blue. "I'd never steal from you." He licked some blood off his lip. "I'd never hurt you, Cora. Remember that."

My heart twinged. Daddy went to hit Brendon, but I held up my hand, shifting my body so I could block Daddy from Brendon.

I placed my hand on Brendon's cheek and turned his face to mine. "Brendon, I want the truth. I know it was you. You stole my journal and used it to get close to me. Please, just tell us where it is. You don't want Daddy to get mad."

Brendon scoffed. "So this *isn't* him mad? How can you defend him? He's turned you against me."

"No." Daddy stood, shoved me away, and kicked Brendon's side. "You are trying to turn *her* against *me!* I love Cora."

"So do I!" Brendon yelled.

My breath caught in my throat and the fire in me exploded, sending heat coursing through my veins. He loved me?

Daddy sneered. "You don't know what love is! You're sixteen!"

Brendon glared at Daddy. "Doesn't mean I don't know love, sir. I'm capable of loving someone and treating them right. Unlike *you.*"

Daddy kicked him again.

"Brendon, please," I pleaded, tears dangerously close to the surface. He was just fueling Daddy's rage, and I wanted Brendon to be safe. "Don't say things like that. Daddy does love me. . . ."

Brendon looked at me, the anger drifting away. All his

compassion and tenderness soared back in. "No, he doesn't. He hurts and abuses you. That's not love, Cora. That's obsession and control."

I shook my head, trying to keep his words from staying in my mind. "No. You're the one obsessed with me. Stealing my journal. Showing up at my house in the middle of the night. Making your father follow me around."

"Cora, go to the van and get my toolbox from the back," Daddy said, his chest heaving in and out. "We need to get the truth out of him." When I didn't move, he shouted. "Now!"

I scrambled to my feet and ran past the fire to the van. Opening the side door, I pulled myself in and reached for the toolbox behind the driver's seat. It was heavier than I was expecting. I dragged it away from the chair and toward the door.

Out of the corner of my eye, I saw a book under the driver's seat. I reached my hand underneath, wrapped my hand around the hardback case, and took it out.

"My journal." I ran my fingers along the top, the indents from the blue and pink swirly design brushing against my skin. The ribbon tucked inside showed how I'd been so close to finishing it. Relieved, I rushed out to Daddy. "I found it! Brendon must have had it on him, and it fell out during the drive."

Daddy's eyes widened when he saw it. "That's good. Throw it in the fire and let's get out of here."

The relief inside faded. The journal had been behind the toolbox. The heavy toolbox.

"How could it slide under there?" I ran my fingers along the pink pages of the journal and noticed a dark brown spot on the corner. I flipped through the pages. Almost all of them had a dark stain, damaged from a liquid. "Coffee."

I'd spilled Daddy's coffee in the van weeks ago.

"It didn't slide under there," Brendon said. "I didn't have it on me because *I* didn't steal it." He sounded so sure, not even the slightest hint of deceit.

"Cora, throw the journal in the fire," Daddy said, pointing his finger at the flames. "We need to get going."

"Daddy?" I furrowed my eyebrows together. "This has been under your seat for weeks." He'd stolen my journal? Daddy? I shook my head. Impossible. "No. You wouldn't do this."

He threw up his hands. "Of course I wouldn't! If I knew you kept a journal, I would have confronted you." He motioned to Brendon. "He probably stashed it there. I wasn't always in the van, Cora."

It was true. Multiple times I had gone to the van and Daddy had been inside the school looking for me. Or Brendon could have broken into it at night.

Brendon hated Daddy. He probably wanted to frame him and get me to turn on Daddy.

"Hate to interrupt your thought process." Noah's voice rumbled in my head. "And you know I hate to side with the boy, but between him and *Daddy.*" His tone went down and slightly snarky on the word. "I'd have to choose the boy."

I shook Noah from my head.

"How could you do this to me?" I asked Brendon. All those nights we spent in his room, laughing and having fun, making the cell phone bands, creating memories. Did they mean nothing to him? "I never did anything to you."

Brendon grunted in pain. "I didn't, Cora. Your dad is lying to you. You can't trust him."

"I can't trust you." I couldn't trust anyone. I lifted the journal, ready to throw it in the fire.

"Stop!"

I whipped around, startled at the voice.

"Mr. Mendoza?" I shook my head, surprised at what I was seeing.

Mr. Mendoza stepped out from the darkness and cautiously approached the fire, his hands held out in front of him. "Cora, put down the journal."

Behind him, another man stepped forward.

Perv man, with the blue eyes similar to Brendon's.

Brendon's father.

CHAPTER 39

I gripped the journal tightly, staring at the creepy man. "What are *you* doing here?"

The man's wide eyes passed over the scene. His soft voice came out a little shaky. "We came to help you." Horror flew into his eyes when he got a good look at Brendon.

I pointed the journal at him. "*Help* me? You've helped your son torture me."

"Who is that man?" Daddy asked, standing so strong that it made him almost appear taller than the other two men, even though he was the shortest of the three.

The man looked between me and Daddy, and then glanced up at Mr. Mendoza. The man's confused eyes finally landed on me. "My son?" He shifted uncomfortably. "You mean my nephew? I lied about that. I don't have a nephew on the basketball team."

Brendon smirked. "Thank you, Captain Obvious."

"Not your nephew." I pointed at Brendon. "Your *son*. You've been helping him. Pretending like you're some perv man. But now I know the truth."

"What?" Brendon asked.

"What?" the man asked at the same time. "I'm not that young man's father. The first time I saw him was at the basketball game."

Brendon tried to sit up but was in too much pain. "I know who my father is, you know, since I've lived with him my whole life." He nodded his head at the man. "That's not him."

"Stop lying to me!" I yanked at my braid and pounded my shoe against the dirt. "Why does everyone lie to me?"

"We don't," Sally and Noah sang at the same time.

"He's not lying," Mr. Mendoza said, his deep tone rumbling through the darkness that surrounded us. I could see nothing past the fire. "This man is not Brendon's father."

"How would you know?" I asked, glaring at him.

Mr. Mendoza sighed, rubbing his eyes. "Because he hired me to investigate you and your father."

"What?" I asked, squeezing my journal. Why would they want to do that?

"What?" Brendon asked, intrigued.

"What?" Daddy asked through clenched teeth.

"Oh, this just got good," Noah rasped.

"Shh!" Sally said. "I'm trying to listen."

Mr. Mendoza put his hands on his hips, pushing his jacket back. A gun sat in a holster at his side. "I'm a private investigator."

"You're a school counselor," I mumbled, my hands loosening around my journal. It slipped a little in my fingers.

"No." Mr. Mendoza stood comfortably, unlike anyone else there near the fire. His slacks, T-shirt, and blazer suited him. More than a dress shirt and tie ever did. "Your principal owed me a favor, so he let me pose as a counselor so I could get to know you. You're the only student I ever saw."

Brendon squinted at Mr. Mendoza. "No way that man's a guidance counselor." The faintest smile touched his bloody lip. "Although, with muscles like those, I'd go to any college he'd want me to."

I paced along the dirt. "Stop! All of you!" What was happening? Who were these people? What did they want from me?

I'd made the biggest mistake of my life going to public school.

"Cora, throw that journal into the fire and let's go," Daddy said, his tone gentle and encouraging. At least, that was what he was trying to do, but I knew him better than that. He wanted to destroy the last piece of me.

Mr. Mendoza rested his hand on his gun. "You're not going anywhere."

"Is that even your real name?" I asked him. "Mr. Mendoza?"

He nodded. "Ford Mendoza, P.I."

"That's the coolest name," Brendon said. He grimaced as he tried to sit up again. "Could one of you gentlemen help me out here?"

Mr. Mendoza moved toward Brendon, but Daddy pulled out a gun from his back and pointed it at him.

"Don't move," Daddy said.

I frowned. "Daddy? When did you get a gun?" I couldn't believe he had a gun. I'd never believed he'd go to that extreme.

"A long time ago, angel," Daddy said "To protect you."

"You're not her father!" the other man yelled.

I took him in. He was taller than Daddy, and a little bit stronger. Daddy had an air about him that made him command the room no matter what. But this man, he reminded me of someone who'd want to be a part of the room, a part of the group – not controlling it. He radiated a calm and peace I'd never seen before in a man.

"Who are you?" I asked. My mind flooded with questions

and confusion. I just wanted it all to end. I wanted my life back.

The man flushed. "My name is Troy Kennedy."

I stared at him, expecting more.

Daddy waved his gun at Mr. Mendoza and Troy. "If either of you want to live, you'll leave right now!"

In a swift motion, Mr. Mendoza retrieved his gun from the holster and pointed it at Daddy. "We're not leaving her with you. In fact, we're not leaving without Brendon or Nora."

"Cora," I said. Kind of a bad moment to forget a girl's name.

Mr. Mendoza kept his gun trained on Daddy. "The name you were born with was Nora."

Noah chuckled. "Oh, I called that one, didn't I?"

My head spun. The flames from the fire lit up the dark night but did nothing to warm me. I was out in the middle of an abandoned field with four men I couldn't trust. No one knew where I was or who I was with. I sat down before I passed out. "What's going on?"

"I'll kill you!" Daddy yelled.

"Not before I kill you," Mr. Mendoza said. Composure sat in his eyes, contrasting Daddy's storms.

"Nora, I know this is all very confusing," Troy said with his hands held out. "But please let me explain."

"Cora!" I clutched my journal close to my chest and rocked, a few notes of a broken melody escaping my throat.

"Breathe, Cora," Sally said with a sweet tone. "Remember, you're in charge of your life. Not these *men*. They can't control you."

Daddy stepped forward, kicking up a rock and some dirt. "You will say nothing to my daughter!"

"She's *my* daughter!" Troy yelled, shoving a finger into his own chest before he pointed at Daddy. "You kidnapped her!"

Even though I was sitting, I swayed, the earth pulling at me. Nothing made sense. Spots danced in my vision.

"Cora?" Brendon whispered next to me. "Cora? Are you okay?"

I turned to him, taking in his bloody body. He was beaten and bruised. Ruined by Daddy. He'd been hurt, and it was all my fault. How could I have let that happened to him? "I'm sorry, Brendon."

Brendon gave a small smile. "Mr. Snow is smart." He glared at Daddy. "If Snow is really his last name." He scrunched his face. "In fact, I don't even know your first name."

"It's Gary," I whispered.

Daddy shot the gun off in the air, getting everyone's attention. My hands flew up to my ears. I'd never heard anything so loud before. My heart pounded against my chest.

"I will not have any of you telling my daughter lies. Filling her head with your nonsense. *I* raised her and took care of her. I fed her and loved her when no one else would."

"That's a lie!" Troy squeezed his eyes shut for a moment. "If I'd known she existed before now, I would have raised her."

I rocked where I sat on the dirt ground, holding the journal and my legs close to my chest.

Brendon scooted closer to me. "It's okay, Cora. Take deep breaths."

Brendon. Still being kind to me. Or was he just using me? Manipulating me? That was all boys did. According to Daddy. I couldn't get him out of my head.

"It's going to be okay," Brendon whispered. "Gary can't hurt you anymore."

I backed away from him, kicking up dirt. I'd had enough. I couldn't take any more of the lies all the men were feeding to me. I wanted answers.

Running toward Daddy, I took him by surprise, wrapped one arm around his waist, and tackled him to the ground. We rolled along the dirt with me clawing for his arm. We finally came to a stop. I yanked the gun from his grip and pointed it at him as I stood back up.

"Back away from me," I said with fury.

Daddy did as I asked. For the first time, he looked afraid of *me.*

I pointed the gun at Mr. Mendoza. "Slowly lower your gun."

Raising his free hand in the air, Mr. Mendoza leaned over and placed his gun on the ground, never taking his eyes off mine.

"Now, kick it toward me."

He kicked it, sending it to my feet, dirt flicking into the air along the way.

I pointed the gun at Troy. "Untie Brendon."

I waited until Brendon was completely free and then made all of them kneel in front of the roaring fire.

"I want answers," I said. "And you're going to give them to me."

I took a few long, deep breaths, calming myself. I was in control of my life. In control of the men before me.

"Or else we're all dying tonight."

The four of them stared at me, wide-eyed, but said nothing. I was through with being a toy or pawn. I was through with men trying to take advantage of me.

Daddy had always said I couldn't trust men.

Each of the guys in front of me had to earn my trust if they wanted to live.

CHAPTER 40

Brendon seemed like the easiest to start with, so I pointed the gun at him. "Did you steal my journal?"

He shook his head, his terrified eyes not wavering from the gun. "No, Cora. I promise."

"Do you know that man?" I pointed the gun at Troy.

He shook his head again. "Never met him until tonight." He shrugged. "Aside from the basketball game where he stalked you."

"I wasn't stalking her," Troy said, his gaze turning toward Brendon.

"Shut up!" I yelled at him. He quickly snapped back to me.

I took a few deep breaths. I needed to remain calm and focused if I wanted answers. I didn't want to lose control like Daddy always did. Anger made someone think and act irrationally.

"The only person who can talk, aside from me, is the one I'm speaking to. Right now, that's Brendon." I looked at him. "Why did you start talking to me at school?"

Brendon licked at the dried blood on his lip. "You want the truth?"

"Yes. That's all I want. No lies."

"Fine." He sighed. "I saw the way your dad treated you at the pizza place. You were terrified of him. I could see it in your eyes."

"So you decided to become my friend?"

Brendon stole a glance at Daddy, who was next to him. "I wanted to make sure you didn't get in trouble." A small smile appeared on his lips. "Plus, I've always thought you were cute, but I didn't know how to talk to you. You were so shy and kept to yourself. This gave me a good reason to talk to you."

"Why did you want to help me find the journal?"

"You're pretty," Brendon said.

Troy smiled, which for some reason made me mad. I glared at him, wiping the smile off his face.

"Why were you so nice to me?"

He sighed. "You're beautiful, okay? I like you. I helped you because I like you. That's all there is to it." He looked at Daddy again. "Well, besides the fact that I was worried about you. Your dad hurts you. He's not a good man. You can't trust him."

"I'm starting to like this kid," Noah said.

"Same here," Sally said. "Not bad for a teenage boy."

"Yes, she can!" Daddy yelled.

I took a step toward Daddy, pointing the gun at him. "I said no talking! Only Brendon can talk right now. I don't care if any of you like or don't like what he's saying."

Daddy opened his mouth, but quickly shut it when he looked in my eyes. He wasn't the only one who brewed storms.

I shifted back to Brendon. "So, you don't like my dad, you like me, and just wanted to help?"

"Yes," he said. "I promise."

"You weren't using me for sex?"

All three men went wide-eyed and turned to Brendon, who flushed.

He shifted uncomfortably. "Since you're pointing a gun at me, I'm not going to lie - I'm attracted to you. But I would never pressure you for sex. I was being truthful when I said you weren't ready for it. Neither am I." He looked me straight in the eye. "I've only wanted to kiss you, and that's it."

I nodded. "Okay."

He raised his eyebrows. "Okay?"

"Okay."

Brendon let out a relieved breath.

I turned to Mr. Mendoza.

"Wait," Brendon said.

I swept the gun to him and Brendon scooted back.

"Never mind," he whispered.

"Just say it."

Brendon shook his head. "Not with you pointing a gun at me."

Clenching my hand around the gun, I slowly lowered it. "Say it."

"You're a good kisser. That's what I wanted to say."

Again, Troy smiled. In fact, so did Mr. Mendoza. Daddy, on the other hand, looked like he wanted to strangle Brendon.

"Thank you," I said.

"You're welcome." Brendon scrunched his face.

"Are you okay?" I asked him.

He raised his eyebrows. "Um, I'm in pain. Your dad beat me up."

"Right," I said, nodding my head. "I'm sorry you're in pain." I changed my focus to Mr. Mendoza at the end of the line. Again, out of everyone, he looked the most relaxed, like he kneeled in the dirt in front of a fire and a gun pointed at him every day. "Troy hired you?"

"Yes," Mr. Mendoza said, his voice deep and rumbly.

"Why?"

He stole a glance at Troy, who nodded. Mr. Mendoza scratched his goatee. "I'm a private investigator. He wanted me to find his daughter."

I tapped the gun against the side of my leg. I really had no other questions for him. I knew who he was and what he wanted.

I turned to Troy on the other side of him. "Why do you think I'm your daughter?"

"Wait a second," Brendon said, holding up a hand. "Ford only gets two questions?"

My left shoulder went up in a shrug. "That's all I had for him."

Brendon lowered his hand with a grimace on his face and mumbling something about it being unfair that he had no embarrassing questions.

I raised my eyebrows at Troy, wanting an answer.

He took a deep breath. "A while back I found out that an old girlfriend of mine had a baby. When we broke up, she never said anything about being pregnant. She died during child birth, so I couldn't ask her about it and see if the baby was mine. The time line matched up, though."

"I searched everywhere," Mr. Mendoza said. I didn't stop him from cutting in. He was adding to the story, not trying to change it or defend himself. "Nora Stewart was bounced around to different foster homes."

Nora Stewart. The name sounded familiar. It struck something deep inside me just like the time Noah had accidentally called me Cora Nora. Or maybe it hadn't been an accident.

"Is anything ever an accident?" Noah asked.

Please be quiet, Noah, I thought. *I need to stay focused.*

Mr. Mendoza had his hands calmly clasped in front of him. "Nine years ago, she disappeared from a foster home and was never found."

Troy clenched his jaw. "The police didn't even look for you."

"They looked," Mr. Mendoza said, eyeing Troy. "Just not very long."

"They gave up on her," Troy said, frustration in his eyes. "They gave up on my daughter."

It had been nine years since Daddy brought me home. That didn't make me Troy's daughter, though. "Why do you think *I* am your daughter?"

"DNA test," Mr. Mendoza said. "We took some of your hair and compared it to Troy's."

"You took my hair?" I scrunched my nose and ran my fingers over my braid.

Mr. Mendoza rolled his eyes. "I didn't rip it from your head. Girls shed hair all the time. The first time you left my office, there were two on the chair."

Troy scooted closer to me, sending a little bit of dirt up around him. "It matched, Nora. I'm your real dad."

I lifted the gun. "No. If that were true, you would have called the police."

"We just barely got the results," Mr. Mendoza said. "These things take time, and we didn't want to make a mistake. We were headed over to your house when the GPS signaled you were out here."

"GPS?" I asked.

Troy looked down at the ground. "I wanted to make sure you were really mine before we did anything. I went to your school so I could see you." He glanced up at me. "And we put a GPS tracker on Gary's van."

Daddy braced as if to lunge toward Troy, so I pointed my gun at him, my finger sliding to the trigger. "Don't move."

Mr. Mendoza grumbled something I couldn't make out. "Can we go over some gun safety? Don't put your finger on the trigger until you want to pull it. We wouldn't want that accidentally going off."

I moved my finger to the side of the gun. I didn't *want* to use the gun – they scared me.

"Also, hold it with both hands if you ever shoot," Mr. Mendoza said. "To stay steady."

I stared at him in confusion. Why was he giving me pointers on guns? His eyes looked like they knew more than I ever would.

"We have the same eyes," Troy said, putting the conversation back on track. "That first night we met, I knew you were my daughter. I could see it." A couple tears slid down his cheeks. "You have Naomi's smile."

"Naomi?" The word felt odd on my tongue. Foreign.

"Your mother." Troy scooted closer to me.

I stared into his eyes and suddenly saw so much of me in him. It was a weird connection I couldn't explain.

"Nora, if I had known I had a baby, believe me when I say I would have taken you in, raised you, and loved you." Troy pushed his shoulders back. "I do love you. You're *my* daughter. If you'll let me, I'd like a chance to be your dad."

"No!" Daddy's jaw tightened. "*I'm* your father, *Cora!*"

I hadn't moved the gun. I'd kept it pointed at Daddy the whole time. Daddy. He wasn't my real dad. Just the man who'd loved me and taken care of me for nine years.

"Why did you take me?" I asked him. "That night, on the lawn. Why?"

The storms in his eyes calmed. He took some breaths to steady himself. He opened his mouth and then closed it.

"Please," I said. "Just tell me why."

He lifted his chin. "I was driving by and saw you all alone on the lawn. Those people didn't take care of you. They let you sleep all alone outside. Any pedophile could have come by and snatched you up."

"Like you did!" Troy yelled.

"I'm not a pedophile!" Veins burst on Daddy's forehead. "I would never touch my daughter like that. I wanted to take care of her, provide for her, and give her a stable home."

"Wait." Brendon glared at Daddy. "Not only did you beat her, you kidnapped her?"

"You beat my daughter?" Troy asked, his stare like daggers being thrown at Daddy.

"No!" Daddy's chest heaved in and out from anger. "I disciplined her, like any loving father would do." The dark gray clouds flew back into his eyes in full force.

Brendon stood, so I moved the gun to him. He held up his hands. "Look at her back. She has scars."

"How would you know that?" Daddy asked, jumping up.

Brendon stepped away from him. "It's hard to hide when every time I hug her, she sucks in her breath from pain!"

Troy pushed Brendon behind him, putting himself between him and Daddy. "You'll never touch my Nora again."

"Her name is Cora!" Daddy bellowed. His hair was disheveled, like it was falling apart with everything else on him.

I shifted the gun between Daddy and Troy. Two men claiming to be my father. One by blood, one by raising and taking care of me. What a true father would do.

But I still had to know one more thing. I lowered the gun to my side and looked Daddy straight in the eye. "You took my journal."

"No." Daddy blinked rapidly. "I . . ."

"Please. No more lying. It was under the driver's seat in the van. It's been there for at least a couple weeks." I patted the gun against the side of my leg. "Why did you take it? When?"

Daddy stood there in silence, staring at me. He unbuttoned the top of his shirt, something he never did in public. But his cheeks had gone red. He fanned his shirt a bit.

All I wanted was the truth. He owed me that much.

He rubbed his hands on his pants. "That night I came in to check on you. You said you were studying for a math test. When I opened the door, I saw you stuffing something in your backpack."

I'd thought he hadn't notice, but I'd been so focused on what was in front of me, not Daddy.

"I wanted to know what," Daddy stammered. "I needed a moment when you weren't attached to your backpack. So when you were in P.E., I went into the locker room and found the journal."

"You went into the girl's locker room?" Brendon folded his arms. "I thought you said you weren't a pedophile."

Daddy glared at him. "I was the only one in there." He took a deep breath. "I read the journal until school ended and then shoved it under the seat. I was hurt, Cora. All those things you said about me – about us. After everything I did for you. You betrayed me."

"Betrayed you?" Troy pointed his finger at Daddy. "You kidnapped her! Beat her! Made her change her name and basically worship you!"

"Stop!" I yelled, the gun heavy in my hand. It needed to end before I lost all control. "Just let him finish."

Daddy stood tall, a slight smirk crossing his lips. "I wanted to test your loyalty and see if you'd do whatever you could to protect our family. See how far you'd be willing to go."

All of this had happened because he wanted to *test* me? All he had to do was tell me he'd found it and pull me out of school. No one would have ever gotten hurt, aside from me. I'd never have gotten attached to Brendon, or Jenna, or Dalton.

Dalton. There was one thing that had been driving me crazy. "Did you tell Dalton I wanted to learn the guitar?"

"I had to see if you followed all my rules at school. I couldn't spy on you in the classroom, so it had to be out in the open. I planted a seed in his head." His nostrils flared. "I quickly learned, you didn't obey my rules. You disappointed me."

Brendon rubbed the back of his head. "So you're the one who knocked me out?"

"Yes," Daddy said with a grin. "It gave me great joy. You tried to take advantage of my daughter. You tried to rape her."

"Whoa!" Brendon threw up his hands. "Rape her? We only kissed." He looked wide-eyed between me and Daddy. "A mutual kiss, wanted by both sides, does not lead to rape." His gaze finally settled on me. "What has he done to you, Nora?"

It was so strange to hear him call me by that name. My real name. The name I had been born with and belonged to me.

"I would never take advantage of you like that," Brendon went on. "I do like you. A lot. But I respect you." He shot a glare at Daddy. "Not like him."

The storms in Daddy's eyes exploded. The final hurricane, blowing in, raining terror on everything in its way.

"I gave her everything my family couldn't give to me!" Daddy roared.

Gary. His name was Gary Snow. Or maybe not. I had no idea who the man really was. He'd taken me in the middle of the night. Kept me locked in a basement. He'd called me broken. But was I?

"My father always said I'd amount to nothing," Gary spat, "but I raised a beautiful daughter all on my own!"

It all came flooding back. He wanted me to change my name. He threw out so many options. After months, I finally agreed to Cora because it was close to Nora.

"My name is Nora," I whispered.

Gary locked me in a basement for a year. He put me down there when he thought I'd been bad. Everything, though, had been minor. Little scratches or a burned meal. I couldn't have friends. Couldn't go outside without him. He locked me in my bedroom when he wasn't home. He had complete control of my life.

"You controlled me," I said.

Gary shook a fist at me. "I *loved* you! That's how a father shows his love. He shelters and protects his children!"

Did I want that? Someone who dominated me? Told me what I could and couldn't do? I'd never have a normal life with him. Never have friends. Never finish high school or go to college. Never have a job or a chance at a career I wanted. Never be a painter.

I wanted to paint. Or write. I was an artist.

But he stopped me from being one. With him, I could never date. Never get married or have kids. Never own a home or a car. Never travel or see new things.

"He's a cancer," Sally said. "A vile disease that will consume you. You need to let him go."

"Let him go," Noah agreed.

They were right. I would never experience *life* with Gary Snow as my father.

"You're my world, Cora." His eyes were feral, contrasting with his words. "The only thing worth living for. I'd do anything for you. You must know how much I love you." He practically snarled the last part, like I should've been grateful for his love.

I clutched the gun in my hand. "I don't know what your father did to you, but you're through playing with my life."

I was strong. I was brave.

I was *not* broken.

Gary pulled at his hair, the wild in his eyes exploding everywhere. He wiped at some spit dribbling down his chin. "I'm the greatest father you'll ever have."

"That's not true," Troy said with a plea in his voice. His whole demeanor was much softer and gentler than Gary's. His eyes held kindness and concern. "Please give me a chance. There's a whole world out there waiting for you. Let me give you the life you never had."

Could he really do that? Would he let me do all the things Gary wouldn't let me do?

Gary lunged at Troy, the storms in his eyes moving in for the last destruction. Somehow, he had a knife in his hands. He must have had it tucked in his pants. He'd kill him. Gary would kill my real father before I could even get to know him.

I wouldn't let that happen.

"Stop him!" Noah and Sally roared.

With a deep breath, I wrapped both my hands around the bottom of the gun and pulled the trigger. Once. Twice. The gun was hot in my hands.

I kept pulling until it ran out of bullets. I'd never used a gun before, and I had no idea if my aim was accurate.

Gary stumbled back, away from Troy. He fell to his knees, his wild eyes searching me out until they stared straight into mine.

The storms in his eyes hadn't calmed. Hadn't stopped. Not until he fell to the ground and the life left him.

I let out a shaky breath as a relieved sob crawled up my chest and into my throat.

Gary Snow would never hurt me, or anyone, again.

CHAPTER 41

*T*he gun fell from my hands, and I landed on my knees. Brendon rushed to my side and wrapped his arms around me. I clung to him, crying and screaming.

I'd killed the only man I had loved. I'd taken the life of the man who had provided for me and raised me.

The man who had stolen *my* life.

Brendon rocked me in his arms, letting me get out all my frustration. I wanted to stay there forever and not face the aftermath. I was safe in his arms. Nothing could harm me.

After a while, sirens sounded in the distance.

Troy knelt in front of me and Brendon. He held out my last journal – the one Gary had found.

"What do you want to do with this?" Troy asked. His voice was soft and gentle. Compassionate.

I took the journal from him. "As much as I would love to burn it and erase the past nine years, I want to keep it."

"Why?" Brendon asked, holding me firmly in his arms.

I turned the journal over in my hands. "As a reminder. Any time I feel pity or remorse for Gary Snow, I can open this and remember what he did to me. What he stole from me."

I still loved him. A part of me always would. While his motives weren't purely good, he thought he had been doing the right thing. He had provided me with a stable home. He had loved me. I knew he did – in his own twisted way.

Police were soon on the scene. Ambulances and fire trucks also arrived. Smoke filled the air, and all I could smell was burning paper. So many people surrounded me and asked me questions. A never-ending stream of men and women wanting to look at me. Get a good look at the kidnapped girl. The girl who had shot the man who'd held her prisoner.

Brendon and Troy never left my side. I was grateful to have them. They weren't overbearing or trying to control the situation. They were just there to let me know they cared and I wasn't alone.

That had always been my biggest worry. If Daddy was ever taken from me, I'd have no one. I'd be all alone in the world. But that wasn't true. I had Brendon and Troy. Wherever I went next, I could make new friends. I'd find another girl who was amazing like Jenna.

A paramedic left me after he'd checked my vitals. For the moment, I was just with Brendon and Troy. But another person would be demanding more from me soon.

I looked at Troy, the gentleness in his demeanor comforting me. "What now?"

He went to take my hand, but then pulled back. He wanted to be careful. I could see it in his eyes.

So I held out my hand to him, and he took it with a soft smile.

"I was hoping you could come live with me and my family."

I furrowed my eyebrows, my stomach sinking. "Your family?"

Troy nodded. "I have a wife and a little girl. Renee is pregnant with a boy. Two more months."

"Oh." I stared down at our clasped hands. "I don't want to intrude on your family."

Troy let out a small laugh, the sound warm and inviting. "Nora, you *are* my family. Renee is so excited to meet you. She's already decorated your room. And Ella, she can't stop talking about her big sister. I'll try to keep her away so you can have some space, but she's five and doesn't quite understand boundaries yet."

I couldn't help but smile. A family. A real family. Just like the ones I daydreamed about in the brick homes around my house. "Where do you live?"

"Utah," Troy said. "If you like the outdoors, there's a lot to do. Hiking, skiing, four wheeling, shooting." He grimaced. "Maybe we'll stay away from guns for now."

Brendon chuckled. "Probably a good idea." He squeezed my arm. "Does she get a cell phone? I'd at least like to keep in touch."

The happiness I'd been feeling faded away. I hadn't thought about the fact that I'd probably never see Brendon and Jenna again.

Troy patted my hand. "Of course. You can Skype, email, Facebook, whatever you want."

I scrunched my nose and heat flared in my cheeks. "We can what?"

Brendon held in a laugh. His shoulders shook a little, so I slapped his chest.

"She has a lot to learn about technology," Brendon said to Troy. "And the world."

"Oh." Troy's eyes saddened. "Gary didn't allow you those things, did he?"

I thumbed the pages of the journal. "No. I've never been hiking or skiing, or any of those things."

"Well," Troy said. "Hopefully we'll find an outdoor activity you enjoy. There are many options." He sweetly smiled. "But we'll take it easy. We won't do anything you're not ready to do. Renee was a high school teacher before she decided to stay home with the kids for now. She can teach you at home if you'd like. Or you can go to public school. Private school."

When I just stared, his smile grew.

"One thing at a time," Troy said.

Mr. Mendoza suddenly stood before us, his hands on his hips, his blazer pulled back so his gun could be seen. "Well, as exciting as this all was, I'm going to call it a night."

Troy stood and shook his hand. "Thank you, Ford, for everything." He glanced at me. "For finding my Nora."

Mr. Mendoza stroked his goatee. "I'm glad we finally found her. This is my favorite part of the job."

Standing, I brushed off my pants and then hugged him. "Thank you, Mr. Mendoza. For giving me back my life."

"Just doing my job." He awkwardly patted my shoulder and then released me. "Take care of yourself." With a nod, he left us by the smoldering pile of journals.

Firefighters had put out the fire and were trying to salvage what they could. Which wasn't much. I'd be surprised if they found anything.

A detective in a suit cautiously approached us, his eyes on the journal in my arms. "Ms. Kennedy, do you mind if we take that for evidence?"

Kennedy. That was Troy's last name. But Mr. Mendoza had said a different last name earlier. Stewart. Too many names. Who was I?

I clutched the journal tightly.

"Will she get it back?" Troy asked.

The detective nodded, his eyebrows set in a stern line. "Once the case is closed, I'll see to it she gets it back."

I looked at Brendon, who stood right next to me. He placed his hand on the small of my back and nodded. "It's okay, Nora."

With a deep breath, I handed the detective my journal. The last piece of my former life. He gave me a simple smile and then walked away.

"Stewart was your mom's last name," Troy said. He'd probably seen my confused expression. "Kennedy is mine. Your birth certificate says Stewart."

"I thought I didn't have a birth certificate."

Troy sighed. "I'm sure there's a lot of things Gary lied to you about." He patted my hand. "You can keep Stewart, or we can get it changed to Kennedy. Whatever you want."

"I think Kennedy would be nice," I said.

"Nora Kennedy," Brendon said. He raised his eyebrows and gave his head a little shake. "I'm going to have to get used to that."

Troy glanced over his shoulder at all the police buzzing around. "I'm going to see if we can leave now. It's late, and I'm sure you're tired."

Before he could walk away, Brendon held up his hand. "Please don't take this the wrong way, Mr. Kennedy, but do you have the actual proof that you're Nora's real father? The last man to claim he was her dad turned out to be delusional."

Troy released the smallest laugh. "Nora's lucky to have a friend who's so concerned about her. I have all the paperwork, the DNA test, and birth certificate, with me. I'll make sure the authorities approve everything before I try to take her anywhere with me."

Brendon released a loud breath. "Good."

"Um, Troy?" I had no idea what to call him.

"Yes?" he asked.

I licked my lips. "There's a bag in the back of the van that says Cora on it. There are four plastic bags in the bottom and a stuffed elephant. Can you get them for me? There's nothing in there the police would need. They're just the only possessions that were all mine."

Troy gave me a soft smile. "Of course. I'll sneak them away if I have to." He left us to talk to one of the detectives.

Brendon hugged me close, and I sank into him, soaking up the warmth. I loved how perfectly I fit in his arms and how he held me with an overwhelming concern. "I'm going to miss you."

"I'll miss you, too," I said, rubbing his shirt between my fingers. I hated that we were going to be separated when we finally had a chance at a real relationship.

He kissed the top of my head, and suddenly all the worry inside me left. From him, it was a loving gesture, not a controlling one. "Call me anytime. I don't care if it's the middle of the night. If you need someone to talk to, or you've had a nightmare, or you don't know how to log onto Snapchat, I'll be here for you."

I slapped his chest. "Why do you say things I don't understand?"

"You have to learn sometime." He rubbed my arms. "I'll have Troy show you how to Skype and then we can use that for me to show you everything else."

"Skype?" Too many things I still didn't understand about life.

"We can talk to each other through a screen. It's like a phone call, but we'll be able to see each other." He squeezed me. "It sucks that I won't be able to see you in person, but I like the prospect of still seeing you blush."

I pushed away from him. "I have a feeling you'll be doing that daily."

He wiggled his eyebrows. "You know it."

I tugged on his Wonder Woman shirt. It was covered in dirt, blood, and a few holes. It was ruined. "I'm sorry."

"For what?"

"For accusing you of all those bad things. And ruining your favorite shirt."

Brendon shrugged his shoulders like it was no big deal. "Don't worry about it. Gary confused you. He made you question everything and everyone. You couldn't trust me." He looked down at the destroyed W. "And I can buy a new shirt. No big deal."

Brendon was undoubtedly the most forgiving person I'd ever met. I'd said horrible, terrible things, and he was still being nice to me.

I hugged him close, his arms embracing me in a gentle hold. "I do trust you. The only time I've ever felt truly safe has been in your arms." His smell reminded me of the ocean, taking me back to simpler times.

"Maybe I'll be able to come visit you every now and then," Brendon said, his fingers running down my braid.

"I'd like that," I whispered. I pulled off my hair band, tucked it in my pocket, and then undid my braid so my hair hung loosely around me.

I couldn't believe how drastically my life was about to change. A chance at a normal life. I would miss Brendon and Jenna so much, but we could keep in touch. It would have to be enough, though I desperately wanted more. Maybe they could visit. Or I could visit them, if Troy didn't have the same attachment issues Gary had.

I'd finally be able to go to school without any worries. Have friends without watching over my back. Hang out with them on the weekend, have a boyfriend, join a club at school, have a family and do things with them. Go on vacations.

A smile spread on my face. I never thought I could ever be that lucky.

CHAPTER 42

I shoved everything the detective sent back into the envelope. I flipped it over in my hands a few times, wondering what to do with it. After a couple minutes, I threw it in the trashcan. Since I had the answers, I never needed to see them again.

The detective over my case sent me all the information he had on the real Gary Snow. His actual name was William Horn, Jr. His mother abandoned them when he was a baby and his dad, Billy Sr., never got over it. He abused William and his little sister every day, physically and emotionally. He'd used it as a tactic to control them. From what the detective could find, William loved and feared his father all the same. His sister finally had enough and ended her life. William blamed their father. Blinded with hatred, William killed his father, changed his name and fled town. On the way out, he found me sleeping on the lawn. From the picture the detective sent, I had a striking resemblance to his sister. She wore a shirt buttoned to the top and had a braid resting over her right shoulder.

The detective had come through on his promise to send

me back my journal. I stuffed it under my mattress. I hoped I never had to look at it again, but there was a small comfort knowing I had the option.

My computer dinged, so I skipped over and sat in front of it, getting comfortable in my chair. I went to fix my hair, making sure it was smooth. I wore my hair down or in a ponytail every day. That was it.

Brendon's face appeared on the screen, making a smile spread across my face.

"How are you doing today?" Brendon asked. A question he'd asked every single day since I'd moved to Utah.

I held up a journal. "I started writing again." I showed him some pages. "Blue ink."

"No pink?" he asked. He bit down on a piece of licorice.

"No pink." I grabbed all my pens and waved them in front of the camera. "Blue and black."

He rolled his eyes. "You're taking it too far."

"I never want to wear pink," I said, "have it in my room, or anywhere in my life. It reminds me of *him.*"

He leaned back, and I finally got a decent view of his shirt. It had an outline of a guitar pick with the initials NK inside.

"What superhero is that?" I moved the pendant on the necklace he'd given me back and forth on the chain. I often found myself doing it in class at school. It replaced my braid tugging.

Brendon grinned. "My new favorite. She's hot, strong, brave, and a really good kisser."

I narrowed my eyes at him, the pendant paused in the air.

His smile grew. "Nora Kennedy: the greatest superhero ever."

With a smile of my own, I released the pendant, letting it fall against my chest.

Dad – Troy – it didn't take me long to call him Dad –

paused in the hallway and then came into my room. He leaned over my shoulder and waved. "Hey, Brendon!"

"Hey, Mr. Kennedy!" Brendon waved back with a few pieces of licorice that were in his hand.

"That looks good." Dad patted my shoulder. "Renee brought some home from the store. I'm going to go see if I can find the stash." He walked to the doorway and then looked back at me. "I always dreaded having my daughter date. But I must say, this is working out just fine for me. I never have to worry about you two being alone."

I threw a pen at him. "We're just friends."

"Even better." Dad left with a smile.

"He seems like a great dad," Brendon said in the middle of chewing.

I twirled a pen around my finger. "He is. Renee has been an amazing mom, too. They've been so nice and patient with me."

"Back to the journal," Brendon said, pointing at it. "What are you writing about?"

"Happy things," I said. "School, Dad, Renee, Ella, and Liam."

Brendon smiled. "How's the little guy doing?"

Liam had been born two months after I moved to Utah. It helped me settle in. They weren't focused on my every move or hovering. All of us were focused on the new baby in the house and getting his room ready. It brought us all together. A common ground.

"Sleeping through the night now, thank goodness," I said. He'd cried for the first few months, waking up everyone in the house. Ella would sometimes sneak into my room and climb into bed with me when Liam was real loud. My room was the farthest from his, dulling the sound somewhat. I'd loved how trusting and open Ella was from the moment we met. She never questioned the fact that I was her big sister. In fact, she told everyone she met, including strangers.

"Dad and Renee are going on a date Friday." I tapped my pen against the desk.

Brendon raised his eyebrows. "Did they get the three of you a babysitter?"

I stuck my tongue out at him. "They're leaving me in charge."

"That's good, right? It means they trust you."

I nodded. "It's really good." I stole a glance at the open door to make sure there were no eavesdroppers. Dad had said he liked Brendon being in a different state, but that didn't stop him and Renee from constantly walking by my room when we were video chatting. They also told me I had to keep the door open at all times.

Since Gary had always kept me locked in, I was happy to leave it open. In fact, the only time I closed the door was to dress.

"I'm nervous, though," I whispered. "What if something bad happens?"

"Nothing bad will happen," Brendon said. "You're a great big sister. Ella adores you. And I've seen you hold Liam. You're careful and protective."

"Dad said I could call if I need help. But I'm going to avoid that if possible. They deserve a date night."

He straightened out his hair, making me smile. He constantly did that when we were chatting. "Any nightmares?"

I shook my head. "It's been a month since my last one."

"Good," he said. "Have you made a fool of yourself at school?"

I sat up tall. "I didn't say one stupid thing today. And I made a basket during P.E."

Brendon held up his palm. "Way to go!"

I air high-fived him. "I even answered a question in class, and it was correct."

"You're always correct. That's never been your problem. The social thing has been your downfall." He twisted his lips in thought. "Let's see. Stolen anything recently?"

It was a habit that had been harder to break than I thought. A lot of the times I had just done it without thinking. The few times Troy or Renee caught me, they made me return it. I held my chin high. "It's been almost two weeks since my last crime, thank you very much."

"That's not that long, Nora," Brendon said with raised eyebrows.

I frowned. "You sound like my therapist."

"How's that going?" His eyes held his genuine curiosity and care that I loved.

"Really good, actually."

When Troy had suggested it, I refused. But after a few late-night chats with Renee, I finally realized it would help me out, which it had. I was still adjusting to so much out in the real world. There were so many things I didn't understand and needed help with. I also needed to get over the verbal and physical abuse from Gary. That was something that would take a lot of time and dedication, but I was willing to put forth the effort. I wanted to overcome it the best I could.

"Good," Brendon said with a smile. "Is your shop still doing well?"

Renee had helped me set-up a business online where I could sell my cell phone bands. It was a nice distraction and helped me earn money for college.

"Yeah. I can barely keep up with orders. Oh!" I sat forward, leaning my chin on my hand. "I made a new friend today in art. His name is Aiden, and he's incredibly talented and said he'd take me to a local art museum and . . ."

Brendon flexed. "A guy? Competition?"

I wiggled my eyebrows. "Maybe."

He lowered his arms and frowned. "I knew this wouldn't last and you'd move on. You're way too pretty."

"Calm down. I was just kidding."

"So, there is no Aiden?" Brendon let out a sigh of relief.

Heat crept onto my face. "I meant about him being competition. He has a girlfriend. Plus, I'm so not dating any time soon. I'm not ready."

"That's right," he said, pointing a bandaged finger at me. "You're not ready. I'll let you know when you are."

I tilted my head to the side. "How very kind of you."

"I try," he said with a shrug.

I picked up a pen and twirled it. "What about you? Dating anyone?"

He waved his hand. "No way. My last girlfriend was way too much drama. I need a break."

"You're lucky I can't smack you."

He clasped his hands behind his head and leaned back in his chair. "That's a perk to this whole living in a different state and video chatting thing. You can't hurt me."

I smirked. "You also can't try to kiss me again."

"You enjoyed it. Don't deny it."

I'd really enjoyed it. I'd probably enjoy it more since I'd had some distance from Gary. I could be worry free and just live in the moment.

I shrugged. "I've had better."

The screen flashed.

"Jenna's calling me. Talk to you tomorrow?"

"Same time," Brendon said. "I miss you."

I put my hand on the screen. "I miss you, too."

Brendon put his hand on the screen where mine was. I wished I could feel the heat from his hand, but it would have to do.

"Later, Nora Kennedy."

"Bye." I blew him a kiss and then switched over to Jenna.

Jenna's big, brown eyes stared back at me, pure excitement pouring out. She was covered in purple. I'd noticed she hadn't worn much pink since I'd moved. "Nora!" She had her hand covering her mouth. "Look!" She lowered her hand and smiled.

Her braces were gone, showing off her shiny white teeth.

"You look beautiful," I said. "Well, you did before, but now you have straight teeth as well."

Jenna clapped her hands. "I have the biggest news! Aside from the braces being gone."

I rested my chin on my hand. "Spill it."

"I have a boyfriend!" She squealed. "A real boyfriend!"

"Was your last one fake?"

She glared at me. "Ha. Ha." She cleared her throat. "You have to guess who it is. I'll give you three guesses."

"Dalton." I opened my journal and wrote down Jenna's big news.

She pouted. "That's not fair!"

I pointed my pen at her. "He's the only guy you've been talking about for the last few months."

"That's true, I guess." Her smile came back. "Fine. I have another surprise!"

"You kissed?" I wrote that news down as well.

Jenna threw up her hands. "Come on! How do you do that?"

I brushed my shoulder. "I'm pretty much amazing."

Someone came into Jenna's room and, by the smile on her face, it was Dalton.

Dalton plopped down next to Jenna on the edge of the bed and waved at me. "Hey, Nora!" He rubbed his forehead. "It's still weird calling you that."

317

"Get used to it," I said. "No one is ever allowed to use the C word again."

Jenna giggled. "Never." She linked her arm with Dalton's and wiggled her eyebrows at me. I so missed her.

"How are your guitar skills coming along?" Dalton asked.

I widened my eyes. "Oh! I have a surprise of my own!" I held up a finger. "Hold on." I rushed to the side of my bed and pulled out my new acoustic guitar from its case. My initials were engraved on the black strap. I brought it back and flashed it in front of the camera.

Jenna gasped. "No. Freaking. Way!"

"Dad got it for me," I said, sitting down in my chair. I placed the guitar in my lap. "A present for not doing anything to embarrass myself at school for two whole weeks."

Both Dalton and Jenna laughed.

"That's quite the accomplishment," Dalton said.

"Right?" I stared down at the guitar. "I wrote a song."

"Play it for us!" Jenna said, bouncing in her seat.

I strummed a few notes. "It's for Brendon. I'm not sure if I should play it for him first, or practice in front of you so you can tell me if it's stupid or not."

"It's not stupid." Renee stepped into the room. Her long, dark hair hung around her shoulders. "It's a beautiful song." She sat down on the bed and smiled at me, reaching all the way to her brown eyes. "Play it for me and your friends."

"Yes!" Jenna said. "Play it for us!"

I was still getting used to playing and singing in front of people. Dad and Renee let me play for them all the time. Ella requested a song every night before she went to bed. It was our new ritual. But I still felt so exposed.

"I don't know," I said, holding my palm against the strings.

Renee gently touched my arm. "Come on, sweetie. You're so talented. Besides, you have to practice for when Brendon and the others come to visit during the summer."

"What?" Jenna's jaw dropped.

Dad shuffled into the room holding a sleeping Liam in one arm and licorice in the other. "You weren't supposed to tell her without me."

Renee waved her hand at him. "You're right there." She raised her eyebrows. "Where did you find those?"

Dad waved the licorice. "I know all your hiding spots."

"They're really coming to visit?" I set the guitar down on my bed.

Dad grinned, handing me some licorice. "We finalized everything last night with Jenna, Dalton, and Brendon's parents."

Every squeal out of Jenna's mouth before that moment paled in comparison. I didn't know it was possible for her to reach that level. Dalton pressed his hands over his ears. Even little Liam stirred in his sleep.

"Shh!" I held my finger to my lips.

"Sorry," Jenna whispered. She silently clapped her hands. "I'm so excited! I've never been to Utah. Can we go to the mountains?"

Dad leaned down so he could look in the camera. "Already planning a camping trip. Hiking, fishing, and s'mores around the campfire."

"No bears, right?" Dalton asked, panic in his eyes.

Dad shrugged. "Probably not." He smiled when Dalton's eyes widened.

I hopped out of my chair and kissed Dad on the cheek. I would have hugged him if he weren't holding Liam. Then I gave Renee a huge hug. "Thank you."

Renee rubbed my back. It was nice to not have it hurt when someone did that. "Of course. I can't wait to finally meet them all in person." She handed me my guitar. "Please play the song for us."

I settled back into my chair, took a deep breath, and

played the song I'd written for Brendon titled *New Dawn*. Through my dark and scary world, Brendon had been a bright light that had steered me toward a new dawn. He showed me that I could thrive in a world without fears and demons and that I could be safe to live.

Later that night, I pulled out my journal and wrote my daily events. Only the happy, positive things. I wanted to focus on the good in my life.

Everything had changed so dramatically for me in the best way possible. I had a life. A family. A mom and dad that loved and cared for me. A little brother and sister. A chance at a life of my own. A future where I got to choose my path. Freedom to be whoever I wanted. I could explore my love of music and drawing without any hesitation or worry. Openly expressing myself through a creative outlet was a newfound passion. One I didn't have to hide.

I had real friends. Friends who cared about me and my wellbeing. Friends who stuck by my side.

The best part of it all?

Fear of being controlled was no longer a part of my life.

It will always have a small part, Noah said.

I huffed. "Says you. I have conquered my fears."

Of course you have, Sally said. *Noah doesn't give you enough credit.*

"I'm not sure I like the fact that you two know about each other." I set my pen and journal on the nightstand and turned off the light.

You need us both, Sally said. *We balance each other out.*

Noah scoffed. *Please, she'd do just fine with only me.*

"Both of you quiet. I need rest tonight." I pulled Noah out from his hiding spot behind my pillows.

Sleep well, Cora, dear, Sally said. She hummed a favorite lullaby of mine.

I braided my hair, tucked it over my right shoulder, wrapped my arms around Noah, and drifted off to sleep.

THE END

If you enjoyed Good Girls Stay Quiet, would you do us a solid and leave Jo an honest review? You can leave one on Goodreads, Amazon, iBooks, Kobo, or any other book retailer or review site online. The more reviews Jo gets, the more visibility she has. Then, she can connect with even more fantastic readers like you!

ACKNOWLEDGMENTS

For the longest time, I never thought I'd find a home for Cora and her story. As weird as it may seem, I loved writing this book and seeing the characters come to life. I wanted to share it with the world, but wasn't sure I could find a publisher who loved it as much as I did.

I believe fate/destiny brought me to Monster Ivy Publishing. They came into my life at the perfect time and from the second I read their website, I knew I'd finally found my people and a home for Cora. Thankfully, they loved my story from the beginning and truly understood my characters and the story.

Mary Gray, working with you has been a dream come true. You shaped Good Girls Stay Quiet into a gripping novel and helped me reach deeper inside myself than I thought was possible. I get all little girl giggly when I think about what a perfect match you've been to my soul. This book wouldn't be where it is today if it weren't for you, so thank you!

Cammie Larsen, thanks for making such a breathtaking cover. It's gripping, perfect, everything I hoped for and more.

You're awesome to work with and I struck the lottery with you!

To Casey Cheney, thank you for championing this book from the beginning. The Lord truly brought you into my life to share in the many different journeys and paths we've been down. You're my sister from another mister (sometimes it's freaky how much we have in common) and I love you more than words can say.

Thank you, Cindy Dorminy, for always being a sounding board and cheering me on. You helped find the plot holes in GGSQ, and I'll forever be grateful for that! I love that writing has brought us together.

Douglas. My true love. You're my heart and soul, and I couldn't imagine going on this journey with anyone else. You're the Brendon to my Cora, the Eric to my Emme, the Coach to my Tammy, the Harvey to my Donna, and the Lan to my Nynaeve. Thanks for being my biggest fan and making sure I never give up. I wouldn't be here without you.

Dad, thank you so much for not being a creep. You're a great father and an even better man. You showed me how to work hard for what I want and I love you for that.

Lastly, to Dr Pepper, for being the best writing companion a girl could ask for.

DISCUSSION QUESTIONS

1. Perfection in dress, speech, food, and manners were a big part of Daddy and Cora's relationship. How would you have behaved in Cora's circumstance?

2. Noah and Sally represent different sides of Cora's inner psyche. Noah was Cora's painfully truthful side, while Sally was Cora's logical side. Why do you think Cora projected these different sides of herself?

3. Cora has a distinctively young yet charming voice, with phrases like "me and Daddy" and "thank the stars." What does this tell you about who she is? What other phrases did you notice?

4. Cora uses writing and drawing as her emotional outlets. What are your outlets?

5. Brendon worried about Cora, but he also didn't want to risk losing her in his life. How do you think he handled what he knew about Cora and her father's relationship?

6. Cora's father (aka "Daddy") was both physically and emotionally abusive, yet he said he punished Cora out of love. While Cora should have told the truth about her situation sooner, why do you think she kept their secret for so long?

7. Do you think Cora will fully heal from what Daddy did to her? Why or why not?

ABOUT THE AUTHOR

Jo Cassidy grew up in sunny Southern California but now lives in snowy Northern Utah with her husband and their crazy cat. She loves all things creepy – Bates Motel, Stranger Things, and Criminal Minds are a few of her favorite shows. She believes Stalker was canceled way too early and would love to see it come back. You can subscribe to her newsletter at www.authorjocassidy.com.

When seventeen-year-old Tessa uses séances to contact her brother and mom, renegade spirits slip through the gateway, taking over her mind and town.

WILLOW MARSH

CHAPTER 1

I'd been trying to contact my mom ever since the night of the crash, but it's difficult to speak to the dead. None of my séances worked. Amá always told me to never give up, so I kept trying, knowing the sound of her voice could solve my worries.

Like most backyards in Willow Marsh, the woods lay behind the property line, filled with thick birch and willow trees. The frosty air pricked at my skin as I stared up at the dark clouds. If it was this cold during the day, I didn't want to imagine what it was like at night. I ducked between a couple trees, wishing I had a jacket. I didn't want to risk sneaking back to get it, though. Dad could come back any minute.

A small clearing opened among the trees, revealing an area of damp soil with scattered grass. When I kneeled, the cold, wet earth saturated my black jeans, sending a shiver through me. I took three red candles out of my backpack and placed them in a triangle on the ground. With shaking hands, I struck a match and held the flickering flame over each wick, waiting for it to ignite.

Closing my eyes, I breathed in the aroma of cinnamon, letting it soothe me.

"Amá, it's Tessa." I waited. She had taught me how to contact the dead when my abuela passed away. It would've helped if I had someone with me, but people tended to freak out when I used the word séance.

Especially my dad.

Staying connected to the dead, honoring them, and always remembering them was part of me. My culture. Everything I loved and held dear to my heart were my family. And two of them were gone because of me.

I needed to focus. I pictured her in my mind. The dark curls. The warm, brown eyes. Her smile, always knowing, always laughing. "Amá, are you there?"

A gush of freezing wind brushed by me and my whole body shook from the cold. A light force, almost like a weight, pushed into me from all angles. My fingers scraped along the damp earth as I hurried to stand, sensing something nearby.

Tessa. My name rushed by with the breeze in a soft, sweet tone.

I whipped around, searching between the weeping branches for Amá. My low ponytail, heavy from the weight of my thick hair and the green scarf holding it back, swished with every sweep of the head.

Tessa.

"Amá?" Had she finally come? I rushed back to the candles, kneeling before them, bouncing and shaking at the same time. "I'm here. Please talk to me."

The flames danced and a chill crawled up my back, snaking onto my neck. Frost engulfed the leaves on the ground and I watched as each one froze over in a slow motion tidal wave. I dug my dirty fingers into my jeans just to have something to latch onto. My ragged, deep breaths created a cloud of mist in front of me.

I stood, my wobbly legs almost making me collapse. My eyes darted around in search for the source of the cold. A bird whistled above me, piercing and loud, the sound echoing through the woods and vibrating my skull.

Swirls of dark colors forced themselves into my mind, followed by a series of images. An old, rusted key. A willow tree etched into stone. White flash. A brown and black bird with black, beady eyes and a sharply pointed orange beak. Black flash.

The intensity of the images shoved me to my knees. A presence drifted at my side at the same time a bone-chilling energy pressed into me. The bitter power ripped out any trace of happiness inside me, leaving something hollow in its place like I'd never experience joy again. My skin tingled all over, fear icing its way through my veins to the point I could barely move. The small bird landed next to me and craned its neck, looking at me with its beady eyes, just like from the image. At the same time it cawed – a lilting song that was captivating – heat radiated under my skin, replacing the cold and thawing my bones.

Lungs burning, I pushed my palms against my forehead until everything stopped. My eyes throbbed, lids twitching with each heart beat. Whatever evil had been there was gone. I took a few breaths to calm down before I peeled my eyes open one at a time, afraid of what possibly awaited me. The forest stood in a contemplative silence, the frost on the leaves gone and the candles blown out. The bird was nowhere in sight.

I wiped away the dirt on my hands, thinking I'd see a change in my body. Something inside felt different. But my brown skin looked the same as always. I traced the long, thick scar on my right hand, running between my thumb and index finger, remembering the crash.

For a while, I stayed rooted on the cold ground in confusion, trying to figure out what I had done wrong. Nothing like that had happened before. My previous séances had been calm and peaceful. This one had felt, well, evil.

When I noticed the time on my phone, I collected my candles and bag and forced myself to weave back through the trees and to the moving trailer outside the house. If Dad found out that I tried to contact Amá, I'd be grounded for the rest of my life. Luckily, he hadn't come back from running his errand, giving me time to collect myself.

He'd tried to get me to go with him, but I wanted some time to have my séance, so I told him I needed to call my best friend back home and wanted some privacy. Dad had taken the car, but left my duffel bag so I had something to sit on. I fished out my favorite maroon hoodie with a Día de Muertos skull on it. My abuelo had bought it for me for my last birthday, and I wore it every chance I got.

I tightened the scarf holding my hair in a ponytail. It was one from Amá's huge collection. I'd started wearing them after the crash to feel connected to her. The scar on my hand glared at me, reminding me of what I'd done. I quickly found another silk scarf in my duffel bag and wrapped it around my wrist, hooking it over the web of my right hand.

I sunk onto my bag, placing my hands over my face. I had to act like my normal self so Dad wouldn't get suspicious. He couldn't know the terror I'd just faced. Even though the evil had vanished, my heart was still trying to find a normal rate. I took deep breaths, thinking of my mom and brother. They always brought me back to my serene place.

Since Amá and Felix's deaths, acting had almost become second nature so I could get the worriers off my back. It was easy to appear fine on the outside, when, inside, I was slowly falling apart.

Made in the USA
Monee, IL
20 November 2022